The Black Mask

Afua:

Thank you for your support. I hope you enjoy this book.

Kim McKenzie
7/13/08

Kimberly McKenzie

The Black Mask

Kimberly McKenzie

Small Fish Big Sea Publications
December 2007

Small Fish Big Sea Publications
Paperback Fiction
P.O. Box 201061
Shaker Heights, OH 44120

PUBLISHER'S NOTES

This book is a work of fiction. Names, characters, places, and incidents either are products of the author's imagination or are used fictitiously. Any resemblance to actual events, locales, organizations, or persons, living or dead, is entirely coincidental.

First Printing

Copyright © 2007 by Kimberly McKenzie

All rights reserved, including the right of reproduction in whole or in part in any form.

Printed in the United States of America

ISBN: 978-0-9801470-0-1

Cover Design by N'DigoDesign

ACKNOWLEDGMENTS

Writing is the easy part, but getting my book published took the effort of several people. I would like to thank my husband, Karleo McKenzie, my entire family, and my friends who have supported my writing endeavors. I would like to thank my editor John Kavouras. Special thanks to Joyce Wallace who has rallied behind my work and has read every one of my books. I want to gratefully acknowledge the incredible cover design by N'Digo Design (www.ndigodesign.com) and BWUnited, formerly (Black Writers Alliance), and Timbooktu (www.timbooktu.com) online writing forums, whose members have given me wonderful advice and support on writing. Thank you.

Chapter 1

Mirah Jones regained consciousness and struggled to sit up in the hospital bed. The straps restraining her arms cut through her skin as she tried to yank them free. "Get me out of here," she screamed out angrily. Two nurses ran into the room and flooded her body with medication. In a matter of minutes Mirah drifted off again.

****

"Nurse, how is she doing?"

"Mr. Whitaker, your wife has not improved. If her prognosis doesn't turn for the better I'm afraid we'll have to turn her over to the psychiatric ward."

"No, not my baby," Mattie cried. "Don't you dare talk this nonsense. For goodness sake she's been through a crisis," her mother cried while Bryce tried to calm her down.

"Mattie, that won't happen. Now I think Mirah would like these beautiful flowers you brought for her," Bryce said handing them to her.

Mattie took the flowers and headed down the hall. Her baby had to get better she prayed. Mattie took a deep breath before she opened the door to room 204.

"Oh, Mirah. What's done happened to my sweet little girl," she whispered stroking her daughter's forehead. She lay lifelessly in the bed, different from the energetic child Mattie knew. When Mattie turned the covers down her eyes nearly ripped from her sockets. She screamed frantically for help; why in the world was her daughter strapped down to the bed like a convict?

"What's wrong?" Bryce asked, rushing through the door.

The nurses were behind him. Mattie grabbed at the straps around her daughter's arms. "Get these damn things off of her," she cried trying to unloosen them with her own hands. Her nerves were too jittery. "Help me," she screamed at the nurses impatiently.

"Mrs. Jones, Mirah has been violent and we want to take every precaution to make sure she doesn't hurt herself or the staff," one of the nurses informed her.

"Violent my ass! You get these off of her right now. Right now," Mattie hollered while her daughter continued to lay lifelessly. "And what the hell kind of drugs are you pushing through her body?"

"Mrs. Jones, what are you talking about?"

"Don't give me that...*what are you talking about*! My girl here has always been a light sleeper and all this noise would have surely awoken her. Now I'll ask you again, what are you feeding through these IV's here?"

"It's just a sedative to relax her," the nurse responded.

"Oh sweet *Jesus*! You're doping my daughter up. She's so high...look at her. Just look at her," Mattie cried. "Bryce, we have to get her out from here."

"Mrs. Jones, it is not in Mirah's best interest to release her at this point," the nurse replied. "I can have the doctor come and talk with you both."

"I don't need no doctor to come in here and tell me what's wrong with my daughter. You think your pompous asses know it all cause you got some nursing degree under your hand. Well... let me tell you something, we've been nursing our own people before we were even allowed to be treated in these here facilities. Now you draw up her release forms because I'm taking my daughter home."

"Mr. Whitaker, is that your wish?" the nurse asked.

"Nurse, why don't you give Mrs. Jones and me a few moments alone." How was Bryce going to talk her out of this

2

idea? Right now, he agreed with the nurse that Mirah needed to be in here.

"Bryce, there's no need to send her out of here unless she's going to draw up those forms. I want my daughter out from here," Mattie replied sternly to her son-in-law.

"Now, Mattie, I think we should all just calm down. Let's get these straps removed," Bryce told the nurse.

"You damn right. Remove these here things because Mirah is coming home with me."

"Mattie, what you're doing is not the best thing for Mirah."

"Let me tell you one thing," Mattie said angrily. "Don't you ever tell me that I don't know what's best for my daughter. Look at her. Can you honestly tell me this is the wife you married?"

Bryce looked at his wife shaking his head. She looked so different from the woman he had married just a few years ago.

"I thought so! And don't argue with me here. Besides, this is your entire fault anyway. My daughter life was just fine up until the day she met you. She was full of life and now she has been wearing this unhappy mask that you don't even seem to care about," she yelled, annoyed by his attitude.

Bryce tried to speak but Mattie interrupted.

"And don't go pretending like you're overly concerned about her now. Give me my daughter back," Mattie demanded, grabbing Bryce by the arms. "My husband and I both made the mistake of thinking all your fancy money could give her a better life. She just needed to be loved. Why didn't I see it before now?" she sobbed feeling guilty.

"Mattie, please," Bryce said. There were no words that could explain his feelings. The nurse undid the straps and left the room while he tried to get a handle on the situation. Maybe Mattie was right. The doctors told him nothing was physically wrong with his wife and maybe her mother could nurse her back to health. He never wanted this to happen. If he released his wife now, it was truly over. There was no way Mirah would want him back after everything that had happened up until now. Quite honestly, he wasn't sure their marriage was worth fighting for. He had enough problems dealing with his own emotions and didn't think he could handle those of his wife. This was the best thing for her, he convinced himself. He walked out to get her release forms signed.

Chapter 2

"Mama," Mirah cried. Her mother came rushing into her room.

"Oh sweetie, you're awake," Mattie called out, sitting by her bedside.

"How did I get home? Where is Bryce? Where is my baby?"

"Mirah, why don't you take it easy. You've been really sick these past few days."

"Mama, I didn't even get to say good-bye. Mirah cried in her mother's arms. My baby is gone. Why has this happened to me?"

"Mirah, sometimes we don't know why things happen to people. I'm sorry," Mattie cried to herself. She couldn't believe she lost her grandchild and her husband all within a few months time. How was she going to cope with this? Mattie was still dealing with being alone herself; now she had to pull herself together and be strong for her daughter.

Mattie spent the next hour getting Mirah cleaned up. She drew a nice hot bath and helped her get into the soapy water, like when she was a baby. Mirah sat there silently while Mattie began to bathe her.

"Mirah, everything will get better. I promise you," she said, letting the water trickle down Mirah's body.

"Where is my husband? I don't believe he let you bring me here instead of taking me to his guarded palace."

Mirah began to cry before her mother could get out any words. "Mama, they treated me so bad in that hospital. They thought I was some crazy nut, shoving medication through my body all day."

"I know, sweetie, and that's why you're home with me. I demanded that the hospital release you immediately when I saw those awful straps restraining your arms; as for your husband, I gave him an earful too."

Mirah smiled taking comfort in her mother words. Finally, someone had realized that her life was not the perfect fairy tale. It was hard to put up such a façade when everyone was looking from the outside in. Mirah had everything she could possible want, but she didn't have the love that a husband and wife should share. Her life over the past few years had been a roller coaster, she thought, as her mother tucked her into the fresh bed sheets. She was glad to be home. A sense of relief came over her; she knew she would be fine here, the home she grew up in. As she began to doze off, she thought back to the day when she first moved out on her own.

****

"I can't believe you're actually going," James said, standing in the doorway of her bedroom.

Mirah body swung around in excitement at the sound of his voice. She never stopped loving James. Tears instantly swelled at the tip of her eyes.

"Hey, what are all those tears for?"

Mirah fled into his arms unable to get any words out.

"Now don't you go all soft on me," James told her, brushing her tears away. "You're just up the highway...not even an hour away," he softly whispered into her ear.

Mirah's grim face turned into a smile while she held on tightly to him. She loved him so much and never understood why they were not together in the first place. They had just broken up over the summer and Mirah would never forget that awful day because it was the week after their high-school graduation and the day before she received her acceptance letter to attend college.

"James I miss being in your arms like this," Mirah said. His strong arms protected her and it felt good. Mirah felt like she was the most important thing in the world when they were together.

"I know," James said, brushing his lips up against hers. He always enjoyed the softness of her lips. The sweetness of her tore at his heart as he broke away from their embrace. He loved her so much, enough to let her go, he thought quietly to himself.

"James, how can you kiss me like that if you don't love me?"

"Mirah, I'll always love you. I really don't want to rehash on old times. I guess I just got caught up in the moment," he lied. He would never forget those crushing words he said to her a few months ago. Mirah had been so devastated and didn't speak to him for a long time. It seemed like an eternity. He was so glad when she finally came around. If he couldn't have her friendship then he might have had to go back on his word. James couldn't imagine his life with her completely out it.

"Old times. Is that all?" Mirah pried, trying to make one last desperate plea.

"Mirah, you know you mean the world to me," James explained, stroking his hand over her lips. "Now is not the time to be thinking about anything but your studies. You have a full scholarship and I want you to make me proud," James told her. He wasn't the emotional kind but he found his eyes tearing up. He quickly embraced her in his arms again; he couldn't let Mirah see his emotions. If he had she would see right through him.

The rapid honk on the horn broke the remaining time they shared together. Her parents never did like him much, which was the main factor of their break up. He hated them so much for that, but he was a man of his word. He closed the door, helping her load her few remaining bags. He couldn't believe he let Mirah go as they drove off. His heart swelled with sadness as if it was the last time he would ever be with her.

****

It was hard starting her life anew, especially without James. At first they saw each other frequently but as time went by it became less often. Mirah met new friends and college life consumed all her time, she thought, as she walked through the hallways of the university. Mirah couldn't believe how quickly two years had passed by. She was so excited about this stage of her life. She had picked a major in Journalism, and she looked forward to the day when she would walk across the stage with her degree. She had worked so hard for this day, not only for herself but also for her entire family. Mirah Jones would be the first in her family to graduate.

"Mirah."

Her roommate, Marcy, came running down the hallway, interrupting Mirah's thoughts.

"Girl, what's on your mind? I've been calling you from way back there," Marcy pointed out.

"I'm just thinking about my life after I graduate from here."

"You certainly don't play around," Marcy said looking at her friend who was decked out from head to toe. Her Liz Claiborne suit was perfectly shaped to her small slender body. Marcy would definitely have to go on a crash diet to get Mirah's model- size figure, she thought to herself. The sharp chocolate color of her suit looked radiant and the silky tan blouse underneath complemented her soft cinnamon tone. Mirah completed her outfit with dark brown shoes; a matching purse completed her look of perfection.

"Well we only have two more years to go and they'll fly by in no time," Mirah replied.

"Tell me about it. So why are you all dressed up?" Marcy asked.

"The English Department had Career Day. I've been so wrapped up into my final exams that I would have forgotten had it not been for my computer reminding me this morning. By the way, you didn't come home last night," Mirah said, wanting to get the scoop.

"That's because Dre and I were talking about this," Marcy responded flashing a diamond ring in Mirah's view.

"Girl, no Andre didn't. You two really engaged?" Mirah asked in disbelief. Marcy hadn't even known Andre that long and now they were already halfway down the aisle.

"Call him Dre, Mirah. He hates it when people call him by Andre. Anyway, yes we are engaged. I couldn't believe it myself. Dre said he had never loved anyone like this before and that he wanted it to last forever. *So romantic*," Marcy sighed. She flashed the ring in front of her face for the thousandth time; she, too, was having a hard time believing she was engaged.

"Well, you go, girl," Mirah congratulated her friend. "So tell me all the details!" Mirah said while they continued walking down the hallway.

"I have to attend this seminar," Marcy said looking down at her watch. "It starts in a few minutes. Why don't you come along with me?" Marcy asked.

"Sorry, I'm going to the step show tonight and I have to change clothes. You know it's going to be some fine brothers up in there. Oh, but I forgot, you're spoken for," Mirah teased.

"Girl, the step show doesn't start for another two hours. Come on, I have to talk about last night or I'll explode," Marcy said convincingly.

"Okay fine, but why is this seminar starting so late? It's Friday for goodness sake!"

"I know. Bad timing, but I have to attend for extra credit. This will boost my grades up. I need all the help I can get to keep this full scholarship."

"Tell me about it," Mirah sighed. She was nearly a zombie right about now, needing some sleep desperately.

Mirah took in every last detail of her roommate's magical evening until she stepped into the classroom. Her eyes stayed glued to the guest speaker, a handsome brother. Mirah stared at him from head to toe, admiring how good he looked. Broad shoulders, chestnut skin, and the most gorgeous smile. Every woman turned twice.

"I'm glad you could make it," Dr. Phelps said, patting Marcy on the shoulder. "This is our guest speaker for the day, Bryce Whitaker," her professor announced, as the two shook hands.

Marcy couldn't get a word out in greeting before professor Phelps interrupted her.

"And who might this young lady be?" he asked, shaking Mirah's hand.

"This is my roommate, Mirah," Marcy said before anyone could speak. "She's majoring in journalism and thought Mr. Whitaker could offer some valuable advice, with his background as one of the leading African-American architectural engineers in this town."

Mirah couldn't do anything but smile as Professor Phelps welcomed her to the class.

"It would be a honor to discuss things further," Bryce said, shaking Mirah's hand. He was instantly attracted to her. "Maybe after the seminar we can meet for a while," he offered.

"That would be wonderful," Mirah lied. She knew she would miss the step show now. Her best friend, Callie, would be so disappointed after Mirah promised her she would be there. She could not cancel with Mr. Whitaker after the lie her roommate had just told.

"Can I have everyone's attention," Dr. Phelps announced. When the class became quiet he formally introduced Mr. Whitaker to the class. Mirah jotted everything down. This would give her a jumpstart on preparing questions for their talk afterwards. Mr. Whitaker took the floor and began his discussion.

"Good evening," Bryce said.

Mirah and every other female in the room were caught up on Bryce Whitaker. He was drop-dead gorgeous and his voice was sexy as hell. Mirah had a hard time concentrating. Her mind kept wandering to the physical allure of Mr. Whitaker. His physique was built to perfection. He must spend many hours at the gym, Mirah thought, wondering about his personal side.

At the end of the lecture applause filled the room. Many of the women immediately formed a line to personally speak with him. Mirah looked at her watch and knew she was definitely going to miss the step show. The thought of Callie being disappointed upset Mirah in the back of her mind. There had been some tension building up between them over the months and her best friend seemed to be going in a different direction with her life. She always thought they would be the best of friends but now she wasn't certain anymore. Their interests were different and the time they spent together was far and too few. Mirah knew she should have been there to support her friend on this special occasion.

"Mirah, just give me a few more minutes," Mr. Whitaker said, while he wrapped up the last remaining questions.

Mirah nodded with a shy smile. She continued her conversation with Marcy and a few other classmates until he was through.

"So, ladies, where would you like to go for this meeting?" Bryce asked, joining the two of them.

"Oh, I'm sorry, but Dre and I are going to our parents tonight to discuss our engagement," Marcy responded. She flashed her diamond in front of Bryce's face.

"Well, congratulations," Bryce said.

Mirah couldn't believe the words coming out of her friend mouth. She was the one who had gotten her into this situation, and now she was bailing out on her at the last moment.

"I guess it's just the two of us then," Bryce said, patting Mirah on the shoulder.

"It seems that way," Mirah replied giving her roommate the evil eye. Marcy knew she was upset as she hugged her goodbye.

"It was great to meet you," Marcy stated, extending her hand to Mr. Whitaker. "I'll catch up with you later," Marcy winked at Mirah before dashing out the room.

"So, Mirah, is there any place special you would like to go?"

"Anywhere is fine," Mirah replied.

"Well lets discuss this over dinner," Bryce said. "I'm starved."

"Sounds great to me," Mirah told him as they headed out the door. She normally didn't go off with someone she hardly knew, but the circumstances were different. Mirah trusted Mr. Whitaker and everyone in class knew they were meeting afterwards. Some of the women had even met her with a jealous eye, wishing they were going along instead. In a way that made her feel special. She hadn't felt that way in a long time, not since her involvement with her high school sweetheart, James Gibson.

Mr. Whitaker was the perfect gentleman; he opened the passenger door and helped her get into his Mercedes Benz.

Mirah was impressed as the moonlight illuminated the shining black coat and chrome wheels.

"Thank you," Mirah said. Very chivalrous, a definite plus in my book, she thought to herself.

"So, Ms. Jones, I've indulged you enough about my life, why don't you tell me a little bit about yourself?" Bryce asked her.

"Well, for starters, I should be honest," Mirah said, filling him in on the real reason she attended today's seminar. Mirah felt relieved to get that off her chest. She was not a good liar and didn't intend to start now.

"I'll surely understand if you want to cancel. I can imagine how valuable your time must be," she stated apologetically.

"I'm glad you were honest," he replied, stopping at a red light.

Mirah's heart began to pound at the thought of her deception. She could have told him the truth even before they got to this point. First impressions were everything, one that she definitely blew. She slowly exhaled, waiting anxiously for his response.

"Well since there is no business to discuss, why don't we relax for a quiet dinner?"

Mirah was relieved.

"That would be great," she replied. They headed up 5th Avenue to 52nd Street in Midtown Manhattan.

Mirah was impressed with his dining selection. The Four Seasons restaurant was spectacular. People were dressed in their finest clothes; thank goodness her attire was on point.

"Yes, I have reservations for two," Bryce stated. The waitress scanned her list before showing them to a table.

The atmosphere was absolutely romantic. Bryce couldn't get over how beautiful Mirah was. Her soft cinnamon eyes had dazzled him into a spell the moment he saw her. However, his conscience was telling him something different. He knew he had to be at least ten years older than she was. She seemed to be around the age of his kid sister. He would take advantage of this dinner to find out more information.

"So, Mirah, you never did tell me much about yourself."

"Would you like to order now?" the waitress asked interrupting them.

"Can you give us a few more minutes?" Bryce replied with his drop dead smile.

"Sure," she smiled, blushing as she left their table. Mirah was sure she would slip him her number if Mirah even thought of excusing herself from the table.

Mirah seemed to stumble over his question while she studied the menu. Everything listed was very expensive; she really didn't know what to order.

"Make sure you order anything you like," Bryce said reading her mind.

Mirah looked up a little embarrassed with a faint smile. "With one meal here, I can buy a whole fridge full of groceries," she teased jokingly.

"Tell me about it. On a college income you can only afford to stack your cabinets with all those flavored Ramen noodles."

Mirah broke out in laughter agreeing. Everyone in college knew about the Ramen Noodle diet. She was glad to see he was down to earth and had a sense of humor.

"Well my life is pretty much simple," Mirah said, getting back to his question.

"I was born and raised in Newark, New Jersey as the only child. I started college nearly two years ago, right after graduating from high school.

Bull's eye! Bryce smiled to himself. It was amazing the information you could find out through a simple conversation. He was right; Mirah couldn't be more than twenty years old. Damn, he thought to himself. Why did she have to be so young? Mirah had not even begun to experience life but she certainly knew what she wanted out of it. She is definitely mature for her age. Hell, Mirah seemed more mature than a lot of the older women he had dated. There is just too much chemistry here, Bryce convinced himself. Besides, age is only a number; he smiled while she continued to talk.

"As you know, my major is Journalism and I will be the first generation of my family to graduate with a college degree."

"That's wonderful," Bryce responded. He was hoping she would say a little more about her personal life. Was she dating or involved in another relationship? He didn't want to come on too strong, but then again he never had to because women always seemed to gravitate to him, whether he was looking or not.

"So, enough about me," Mirah said, taking a sip of sparkling water. "I'm curious to know more about you...the personal side," Mirah said in her seductive voice. She had not felt this interested in anyone since her break-up with James. It had been too long since she had been intimate with another man and her hormones were jumping through hoops while she sat there conversing with Bryce Whitaker. He was so handsome and his older charm was very appealing, Mirah thought quietly to herself. Many of the guys her age did not have any direction and the one's who did were always snatched up or spoken for. Why was Bryce available? It's hard to imagine no woman had claimed him yet. There was no ring on his finger. Thoughts were racing through Mirah's mind. She was getting a little ahead of herself. Heck, this was just dinner and he probably would drop her off and then go home to his girlfriend.

"Hold that thought for just one moment," Bryce said, placing their order.

The waitress was just too giddy as she left with their order and a huge smile on her face. Mirah could have sworn she gave him a wink. Some women were just outright disrespectful. She turned her attention back to Bryce; she was not about to ruin her evening worrying about a man that wasn't even hers...not yet, anyway.

"Now, answering your question, I was born and raised in Cleveland, Ohio. I have a younger sister named Briana," Bryce told her purposely skipping over her age. He wouldn't divulge that information unless she asked. For some reason her age bothered him. It made him feel ancient, but at thirty-five he was by no means an old guy. He was very sophisticated and many women thought that was charming. Mirah wasn't the only young woman he had ever dated but something about her ignited a fire within him. He cared about what she thought of him and he could definitely see a relationship with this beautiful woman. Mirah just took his breath away. He gathered his composure; no one had ever made him stand hard by just sight alone. Damn, Bryce wanted her in his bed. The thought of making love with her consumed his mind.

"Sometimes, I wish I had some siblings," Mirah responded. "It was hard growing up as the only child."

"Well having siblings can be just as hard. I love my sister to death but she got me in trouble many a day," Bryce laughed thinking of his childhood.

"I'm intrigued. You have to tell me all about that one day," Mirah replied.

"Sounds good to me." This was a definite plus that he would be seeing her again. Silence fell between them while they dove into their dinner plate of delicious food. The atmosphere was perfect and they both enjoyed one another's company.

"Tonight was wonderful," Mirah said as they pulled off from the Four Seasons. "It's the best time I've had in a long time," she added while he flipped his CD on.

"Well, the night is still young. Do you want to go somewhere or go back to my place to relax?" he asked.

"Relaxing sounds good to me," Mirah replied before she even had a chance to think. She really should have told him to take her home but the idea of going back to her dorm room did not seem that appealing. Besides, she knew her roommate would not be back tonight and she'd rather spend more time getting to know Bryce. He was definitely a catch, someone she didn't want to slip away. The soft jazz rippling out the speakers was soothing. Mirah took comfort from the cool breeze that swept gently against her face. It wasn't long before she drifted off into a light sleep.

"Mirah, we're home," Bryce tapped her lightly on the shoulder. He actually felt good saying those words.

"Sorry, I drifted off." Her mouth literally flew open as she adjusted to the sight of the gorgeous high-rise condominiums. It was one of those classy buildings that the Hollywood rich and famous lived in.

"Oh, it was no problem. If you're tired I can take you back to your place."

"I'm fine," Mirah replied. "I must have been a little tired from being up so early. You know there's something about the motion of these cars that will put you right to sleep."

"Yeah, that's what they say," Bryce said, turning the ignition off. "I'll be right around to help you out," he said grabbing his jacket. Mirah just waited patiently, a twinge of excitement rippled throughout her body.

"Wow, this is gorgeous," Mirah, said, walking into the front lobby.

"It's only great if you have someone to share it with," he told her, as he greeted the receptionist sitting behind the desk. They headed towards the elevator and he held the door for her before pressing the top button "P" for the penthouse suites.

Mirah was equally amazed by the inside of his place. She stood in the middle of the foyer, admiring the most radiant crystal chandelier she'd ever seen. The hardwood floors were spotless. She followed Bryce into the family room.

"You can unwind here," he said, flipping the television on. "Just give me a few moments to grab some wine and check my messages," he told her with a wink. "Make yourself at home," he added before disappearing out the room.

Mirah sat on the mahogany leather sofa, glaring at the big screen television mounted on the wall. It was just like being at the movies. A girl sure could get used to this, she thought, stretching her feet out. This one room was bigger than the whole dorm room that she shared with her roommate. Wait till she told Marcy about this. You don't see too many brothers living this kind of lifestyle, and single to top it all off.

"I hope I didn't keep you waiting too long?" Bryce asked.

"Not at all," Mirah responded as he sat next to her. He had changed into some black jeans and a silk short-sleeve shirt to match. This brother was past fine, Mirah thought, gawking at his masculine features. "I was just admiring your home," she answered.

"Well I'll have to give you the grand tour." He filled up the wineglasses and handed one to her. "Shall we toast?" he asked her.

"Sure. You do the honors," she told him holding up her glass. This was the first time that she ever found herself at a loss of words. He definitely had her emotions jumping through hoops.

"Okay. Let's toast to new beginnings," he said, as their glasses came together.

He gulped down nearly the whole glass while Mirah took a few small sips. She was so sexy. He put his glass down and eased closer to her. Before she knew it he had set her glass down next to his and he began kissing the softness of her lips. First, he slowly teased her before entering in to taste the sweetness of her. His tongue nearly melted as it traced magically over hers. The softness of her hands circling around his neck only made him lust for more. Bryce's deep embrace caused Mirah to slide back further into the leather sofa, his body nearly lay on top of hers. He pushed all of his weight into his arms unable to control the weights through his pants. Her lips were so full and tender; he ventured down to brand her neck. The soft scent of her perfume and her low pitched moan sent his pulse racing even faster. Things begin to spin out of control. He never actually thought he would be making love to her as they headed up to his room.

Mirah's clothes were stripped and thrown throughout the big mansion by the time they made it to his bedroom. She stood in her lace bra and panties to match. Mirah watched Bryce with lust in her eyes while he turned on some soft jazz. His physique was absolutely perfect. He headed back to embrace her.

"You are so beautiful," he whispered as he lowered her into the bed.

The silk sheets felt wonderful against her body. He joined her; Mirah couldn't believe she was in bed with somebody she had just met hours ago. What in the world was she thinking? This was no way to catch a man. He would just hit it and leave, but for some reason she didn't care. All her beliefs had been thrown out the door. She wanted to feel him within her. She hadn't been passionately made love to since

James. That was nearly two years ago with the exception of the few times they were together here and there. Maintenance is what some would call it but she even cut that off at his nonchalant attitude of not committing. Damn, her body couldn't go another minute, she thought, convincing herself this was the right thing to do.

"Do you have protection?" Mirah asked, while he slowly unsnapped the buttons to her bra. Her breasts fell freely; he cupped them into his hands.

"Yes," he replied, slowly tracing his tongue around the tip of her hardened nipple. "I always practice safe sex," he moaned. He continued to suckle on each nipple before sliding down to kiss the softness of her belly button.

"What about you?" he asked, making his way back to kiss her tender lips.

"You're the second person I've ever made love to," Mirah responded softly. "I'm perfectly okay, I guess maybe we should have talked about this before hand," she whispered heatedly against his ear.

Bryce could hear the uncertainty in her voice. He looked into her cinnamon brown eyes. "Mirah, are you having second thoughts about this?"

"No. It's just not my character to hop in the sack with someone I've just met but you're different."

"I feel the same," Bryce replied, kissing her again with assurance. They both wanted each other. She ran her soft hands around his back. She wanted him and he would give her the loving that she deserved.

Mirah could hardly keep control as a series of moans escaped. Bryce loved every part of her body. He eased off her lace panties. Mirah lay in bed completely nude; he took a few moments to take all of her in.

Bryce threw the empty condom package to the floor and joined Mirah again. He teased and played with her until her body arched for his to join her. Their bodies fit together perfectly. Heat filled the big room while he pleasured Mirah. It delighted him that she had not been around the block. She was special and he was going to teach her how a man really made love to a woman. His slow sensuous movements increased, and their bodies beaded with sweat.

"*Bryce, ooooh Bryce,*" Mirah called out in sheer gratification. With each thrust her body was spinning higher. She was about to explode. She wrapped her fingers tighter around his waist and he intensified with each thrust. The backward and forward motions sent her body into a shivering state. She reached her pinnacle, and soon after Bryce shared in it before wrapping her in his arms.

Chapter 3

Mirah let the warm water trickle down her body, thinking about the events of last night. She couldn't believe she had had sex with someone she hardly knew. Unlike before, her conscience was now getting the best of her. How many partners had he been with? Did he really practice safe sex? She had asked him that question in the heat of the moment and of course he would tell her what she wanted to hear. What in the world was she thinking? Although they had used a condom, she knew they weren't full proof. Sexually transmitted diseases did not have prejudice against class, gender, or race. And what if he had children? He was older and probably did have some children of his own. And if that were the case then there would certainly be another woman involved. All these types of questions were racing through Mirah's mind as she stepped out of the shower.

She actually enjoyed the quietness of her room. She had to get her thoughts in order. Her biggest fear was that she would never hear from him again. She had made it easy for him and most men did not respect women who jumped into bed with them at the drop of a dime. Mirah knew the names women were given for this, but she wasn't like that. Mirah was a girl that a man would bring home to meet his parents.

Mirah wanted to pick up the phone and call Bryce. She didn't even have his number. She flopped down on the bed upset with herself. She grabbed the cordless phone and dialed information.

"Operator," the voice rang through the receiver. "How can I help you?"

"Yes, I'm trying to find the number for a Bryce Whitaker."

"Do you have the street address?" the operator asked.

Mirah just held the phone looking dumb-founded. She didn't even know the man's address. She had gone to sleep on the ride to his house yesterday, and she was to busy running her mouth on the way home. All she really knew about the man was his career background and that he was born and raised in Cleveland, Ohio, with a younger sister named Briana. She doubted that would be helpful to the operator.

"No, I don't have an address. All I know is it's in Manhattan," Mirah replied, listening to the pecking of computer keys in the background.

"I'm sorry ma'am. There's not a listing for a Bryce Whitaker."

"Thank you," Mirah said, hanging up the phone.

She was glad to hear the key turning. Her roommate Marcy came into the room. Right now she needed the distraction.

"Girl, I just had the most wonderful night ever!" Marcy said, plopping her bag on the floor. She came over and sat at the foot of Mirah's bed barely able to contain her excitement.

"All right, out with it then," Mirah told her.

"Yesterday I was so nervous when we went over to Dre's parent's house to tell them the news. I'm sure they already knew but I was dying with fear of whether they would like me or not. You know we haven't really been dating for all that long, so I had already prepared myself for the worst."

"That was smart thinking."

"Yep. You know how paranoid I am about everything, but things could not have gone more smoothly. They even took us out for dinner to celebrate. Dre's parents, especially his mom, were so excited. They asked when both families could get together so they could start the planning."

"Marcy, that's great. I'm happy for you," Mirah said, giving her a hug. Marcy had been through some really difficult times and deserved all the joy life could bring her.

"After dinner we went back to Dre's place and... well you know."

"Girl, do I ever!"

"So enough about me," Marcy said. "How was your so called interview with Bryce Whitaker?"

"Well let's just say I came home a little over an hour ago."

"What! Girl, spill it out. I want all the 411," Marcy gasped in disbelief.

Mirah filled her friend in on all the details. Marcy didn't say a word as if she was caught up in her favorite movie or something. It was so funny seeing the shock on her face. She covered her mouth, flabbergasted at the information she was hearing.

"Girl, no you didn't. I can't believe this shit. This is not like you," Marcy said putting her hand on top of Mirah's forehead. "Are you feeling okay?"

"Yes, I'm fine," Mirah, replied. "I'm just wondering if I did the right thing."

"It must have been," Marcy assured her. "You've always had good judgment about everything. The timing, well sometimes things happen quicker than you think. Look at me and Dre. Can you believe we will be getting married soon?"

"That's different," Mirah said. "I really don't know anything about the man."

"You will."

"I'm not so sure. I hope he calls me again."

"Girl, don't worry. He doesn't look the type to just hit it and leave. Bryce really seemed like a decent guy from what I've gathered."

Mirah felt a little assurance at those words. She had to think positively; she looked forward to seeing Bryce Whitaker again.

****

Mirah spent the next few days packing. She would be going home for winter break the day after tomorrow. Mirah pulled a single rose from the beautiful arrangement Bryce had sent. He had to suddenly go out of town for a few days on business. Bryce had left her his cell phone number on the card. *"Mirah, to new beginnings. Until we meet again...Bryce."* After reading that, Mirah had a need to hear his voice. She hadn't spoken to him since the night they made love. She picked up the phone and dialed his number, anxious to hear his voice.

"Hello."

"Bryce, it's Mirah," she said happy to hear his voice.

"I'm glad you called," he told her, while he calculated his projected year's income. Three million dollars, not bad he thought quietly to himself.

"I just wanted to call to see how you're doing. I hope I'm not disturbing you."

"Not at all. I've been long overdue for a break. All these numbers are starting to look the same," he told her. "So how are you doing?"

"Good. I'm just packing up a few of my things to take home for winter break."

"Wow, it's that time of the year already. When are you leaving?"

"The day after tomorrow," Mirah said, hoping he would be back so she could see him.

"Damn. I'm not going to be back for a few days. I really want to see you," Bryce said. Memories of their lovemaking flooded back to his mind. She felt so good and the thought of being inside her again sent him rock hard. For some reason she had that ability; he couldn't get her off his mind.

"Mirah, I really want to see you again before you go home for break. Can you wait a few days for me? I'll try to make it home on Sunday and maybe we can spend some quality time together. I promise to take you home," he said, hoping she would say yes.

"I would love to, but everyone has to be out of the dorms by then. They're doing some type of extermination," she replied.

"Well I'm determined to see you. Do you have some cash on you?"

"How much are you talking about?"

"Just enough for you to take a cab over to my place. I have a spare key," he said, giving her all the information she needed.

Mirah jotted down everything. She couldn't believe he wanted her to stay at his home while he was away. She sure felt special. Her stomach fluttered with butterflies. She could hardly wait to see him again. She turned her attention back to the phone.

"I'll see you when you get home."

"Well, I'm certainly looking forward to it," he told her. "Until then…thoughts of our night together will be on my mind," he told her before hanging up.

Bryce didn't waste any time getting back to work. His assignment normally would have taken him a week but he knew he could wrap things up by Sunday. He would work double hours so he could hurry back home. The thought of Mirah waiting there for him was all he needed. Bryce was finally stable enough financially to start his own business. Now it looked like he would have a beautiful woman to share his dreams with. Everything was perfect, he thought, smiling quietly to himself.

****

"Well, Mirah, I'm all packed to go," Marcy said. She came into the room followed by her fiancé Dre.

"You two have a safe trip," Mirah said, giving them both a hug.

"We will," Dre responded picking up the last of Marcy's bags. "You women certainly pack a million things," he teased, heading towards to the door.

"Ha, ha," Marcy quipped, giving him a tap on his derriere. "I'll be down in a few minutes," she told him before he left.

"So, Mirah, have you heard from your new beau?" Marcy asked.

"Yep. We just got through speaking with one another. He's coming home Sunday and wants me to wait for him before I leave for break."

"Girl, you know you have to be out of here by tomorrow, no later than Saturday by noon."

"I know. Bryce wants me to stay at his place until he gets back on Sunday."

"Wow, you must be something really special to him," Marcy told her. "I told you he was a good man."

"Yeah it seems that way. I have to admit I was a bit worried at first."

"Well you must tell me everything when we return," Marcy said before leaving.

Much of the dorm was now empty and the quietness was too much. Mirah picked up the phone and dialed home.

"Hi, Mom," Mirah said, plopping down on her bed. The boredom was already beginning to kick in as she called to tell her mom her change of plans.

"Well how is my daughter?" Mattie asked. She was glad Mirah would be coming home for a few weeks.

"I'm doing fine."

"Good. Your dad and I are planning a wonderful home cooked meal for you. You must be sick of all that cafeteria and fast food," she stated, jotting down her grocery list.

"Yes, I am," Mirah replied.

"Well, Mamma is going to fix that. I'm planning on going to the grocery store this afternoon."

"Mamma, that's why I called. I'm not coming home until sometime next week."

"What...but why? I was looking forward to seeing you sooner. Besides, I thought you had to be out of the dorms by tomorrow."

"We do, but I've arranged to stay here a few more days," Mirah lied. She felt shameful but could never tell her mother she was spending the next few nights at the house of a man she barely knew. Her mother would go nuts if she knew what her daughter was doing down here. Mirah wasn't raised that way and decided it best to leave the details of her relationship with Bryce to herself.

"What on earth do you want to stay a few extra days for? The last we talked you were so exhausted that you couldn't wait to get home."

"Mom, there's someone I want you to meet," Mirah told her.

There was a moment of silence that registered over the phone. Mirah didn't know what to expect as she waited for her mother's response.

"Honey, he must be something special if you're bringing him home. You never mentioned being involved," Mattie said. She sure hoped her daughter hadn't gone down there and fallen in love again. They had enough trouble getting their daughter's first boyfriend to break things off with her. She knew James's plans of wanting to marry her daughter, which would have messed up Mirah's whole future. Mattie wondered who this person was and what his intentions were toward her daughter.

"I know, Mom. I just wanted to make sure he was the right person before bringing him home to meet the family."

"Mirah, are you in love with him? And for heaven sakes what is the man's name?"

"Yes, to your first question," Mirah lied again. "His name is Bryce Whitaker," she told her mother.

"Well, is that boy in school, too?" Mattie asked. "And I sure hope you're not letting this supposed love interfere with your studies, gal."

Mirah knew her mother was getting upset from the southern tones in her voice.

"Mom, he's not in school now."

"What! We're trying to get you from out of this ghetto. You will be the first to graduate from this family, so don't you go and get blind-sided, Mirah."

"Mom, what does going to school have to do with anything?" Mirah asked. They never did too much care for her first boyfriend James, but when they found out his plans for not going to college, they really showed their outright disapproval.

"Gal, don't get sassy with me," Mattie quipped.

"I'm just saying that a lot of successful people don't have degrees. Look at Bill Gates, he's one of the richest men in the world."

"Well, you're not Bill Gates. And besides it's always been a dream of ours that you graduate and become something."

"Mom, don't worry," Mirah assured her. "I have to go now and return the last of these books before the bookstore closes."

"All right, but we're not done with this conversation," she told her.

"Okay, we'll talk later," Mirah said before hanging up. Mirah grabbed her books and headed out the door.

Chapter 4

Mirah stepped into the cab while the attendant placed her suitcases in the trunk. They headed off the campus and into the busy streets of New York. Normally she would have been annoyed by all the traffic but today she didn't care. Bryce Whitaker had asked her to wait for him at his home. He must have trusted her a lot, she thought, leaning her head back on the seat and taking in the beauty of her surroundings. Mirah didn't particularly care for the cold weather, but the hint of snow covering the city was absolutely breath taking this time of year. She even paid close attention to directions as they made their way into Manhattan.

"I'll be back in just a moment," Mirah told the cab driver. She ran into the lobby to the receptionist desk. As promised a key was waiting for her. Mirah slipped the key into her purse and joined the taxi driver out front who had already unloaded her bags. He helped her carry them to the front door. Grateful, Mirah reached into her purse and handed him the last of her money.

"Thank you," the driver replied.

"You're welcome," Mirah answered, watching him disappear into the busy traffic again. Excited, she hurried up to Bryce's penthouse suite and settled her bags in the foyer. She decided to take a grand tour of the place again, this time taking as much time as she wished to marvel in its splendor. This was a girl dream come true, a palace fit for a queen.

Mirah liked the idea of living this lifestyle. This could all be hers but first she had to win Bryce over, and like her mother said, the way to every man heart is through his stomach. Mirah began to prepare dinner since Bryce's plane would be arriving shortly. Their meal would consist of a Cesar Salad to start, followed by one of her mother's delicious homemade lasagnas.

Mirah had learned to cook over the years. She even prepared a light strawberry whipped cream blend for dessert and a bottle of red wine to wash everything down with.

Mirah decorated the kitchen table with two of the crystal candleholders that sat on the dining room table. She decided to wait before lighting them. Mirah certainly didn't want to give him the impression that she had taken over his place and moved in. She was sure other women had tried it but not her and that's why she settled her things in the guestroom while he was away. Mirah by no means wanted to intrude on his personal belongings as she gave the room one last glance. Everything was perfect; all she needed was some music. She switched on some soft jazz. The ambiance of the room caused her stomach to knot up with butterflies thinking what lay ahead for the two of them. She could certainly get used to this, being the lady of the house.

Mirah's thoughts were interrupted by the sound of the doorbell. By the time she made her way to the foyer, Bryce was already setting his luggage down.

"Bryce, you're home," Mirah said, running into his arms.

"It's good to be back," he said kissing her gently on the lips. Damn, he could sure get used to this shit. The feeling of being missed and greeted like this felt good. The scent of her perfume moved him; she still looked as beautiful as the first time he met her.

"Something sure smells good," Bryce said stealing another kiss.

"Well I hope you're hungry because I've prepared one of your favorite dishes."

"*Mirah a la carte*. That sounds good to me," he said lifting her into his arms. "I'm hungry as hell. Can't you tell?" He ventured his mouth over the hardened nipples that sprang forth through her cotton blouse.

"Bryce, don't get me all worked up. Not any more than I already am," Mirah teased, motioning for him to put her down.

"Now, come on, so I can feed you dinner," she said, grabbing his arm and leading him towards the kitchen.

"All right, all right," Bryce motioned with a shrug of his shoulders. "You can't blame a brother for trying. Damn, Mirah, don't you know you are sexy as hell. And very intelligent, I must add."

"You sure are racking up those bonus points. I'm definitely going to have to throw in something extra," she told him.

"Do please..." Bryce lit up like a little kid waiting in anticipation of playing with his favorite toy.

"Now have a seat and unwind," she said, filling his glass with red wine. "I'll be back in a few moments," she told him before disappearing from the room.

Bryce took a few moments to relax, thinking back over the last couple of weeks. *And to think, I was going to cancel my seminar at New York University,* he thought quietly to himself. *If he had done that then he would have never met Mirah. His schedule had been so crazy, but he decided at the last minute to stick with it no matter how tight things were. He felt the students needed some kind of encouragement. It's hard to imagine how all those textbook theories really apply to real life experiences.* Bryce wanted to show them that they really did. If you work hard at anything for long enough, you're bound to succeed if you set your mind to it.

"*What in the world!*" Bryce gasped as Mirah walked into the room interrupting his thoughts. She was nearly naked wearing a little silk and lace maid's negligee.

"May I give you a refill, sir?" she offered, picking the bottle up in her hands.

"You certainly can," Bryce said, his eyes glued on her.

Mirah filled two wineglasses before serving dinner. Bryce still could not take his eyes off of her. He had already lit the candles she had set on the table and the mood was perfect.

"So, I take it everything is to your satisfaction?" Mirah teased seductively.

"Yeah…in more ways than one," he told her between bites of food. He would rather be nibbling on her hardened nipples that peered through the soft silky lace of the negligee. It took everything in him not to shove everything to the floor and feast on her instead.

"You look really stunning, and the food is delicious too."

"Thanks," Mirah replied. "You don't know how good it is to be in a kitchen. Sometimes I get so tired of microwave food."

"I can imagine. We'll just have to rectify that problem," Bryce stated as he continued eating. He sure appreciated a woman who listened. On their first date he had mentioned to her that lasagna was one of his favorite meals. No woman he had been with before had ever done this for him. They were so into themselves, more concerned about what he could do for them, with their hands always stuck out for something. Mirah, on the other hand, seemed different. She was sweet and caring with a beautiful innocence to her.

"Okay, I have a surprise for you," Mirah told him, clearing the table.

"Surprise."

"Yes. Now close your eyes," Mirah demanded with a hypnotic wave of her finger.

"Your wish is my command," Bryce stated as he quickly complied. He wondered what excitement she had in store for him next as his pants nearly exploded from anticipation. Damn, he was really enjoying this evening. Why in the world hadn't he met her sooner?

"All right, you can open your eyes now," Mirah said. She positioned herself on top of his lap.

"See I told you we would have plenty of time for dessert," she motioned, pointing out the strawberry whipped cream delight on the table.

"Now lets play *Truth* or *Dare*," Mirah explained setting the rules. This was a fun way to get to know one another better, she thought, as she wiggled on his lap enticing his hard shaft even further. The rules of the game went as follows: questions asked by each partner will be answered truthfully, while afterwards taking a spoonful of the strawberry delight dessert she had prepared. If one partner wishes to skip the question than he must oblige to a dare by the other partner and misses his dessert. The dare is only to last one minute and whoever finishes the dessert first gets anything. *No holds barred…anything goes.*

"Okay, I'm ready," Bryce motioned excitedly. He felt like a little puppy waiting for a treat. *No holds barred…*now he was beginning to like this even more, his heart began to beat a bit faster. Mirah just had that effect on him.

"First question, how old are you?" Mirah asked.

"Thirty-five."

Mirah spoon-fed Bryce a spoonful of the cool refreshing strawberry delight.

"On a rate of one to ten, how would you rate our sex compared to your prior lover?"

Damn, that's just like a man, Mirah thought to herself. "Bryce there's no way I can answer that question," Mirah responded honestly. James had been her first love and she held him in too high regard to compare him in this fashion.

"So, then you miss your dessert and take my dare. I want you to table dance for me," he whispered softly in Mirah ear.

"All right," Mirah replied, taking off her black heels. What in the world did she get herself into? She eased her way on top of the dark cherry-wood table feeling a little shy. She started to twist her body to the sounds of the soft music while Bryce took pleasure.

"Woooo Weeee! Shake that ass," Bryce hollered, unable to contain his excitement. Mirah had it going on. Damn, damn, damn! The slow turns of her body revealed all the curves of a woman, and Mirah wasn't lacking in any place. She had the picture perfect body as he sat back and watched in excitement. This shit was off the hook. He felt like he was right at home in Cleveland, where they used to sneak into some of those strip clubs back in the day with their phony IDs. He was quite impressed that Mirah could feed his fantasies. It's not many women who could fill all a brother's needs, but Mirah was different and he began falling for her with each passing moment.

"Okay, times up," Mirah said, easing back on his lap. "My turn. Do you have any kids?"

Bryce's face immediately became serious; the glare in his eyes was more of a sad look. Mirah looked at him knowing the answer. She knew she would never have him all to herself. That might sound selfish, but things were just too good to be true.

"Yes. My son, Bryce Jr., was born premature and died on his third day in this world."

"Bryce, I'm so sorry. I had no idea."

A terrible guilt rushed through Mirah's body because of her selfish thoughts. She didn't know what to say to him, tears beaded up in the corner of her eyes. The thought of him suffering that type of pain was unsettling and her heart even went out to the woman, though she didn't even know her name.

"Mirah…"

"I'm sorry Bryce. Maybe we shouldn't play this game," she said cutting him off.

"Mirah, it's okay. Your intentions were good and we were bound to talk about this sooner or later. I really care for you," he said, wrapping her in his arms. They sat there in silence for a few moments. Bryce massaged the back of her shoulders; he had never talked openly about his son before now. For some reason, he felt a load lifted off his shoulders. All the pain and anguish seemed to heal in some way when he shared private matters of his life with her. Mirah seemed to have that effect on him. This relationship was definitely something special. He parted from their embrace and lowered his lips over hers. Mirah's lips were so full and vibrant; he entered in to taste the sweetness of her. Her kisses reminded him of times when he relished over his favorite dessert. He would take his time savoring every morsel because he didn't want his gratification to end. Her feeling, her taste, her smell were all so intoxicating. He never wanted to let her go, tracing his tongue slowly over hers. The intensity between them exploded, she responded back with the same urgency.

"Bryce, I think I'm falling in love with you," Mirah whispered between kisses. Just yesterday she had felt so guilty when she told her mother she had fallen in love. It wasn't a lie, after all, Mirah thought, trying to fit the pieces together. How could she be in love with someone she barely even knew? Some things just don't have a rationale. Her heart began to beat even faster. She hadn't experienced this feeling in so long. It truly was love…love at first sight.

"I love you, too," Bryce said, lifting Mirah into his arms. He blew out the candles and they headed off to bed. There would be no lovemaking tonight. As much as he wanted to make love to her, he was more interested in getting to know Mirah Jones. They spent the next few days doing just that.

Chapter 5

Mirah was excited and nervous on the ride home. Today she would be introducing Bryce to her mother. From their previous phone conversations she knew her mother wasn't pleased. For some reason her mother thought having a man in her life would destroy her chances at earning her degree. How foolish, Mirah thought to herself. How in the world was she going to persuade her mother of this? Some folks were just stuck back in time, and Mirah's mother was certainly one of them. Couldn't her mother see that things had changed? Women weren't sitting at home all day like they used to. They were out working and maintaining a whole new spectrum in life. If only she could see it, Mirah thought quietly to herself.

"Hey, you're pretty quiet over there," Bryce stated, giving her leg a gentle squeeze.

"I know, just thinking," she replied.

"You really are worried," Bryce said, coming to a stop at a red light.

"I warned you that my parents could be very difficult. My mom seems to think that being in a relationship will ruin my chances of earning my degree."

"We'll just have to persuade her otherwise. With your good looks and my charm, how can we go wrong?" Bryce laughed jokingly.

Mirah smiled. Bryce knew just what she needed to break the tension in her mind. With each moment she was falling more in love with the man sitting beside her. They spent the rest of the ride enjoying the sounds to the latest R&B music. Bryce could even hit a few notes as they sang in unison at times.

****

"Bryce, this is my father, William," Mirah said formally introducing the two.

"Mr. Jones, it's good to meet you," Bryce replied giving him a firm handshake.

"Same here and call me Willie. Do you need help bringing some of your things in? I know Mirah packed plenty of things," he laughed, kissing his daughter on the forehead.

"Dad!"

"Mirah, you know I'm speaking the truth. Now go give your mother a hand in the kitchen while we bring your things in. That woman is driving me crazy. I'm glad you're home for a few weeks."

Mirah nodded and headed towards the kitchen. She sure prayed her parents weren't going to run him off like they tried to do so many times with James. Didn't they know that just made the relationship even stronger? Mirah never could understand why James broke things off in the first place. They had the perfect relationship but that was in the past. She was looking forward to her future, hoping Bryce would be a part of it.

"Hi, Mom," Mirah said giving her mom a kiss on the forehead. She was wearing the same raggedy old flower apron that Mirah begged her to get rid of. She couldn't count all the new aprons her mother had hanging in her closet but she insisted on wearing this thing time and time again.

"Mirah, I'm glad you finally made it home. For a moment I thought your new beau would keep you away for the holidays."

"Mom."

"Girl, don't get sassy with me in that tone. Now reach in the refrigerator and get me two eggs."

"All right, but, Mom, I want you to be nice," Mirah pleaded with her mother. "Please…you know I came home late because I was waiting for Bryce to get back in town. He really is looking forwarding to meeting my family."

"Mirah, just settle down. You know I'll be on my best behavior. Can't you tell? I've even dressed up in one of my Sunday suits. I promise not to embarrass you."

"Mom, you don't embarrass me. It's just..."

"Now stop all that fibbing and hand me some milk," Mattie stated, stirring all the ingredients together.

Mirah always enjoyed watching her mom cook. She made some homemade cornbread. When she put the last of her meal in the oven, she snapped her apron off and swung it over the kitchen chair.

"Now come introduce your mother to this new love of yours," Mattie said, smoothing her hand over her skirt. She must say her daughter was certainly glowing while she followed down the hallway behind her.

"Bryce, this is my mother," Mirah said nervously introducing the two. She just knew something was going to go wrong. Maybe she should have waited a little longer to see where their relationship would end up over the next few months. Bryce did say he loved her. If he really meant what he said, then she was certain they could get through this evening.

"Mrs. Jones, it's a pleasure to meet you," Bryce said, shaking her hand. He reached beside the couch and handed her a vase full of beautiful flowers.

Mirah was shocked, looking at the beautiful holiday assortment. Her mother's face lit up.

"These are beautiful," Mattie said, taking the vase. "Thank you. These are going to look wonderful on the dining room table," she added. She put the flowers up to her nose and inhaled, she loved the smell of fresh flowers.

"Well, dinner should be ready shortly," Mattie said, motioning Bryce to sit down on the couch.

"Mirah was just about to sit next to him when her mother literally bumped her out of the way taking her spot.

"So, Bryce, I gather my daughter must care a lot about you to bring you over," Mattie smiled. "Quite honestly, I was a little surprised because we didn't even know you existed up until a week ago."

"*Mattie*."

"Now, Willie, don't you go flying off the handle. I'm just being honest here," she said, looking at her husband while his eyes swelled with embarrassment.

"Mom, I explained to you..."

"Gal, now don't go getting into grown folks business. I done told you about that a thousand times," she motioned, twitching her finger in the air.

Bryce obviously didn't know what to say. He saw Mirah put her head down in embarrassment, shaking her head.

"Now Bryce, how did you here meet my daughter. Mirah said you're not in school," she said trying to figure out his age. He definitely looks a few years older, she thought to herself. "Lawd" help her if she asked him his age. Mirah probably would run out the house she imagined trying to control the words coming out her mouth.

"I've already graduated from college. I attended Wilberforce University for my undergraduate degree and then went on to graduate from Case Western Reserve University to get my doctorate degree in Architectural Engineering."

"Doctorate. Willie, did you hear that? This nice young man is a doctor. Thank you sweet Jesus!" Mattie clapped out in the air.

Mirah just smiled, sinking further into her chair in humiliation.

"Mirah, why don't you sit up straight gal? You act like you have no class. 'Lawd' have mercy, we done show raised her better than that," she said, patting Bryce on the leg. "You ought to be used to your mamma embarrassing you," she added, looking over towards her daughter.

Mirah wanted to grab her bags and head for the door. Why in the world did she ever think this was going to be a quiet evening? At least her mother enjoyed the fact that he was a doctor, but does she have to act so country, she thought to herself. Bryce probably thought her family were nuts. He sat there trying to socialize with her mother, who was dominating the whole conversation. What a disaster, Mirah thought to herself.

"So, Mrs. Jones, I'm interested to hear more about yourself and the family," Bryce stated, trying to change the subject with his million dollar charm.

Mirah thought her mother was going to flip out of the chair and do cartwheels. A huge smile appeared on her face. She loved to indulge in conversations and the fact that Bryce was asking about her was a sure plus…but he didn't know what he was getting himself into. Mattie Jones could outtalk anyone, anywhere, and any day. Mirah laughed quietly to herself.

"Well, first of all, call me Mattie." She sank back into the sofa, crossed her legs, and smoothed out her skirt before folding her hands in thought, trying to figure out where to begin.

"Now, continuing on," Mattie exhaled, taking a deep breath before her award winning speech. "Both Willie and I are from Mobile, Alabama. We met over thirty years ago and decided to move up to the industrial north.

"Wow, that's something else. My father's family is from Burntcorn, Alabama. He also left a life of farming to work in the industrial city. He moved to Cleveland, Ohio."

"Yes, siree! Plenty of folks migrated from the South back then. It was money to be made in the North and folks were getting jobs as fast as they could come. Willie here walked into

Steel United to fill out an application and was hired right on the spot. Ain't that right Willie?"

"Yes ma'am and I've worked that job for thirty years and looking forward to my retirement."

"Well, you deserve it, honey. That there factory done gotten plenty of good service from you. They sure don't come that way no mo'. People are quitting these jobs before they can get settled in them."

"Mom, that's because a lot of companies are downsizing or merging with other companies. I hear so many stories where companies switch over names so they can get rid of good workers like dad so they can hire cheap labor with little or no benefits. Heck, and many of these companies are shutting their doors and moving across seas where they can get even cheaper labor."

"You're right. That's just sad, especially for those people who have dedicated their life to these companies. It ought to be laws in place for that. It's just not right and that's why it's so important for you to get that degree. We want you to do better for yourself."

Mirah nodded, glad the conversation turned into something everyone could speak on. Now if only her mother would keep it this way, she thought, crossing her fingers, hoping for good luck.

"Woo, I done forgot about my cornbread," Mattie said, jumping up from the coach. "Lawd have mercy...don't let this dinner be burnt," she called out before she quickly disappeared out the room.

"I'd better go help her," Mirah replied, standing up. "Don't worry, everything will be just fine," she added while her father shook his head.

"I know. Mattie has to have everything perfect to a golden brown. 'Lawd' have mercy if it's not," he laughed out loud. "Mirah I'm glad you're home," he waved while she headed towards the kitchen to help his worrisome wife. That was Mattie, but he sure did love her. He smiled, wondering what was going through Bryce Whitaker's mind.

"Mom, is everything okay?"

"Yes, thank heavens!" she stated, setting the cornbread on top of the stove. "Woo…that was just in the nick of time. Mirah, why did you let me run my mouth for so long?"

"It didn't seem like we were talking all that long," Mirah replied. She grabbed the dinner dishes out the cabinet.

"Not those dishes," Mattie called out without turning around. "Honey, get the fine china from the curio cabinet. And set the dishes up on the dinning room table. We'll be eating in there today," she added, giving her simmering greens one last stir.

"Okay. Everything smells wonderful," Mirah said as she left the kitchen. She picked up the pace, the aroma of the food traveled throughout the house. Mirah was starved and there was nothing like your mamma's cooking she thought as her stomach growled in anticipation.

Mirah spent the next ten minutes running back and forth from the kitchen to the dinning room to set up dinner. Her mother had prepared a feast, looking at all the food on the table. There was a succulent honey baked ham with collard greens, macaroni and cheese, potato salad, yams, and her mother's homemade cornbread. She even baked a sweet peach cobbler and had ice cream to scoop on top for dessert.

"Mom, you didn't have to do all this," Mirah said, patting the perspiration off her forehead with a cloth.

"It was no trouble. Don't you know by now I'll do anything for you? You are my pride and joy," she said giving her a slight squeeze on the cheeks.

"Thanks, Mom," Mirah replied giving her mother a kiss. Even though it didn't seem like it sometimes, her intentions were good. She went to tell the others that dinner was ready.

When everyone was seated at the table, Mirah was shocked when her mother asked Bryce to give the blessings. He nodded to her, seeing the worried look in her eyes.

"May we bow please," Bryce said, taking Mirah hand. With his other hand he held on to Mattie while everyone did the same. When the circle was complete he began the blessings.

"Dear Father, we gather here today and ask for your blessings for the wonderful meal in which we are about to receive. We ask that you thank the hands that prepared this food and pray that our bodies continue to receive nourishment that you so heavenly provide. I would like to thank the Jones family for inviting me into their home and ask that you continue to bless each and every one of us here today. Lord we know that if we keep you before all others we are following in praising your glorious name. And we ask that those who hath turned from your glory will one day see the light because with you all things are possible. AMEN."

The consensus of *"Amens"* followed. Mirah looked at Bryce surprised. He gave her a quick smile as her body warmed throughout.

"Well that was certainly a wonderful prayer," Mattie stated approvingly. "Anyone who put the Lord first is certainly all right in my book."

"Thank you," Bryce replied. "It's so wonderful to be here today. It really makes me miss my family all the more," he stated, piling his plate full of food.

"Yes, family is very important," Mattie, responded between bites of food. "So, tell me a little more about your family."

"Well, like I said earlier, my father is from Burntcorn, Alabama and moved up here to Cleveland in the early 1950's.

He worked the factories for a while but his true passion was drawing. He drew some of the most spectacular homes ever," Bryce said, sipping some of the best homemade lemonade he'd ever tasted. This would sure be perfect on a hot summer day he thought wishing the winter would be mild this year.

"Anyhow, my father would draw any chance he had, on his lunch break or rest break. One day his boss caught eye of his work and was absolutely amazed at my father's talents. From that point on my father would work on the side designing homes for many of the white families. With the money he made from his designs, he enrolled in college where he would meet my mother. With the racial resentment of blacks, they helped each other through school and married a short time afterwards. I'm the only son and I have a sister named Briana. When I was a young boy I immediately took interest in my father's work and pursued in following in his footsteps."

"Wow, that's really something," Willie stated. "Your father must really be proud," he added, piling more collard greens on his plate.

"So who is it you work for again?" Mattie asked being nosy.

"I work for New Edge Technologies. They are the umbrella-company for many of the architectural firms throughout the states."

"Oh, that's just wonderful. Maybe you can design our dream home," Mattie suggested.

"Mom!"

"Mirah, now hush up, gal. How often do folks like us run into someone who designs houses?"

"Mirah, it's okay," Bryce nodded. "If you are really serious just let me know and I can draw up a few sketches for you."

"Well I am definitely serious. We have been in this old shack for too long! We've been ready to go but we were waiting for you to get out of school. You've been gone for over two years and we're still here."

"Whenever you're ready just let me know," Bryce stated, helping himself to some delicious cobbler. He scooped a big hunk of vanilla ice cream on top and enjoyed every last morsel of the dessert. Thoughts of Mirah table dancing shot through his mind as she ran her hand along his leg. He immediately became heated, trying to focus on the conversation at the dinner table. If Mattie only knew what her daughter was doing she probably would have a heart attack. He hadn't believed Mirah when she explained why she forwarded her dorm phone to her cell number. Thank goodness for technology because now that he met her family she would never understand Mirah spending days and nights over at his house.

"Well, Mom, you done certainly out did yourself," Mirah stated rubbing her full belly.

"I agree. Dinner was wonderful," Bryce complimented.

"Wonderful. I'm glad you all enjoyed," she said getting up from the table. Everyone pitched in and the dining room and kitchen was cleaned in no time.

Bryce stayed a little while longer before leaving. It's hard to leave her behind, he thought, pulling out the driveway to head back home alone to New York.

Chapter 6

Bryce pulled into his driveway exhausted from the day's activities. He was looking forward to climbing into his bed and relaxing to the sports channel that he rarely had time for. He changed into his silk pajamas, and flicked the television on. Just when he was about to crawl under the warm covers the doorbell rang.

"Candy, what are you doing here?" Bryce asked, standing in front of the door.

"It's not exactly warm out here in this hallway," she responded, pushing her way through the door.

"You really should have called. I've had a long day," Bryce told her, so she wouldn't get comfortable. Those days they shared were long gone. He couldn't believe she had the nerve to bombard her way into his home without even calling after what she had done.

"Call. For what! So you can give me some excuse of why you can't talk."

"Look, Candy, I've been busy."

"Yeah, you've been busy all right. What, you playing house already? You sure as hell didn't waste any time in letting your bed get cold."

"What are you talking about?"

"Oh, I guess I'm going to have to spell it out for you," Candy said waving her finger in his face. "Since you wouldn't return any of my calls, I stopped by here on Saturday to get a few of my things. I tried to call your ass at work but they said you were out of town. Anyway, I couldn't believe you changed the damn locks, so I left. Just when I was heading down the hall to leave, I saw some young girl letting herself into your place with a bunch of luggage in her hands."

"What did you do?" Bryce asked, motioning for her to get her hands out his face. Mirah hadn't mentioned anyone stopping by. He swore if Candy even so much as hollered at her, she would pay the consequences.

"I'm touched…protecting the poor little bitch. She looks young enough to be your sister. What did you do this time to make her fall prey?" Candy asked, while she slid her fingers across his chest.

"Look, Candy, I don't have time for your stupid ass games," Bryce said grabbing her by the arms.

"Okay, Bryce. Let me go," she called out, trying to break her arms free. His hold was too tight and the fierce look in his eyes was beginning to bother her.

"I didn't do anything to her," Candy screamed, demanding that he let her go. "She didn't even know I was here."

"Good."

"Bryce, I don't need any more trouble. All I came for was to get my things. Are you going to deny me that too?" Candy asked. Tears began to flow down her eyes.

"Look, Candy, I'm not trying to make your life harder. I would have given you anything, but for you to steal from me."

"Bryce you know why…"

"Candy, stop!" Bryce said cutting her sentence off. "You didn't trust me enough, which meant you must not have loved me much either. There's no going back and you have no right coming in here questioning me about my life."

"Bryce, I was just too ashamed of the whole situation. I didn't want to get you involved in all that mess and have your name smeared across the headlines. That's why I didn't tell you. I was just hoping that you would have taken these few months to cool down. So I imagine there's no hope for putting things back together?"

"No, there's not. Let me get your things," Bryce stated before he disappeared out the room.

Candy sunk to the floor in tears. How in the world did she mess this up? She loved him too much so why hadn't she trusted him enough. He was torn up when he found out that she had hocked his grandmother's ring. She stole it right from underneath his eyes. Candy thought that she would one day be wearing the ring so it would not hurt to borrow it for a few days. Besides, she thought she would have the money to get it out without him ever knowing, but things didn't work out that way. Her son's legal problems had snowballed into much more and she had to break down and tell Bryce.

Candy never would forget that moment. It was the first time she'd seen him in tears. He was so devastated and angry; his eyes were so cold, just like they were now. It bothered her but even more because it was she who turned him against her.

After that, everything pretty much spiraled down hill. They argued ninety-nine percent of the time. She tried everything to win his trust back but one night he just told her to get out. He didn't even let her pack her belongings and told her she better be glad he didn't press charges against her.

Candy had laid low for a while hoping he'd have a change of heart. They had a good thing together and he had even accepted her son into his home. Everything had been perfect, but now that Bryce had kicked her out she had to move back at home with her mother. She kicked herself every damn day for messing this up, and it hurt like hell to see that he had moved on so quickly.

Bryce walked back into the foyer to see Candy on the floor in tears. She hadn't even noticed his appearance. He set her suitcases on the floor.

"Candy."

"Bryce, please don't make this any harder than it already is," Candy cried, standing up. It was truly over and she wanted to just get her things and leave with the little dignity that she had.

"Candy, let me finish," Bryce told her wiping the tears from her eyes. Although things had not worked out for them he still cared for her. He didn't want to see her suffer any more than she already had.

"I've had a lot of time to think," Bryce continued, while she gathered her composure. Her dark charcoal eyes still penetrated his soul, as she looked at him heart stricken. "With everything that has happened we can't go back to the way things used to be."

Candy began to cry all over again. He hated to see a woman cry. Over the years they had shared so much happiness together and it was a shame the way things had ended. He had to admit he had been cruel to her over the last few months but now he really had a chance to cool down. "Candy, look, I'll always care about you," he told her tracing his finger across her cheek. "Here, this is for you," Bryce said handing her an envelope.

"What's this?"

"Just open it later," Bryce stated. She ripped open the envelope anyway.

"Fifty thousand dollars! I can't accept this," Candy told him, handing the envelope back.

"Candy, please, let's not argue about this. I want you to take this money and pay off your son's legal fees and get your own place to live in."

"Bryce, I don't want you to think our whole relationship was all about money. These last few months have been hell for me and I turned around and did the same thing to you my son did." How could she stoop so low? She just wasn't thinking.

Everything happened so fast and she couldn't believe she ruined the best relationship she ever had. She was surprised Bryce would do this for her after everything that had happened.

"Candy, I know our relationship wasn't based upon money and that's exactly why I don't want to leave things on a sour note," Bryce replied. "We really did have some good times together and that's what I'll remember," he told her.

"Bryce's, I'll never stop loving you," Candy said kissing him goodbye. She wanted to savor the fullness of his lips as she slowly traced her mouth over his.

Bryce arms circled around her body, he responded to her kiss, letting his tongue trace over hers. Something about Candy made him shake at the knees. She definitely knew how to fulfill his needs, but at the end of the day that wasn't enough, so why in the world was he leading her up to his bedroom? He wanted to touch, taste, and smell her presence one last time. He knew it was wrong but he had to have her. She rode him like a wild stallion, like there would be no tomorrow. The sex was good, it was passionate and they held on to each other tightly, knowing it would be the last time.

When the sex was over she rolled over into his arms. Damn, what the hell did I just get myself into, he thought to himself? This wasn't supposed to happen. He wasn't in love with her anymore.

"Bryce," Candy called out before the phone began to ring. He let it continue to ring and debated whether to answer it or not.

"Aren't you going to get it?" she asked. He probably was scared she would pull some stunt if that were his new lady friend. It's funny how she was always on the watch for other women when they were together. Bryce was a good-looking man and wealthy too. Candy had to be on the defense at all times and always went the extra mile to please her man because, if not, somebody else would be all too happy to fill her place. Now isn't that something she thought as she became what she feared most...the other woman. Go figure, she thought, while Bryce picked up the phone.

"Hello."

"Bryce, its Mirah. I was just calling to make sure you made it home safely."

"Yeah, my tired butt just made it in a little over an hour ago," he replied yawning into the phone.

"I know. It has been a long day for the both of us. I'll be dreaming of you in my sleep," Mirah told him. "Usually I enjoy coming home on our breaks but I can't wait to get back there. I miss you already," she added wishing she were in his arms. "I love you, Bryce."

"Right back at you," he stated, lying on his side for some privacy. Bryce was hoping Candy would not go on one of her rampages. She was a jealous woman, one you dared not mess with.

"Well, you get some sleep," Mirah told him before hanging up the phone. When Bryce turned over he was in the bed alone.

"Candy," Bryce called out loud.

"I'm in the bathroom," she answered, joining him again.

Bryce was surprised to see her fully dressed. She came over to his bed.

"Are you in love with her?" she asked, looking him directly in the eyes. She already knew the answer but had to hear it from his mouth.

"Yes, I am," Bryce, replied feeling guilty for letting things go this far. He knew better...for goodness sakes he just came back from meeting Mirah's parents and now he turned around and did this. He had to get control of his life. It wasn't right to dangle Candy's feelings on the side when he didn't feel the same for her anymore.

"Candy."

"Bryce, it's okay," she lied trying to hide her hurt. She knew what she was getting herself into when she came to his bed. Candy could have said no but she thought if he could see how good things used to be he might change his mind. The fact is things had changed. The intimacy they once shared was gone. There was no chemistry there and their lovemaking was nothing more than a fun night of sex. Candy felt like a whore and she had to get out of here with what little dignity she had left.

A moment of silence fell between them. She glanced over the room one last time. She knew it was really over when she saw Bryce's face light up when he answered the phone. She could tell he was somewhat nervous about what she was going to do but she handled herself well. That protection and love he once shared for her was now for another woman.

"Bryce, let's just think of this night as our last goodbye together," she said, kissing him on the forehead. "All I want is for you to be happy," she told him before leaving the room.

"Candy, wait. Let me walk you to your car."

"That's okay, I know my way out," she said, heading out of the room and his life for good.

Bryce stood at the window watching her put her bags into the car. When she pulled away from the curb, he crawled back under his covers like he wanted to do when he first came home. Damn, this has been a helluva day, he thought before drifting off to sleep.

Chapter 7

Mirah awoke to the sound of her cell phone. She wondered who would be calling her this early in the morning. She didn't recognize the number as she flipped open the phone.

"Hello."

"Mirah, it's James," he announced shocked she hadn't recognized his voice.

"James, I'm surprised to hear from you. How did you know I was home?"

"A man never tells his secrets," he told her. "So you want to go out for some breakfast?"

"You always were an early bird," Mirah said. She sat up in bed; Mirah hadn't heard his voice in a while and wondered what in the world he was up to. Mirah was reluctant to accept but this would be a good time to tell him of the changes in her life. She quickly dragged herself from her warm covers and showered and dressed in record time. She decided not to awaken her parents and went downstairs to wait.

"Mirah, is that you up already?" her mother called out from the top of the steps.

"Yes Mom. I'm just about to leave out."

"Gal, where you heading off to so early in the morning? I haven't even had time to fix you breakfast," she complained coming down the steps.

Mirah could tell by her brisk steps that her mother was up for a brawl. "I'm not hungry," Mirah lied wishing her good morning. The scarf wrapped around her head was nearly half off as the bright green rollers dangled from the sides.

"Where are you headed off too? Nothing's open this time in the morning," she said sitting on the sofa.

"I'm going out with James," Mirah said, wishing he had picked her up already.

"*What*! Are you out of your mind child?"

"No, Mom," Mirah replied with a long sigh. She hated the fact that her mother still treated her like a two-year old child.

"*Oh*, the devil is sure trying to get in this house this morning," she proclaimed throwing her hands up in the air. "*Jesus*, please keep him out," Mattie called out loudly asking for help.

"Mother, I swear, sometimes you are just too much," Mirah told her.

"Gal, don't use that tone with me…and certainly you know better than to swear to things you know ain't right. Tell that boy to stay out of my house," Mattie proclaimed putting her hands on her hips. "He ain't nothing but trouble. Don't see why you're going out with the likes of him when you just introduced us to your doctor friend."

"Mom, that's why I'm seeing James. I want to tell him myself of what's been going on in my life. Besides, were just friends…I don't know why you are getting all bent out of shape."

"What in the world is going on?" Willie asked, coming down the steps. He rubbed his eyes trying to focus on all the chaos that was going on so early in the morning.

"Dad."

"Willie, this gal here has gone nuts," Mattie proclaimed cutting her sentence off. "Look at her all dressed so early to sneak out with that hoodlum James."

"Mom, that's not true and why do you have to call him out of his name?" Mirah asked angrily. This was just too much. Her mom had crossed over the line and she was fed up with all her outbursts. Mirah was grown; she was a woman who could take care of herself. "I left you a note on the refrigerator. I didn't want to wake you so early after everything you did for me yesterday."

"Hmmph," Mattie said.

"Mattie, now come on back to bed. Mirah is grown," he told his meddling wife.

"Thank you *Jesus!*" Mirah called out loud. For once her father had hit the bull's eye. When was her mother going to realize that she was not a child anymore?

"Oh no, not in my house," Mattie quipped throwing her hands up in the air again. "As long as you're under my roof then you have to abide by my rules."

"You mean our rules," Willie corrected, putting his foot down. "Mattie you have to let her go. She's not a child anymore," Willie said putting his hand over her shoulder.

For the first time in Mirah's life her mother didn't say a word. The silence cut through the room like a surprise tornado coming down the path. Its silent winds could spur into a fury devastating anything in its path. Mattie did just the same. She turned and walked up the stairs. Not one word. She left as if nothing happened although the aftermath devastated Mirah's inner most thoughts.

"Dad," Mirah cried upset.

"Honey, now don't you worry," he told her with a fatherly hug. "Your mother just needs a little time to adjust. She's gonna have to let you go sooner or later and its about time that she does it now. My baby is all grown up," Willie told her, assuring her everything would be okay. When he heard a car pull up in the driveway, he told his daughter to have a good time.

Mirah jumped in the car before James had a chance to get out and open the door for her.

"Hey, is everything all right?" he asked, backing out the driveway. He could see her eyes glistening with tears and wondered what was going on.

"You know how my mother can get me all upset," Mirah replied.

"Boy, do I ever," James smiled giving her a wink. He was happy to see her laugh knowing how crazy her mother could be. Her parents were the reason they were not married right now, but that was all about to change, James thought, rubbing against his pocket to make sure the ring was there. After Callie told him Mirah had missed her Greek step show because of some man he decided it was time to claim what was his. He had to put his plan into motion; he had already waited too long. He thought about the ring he had purchased for her while they were in high school. James had a good job now and had upgraded her ring. He wasn't about to let her go and could hardly wait to see the surprise on her face.

Everything would take place tonight. He wanted to meet with her this morning to tell her to prepare for not coming home for the rest of the night. Even though she was grown, he knew her mother would try to sabotage their being together. James could just about picture what she would say, he thought, coming to a red light. "Lawd, Lawd, Lawd! Now why you wonna keep seeing that heathen. *Gal*, he ain't got no education, so how in the world do you think he's going to provide for you?" James couldn't help but laugh out loud while Mirah looked at him curiously.

"What's so funny?" Mirah asked.

"Nothing," James replied, continuing to laugh. He wasn't the shy boy she had known over two years ago. He was a man now and he knew exactly what he wanted and how to deal with Mattie Jones. She would not come between them anymore and this new guy Mirah was seeing didn't have a chance. Their little short week acquaintance is soon about to end, he thought, asking Mirah what she had just said.

"I said you can't be laughing about nothing, so out with it," Mirah told him.

"Okay fine. I was just imagining what your mother was saying," James laughed mimicking her mother.

"Ooh James. I'm going to tell," Mirah laughed hysterically.

"So I'm right?" James asked giving her leg a soft massage.

"Close enough," Mirah responded, tilting her head back to relax. Mirah was having such a good time with James that she didn't even bring up her relationship with Bryce. Right now she didn't want to think about anything, especially the argument with her mother. James always did know how to make her feel better. It was just like old times and it felt good. There were no expectations of her. She could be herself, relax, and unwind. There were no lies hanging out in the air. Their friendship was unbreakable and Mirah couldn't figure out for the life of her why they weren't together. Sure James had explained that he wanted her to finish her education. Mirah saw that as no reason why he would sever their relationship. They were connected in a way that would bind them together forever, like two parents apart but tied by a child. She knew James would always be there for her and maybe that's why it was so hard for her to explain. How could she tell the only man she ever loved that she was in love with somebody else? Was it possible to love two men? This is all too damn confusing, she thought, bewildered at how she felt about the men in her life.

"Hey, what are you thinking about over there?" James asked.

"Just thinking about you and the real reason we broke up. James, it's been over two years and things just don't make any sense.

"You're right. There's so much we need to talk about and we will do that tonight."

"Tonight."

"Yes. That's why I came to get you so early. You need to prepare an over night bag," he told her, pulling into the parking lot of the Marriott hotel.

"James, I don't think that's such a good idea," Mirah told him. Not only would her mother freak out if she wasn't there but she was afraid of being alone with him. The chemistry they once shared was still there and she didn't want to think about what may happen if they were alone again. She couldn't give in to those feelings; she was moving on with her life and she would always remain friends with James. She wondered what in the world he wanted to speak with her about and why now? James always wanted to move to the West Coast. Was he leaving her? She couldn't imagine them being so far apart. She agreed to meet him tonight.

"Come on, let's eat," James said, rubbing his hungry stomach.

"All right, but promise me you won't eat the whole buffet," Mirah teased. If she ate the way he did her body would bust right open; she wondered how he stayed so fit. His appetite had always been that way. They walked through the revolving door together.

"So, how is school going?" James asked as they returned to their table.

"It's going fine," Mirah replied. She couldn't believe all the food James had piled on his plate. "You sure you can handle all that?"

"Piece of cake," James said stuffing his mouth with a slice of golden hot pancakes. He never put more on his plate than he could handle and he would devour the crisp bacon, sausage patties, potatoes, omelet, and grits he had on his plate. He wanted this meal to carry him throughout the rest of the day so he could concentrate all his attention on the beautiful lady that sat before him. Mirah had sure matured over the past few years. Her body was curved to perfection; definitely different from the girl he met when they were in high school. He was looking forward to having her for dessert tonight.

"I'm really curious to what you want to discuss with me tonight," Mirah said in between bites of food.

"Well you'll just have to wait until tonight to see," he replied reaching into his pocket. "Here is the electronic key card to the hotel room," he said sliding it to her.

"James, you know I don't like to wait. Just give me some kind of hint?"

"It's something that I've wanted to do for a long time," James responded. He should have never listened to a word her damn parents said to him two years ago. He had tried to be a respectable man. They said if he really loved her than he would put her needs first. *'Well how is she going to finish school if you all have children? It's not often our kind get a full scholarship,'* they reminded him. They had a damn answer for everything. Her mother nagged the shit out of him until he finally caved in. He had never seen that woman so happy. She said: "It's about time you get your life together. Time will have flown by and Mirah will be out of school. If you two feel the same way about each other, then you will have our blessings in marrying our daughter." For some reason James needed her approval back then. He knew she had never too much cared for him but the idea of her giving him their blessings meant a lot. Besides, a lot of the things they said did make sense. Hell, he was just out of high school with no job. He couldn't take care himself let alone a family. All he knew is he loved Mirah and wanted to be with her forever.

Chapter 8

James dropped Mirah off and headed back to the hotel. He would have liked to come in so her parents could see the real man he had turned out to be. Their very first impressions of him wasn't good; ever since they had been together her parents had treated him coldly. He was referring to Mattie Jones in particular, remembering the first time he'd meet her. She was out right demanding, wanted to know all his personal business. Who were his parents? Where did they live? What church did he belong to? What were his intentions with their daughter and what did he plan to do in his future?

James could vividly remember the heat building in his body from anger. You'd think that information would be learned over time but not with Mattie. She was outright direct like a viscous snake preying on her next meal. For goodness sake, they had just started dating. It wasn't like he had been asking for her hand in marriage, like he was going to do tonight. What a sight this was going to be, James thought to himself. Mattie Jones would probably throw her hands up in the air and ask the good 'Lawd' to take her right now. *'Lawd, why did my daughter have to meet this heathen?'* he imagined her saying. That was her signature line and back then those words really hurt him as a young boy. She called him 'no good' right in front of his face. Damn, can you believe the nerve of that shit?

James felt like he'd done pretty well with his life considering the awful circumstances he had to deal with as a child. He never knew who his biological father was and remembered, at the age of five, his mother dropping him off to the state to grow up from home to home in the foster care system. Most of the foster parents were nice but he always felt like the oddball because he was different. He wasn't their natural child, always getting the leftovers from food to clothing of what their children didn't want. That shit was hard enough but to learn your mother had dropped you off to run the streets smoking crack was just downright cruel. It stripped his emotions away in every sense and he became outright angry towards everyone. He was getting into fights, skipping school, and hanging in the streets selling reefer at the age of fourteen. Damn, his life was fucked up and it almost went straight to hell when he was busted. He was sent to the juvenile courts and thought he would be facing time behind bars. God surely sent angels down that day because the judge decided his life was worth saving and sent him to the best foster parents ever, Cynthia and Matthew King.

The day James stepped into that house he felt loved. At first it was hard to come to grips with because he never had a real father figure in his life before. Matthew, his dad, would spend as much time with him as his own biological son, Will, short for William. His father encouraged, enlightened, and educated them on everything from politics to social problems. Sometimes he had wondered if he was dreaming. His father showed him how to be a man and he was glad somebody showed him the good side of life. He left that negativity bullshit behind him, starting his life anew. He had a new family, home, school, and a new girlfriend, Mirah Jones, who he fell crazy in love with. It was love at first sight and he never imagined her parents to be so bitchy. And getting back to when he first met them he still couldn't believe all the questions they had asked him. Hell, he felt like he was on some kind of interview and didn't even have a job. The questions were too personal and he told them that after Mirah grilled her mother with the most upsetting *'how could you'* look.

Mattie stood straight up and spewed venom at both of them, especially her daughter for acting so disrespectful. 'What kind of secrets was he hiding if he couldn't even be honest.'

Mattie Jones threw her signature hands up in the air saying 'Lawd, Lawd, Lawd, please don't send no *no good* boys up in my house again!' It was unbelievable and her father Willie looked just as embarrassed as Mirah, but he never stepped in to tell his wife otherwise. Mirah was so upset; he had never seen her snap like that before. She attacked her mother like a vicious lion protecting her cubs. He respected her even more for that and, thanks to Mattie Jones, it made their relationship even closer. It had been unbreakable he thought pulling back into the parking lot of the hotel. Enough about thinking about crazy Mattie Jones. He would have a lifetime of doing that. He went up to his room to relax for the rest of the afternoon.

Chapter 9

Mirah waved goodbye to Callie, who had dropped her off at the same hotel she had eaten breakfast at earlier today. It was now seven 'o clock and Mirah was glad to get away from home. She had only been back one day now and her mother was already starting all kinds of drama. The worst of it all was her father was caught right in the middle. Her mother didn't speak to him or her, which was a good excuse for Mirah to get out of the house. Her mother just said, *'Do as you please,'* so Mirah packed her bags and left. It wasn't like she was trying to be disrespectful or anything but she was tired of being embarrassed. She endured that humility growing up and definitely didn't want to go through this crap in the future. Mirah was grown and it was about time her mother treated her that way. It doesn't mean that she loved her any less but she was glad her father had finally put his foot down.

Hopefully, this time away would give her mother a chance to cool down. They both needed time to get their thoughts together but Mirah had to deal with another issue right now, James. She wondered what he wanted to talk with her about. His mood today was different; it was the serious look that concerned her. Whatever it was she knew it was big. It was something that was going to change her life. The only plausible rationale she could think of was that he was planning on moving. It wasn't just any move it was to the West Coast. He always used to tell her how he wanted to move to Los Angeles. James boasted how nice it was when his parents took him down there on vacation once.

As selfish as it might seem, Mirah didn't want him to move far away. What right did she have when they weren't even together, besides she claimed to be in love with another man? That's what she had planned on telling him tonight. She would have done it this morning but chickened out with a bunch of excuses. Mirah hadn't been in the mood to talk about anything then, but she was going to get it out now, she thought, pushing the elevator button. She was actually relieved to take the few second ride to the eleventh floor by herself. She took a few deep breaths and exhaled, getting her thoughts together. Out of all the years they had been together, he still had that effect on her. She loved James but she could not continue to live her life in limbo. Mirah needed some stability, one thing that really attracted her to Bryce. She didn't know if his age had anything to do with it. Quite honestly, it probably did. He was more mature, not saying that James wasn't but it was on a different level. He had everything going for him…looks, a great personality, plus a career, which afforded him lots of money. Now, to be real, that really excited Mirah. She had never been in a home that big before, and to think, all that could be hers if she played her cards right. She was definitely going for the gusto, not that money meant everything, but a girl would be a fool not to want that she convinced herself. She only hoped James and she would remain close friends, especially since he would be moving so far away.

  Mirah stepped off the elevator and walked down the long corridors until she got to room 1170. She took another deep breath and knocked on the door. James had nothing on except for some silk boxers. He was looking fine, good enough to eat, but Mirah didn't come here for that tonight. She had to stay focused. She entered the room trying to avoid the physical chemistry building up inside of her.

  "Prompt as always," James said, closing the door. He couldn't help but notice Mirah scanning his body, from head to toe. Yeah, he knew he had it going on but it still felt good to be looked at this way, with those big beautiful brown eyes. That chemistry alone made his senses heat. It was going to be hard waiting, after he proposed, before they made love. This night was going to be special and it was definitely worth the wait. He licked his lips seducing her more of what she was going to have for dessert tonight.

"Are we going out?" Mirah asked foolishly. She already knew the answer, giving him a hint of what was not about to happen.

"No, I thought we'd just relax. After the morning you've had it just seemed sensible. I've drawn up some water in the hot tub," he told her. James already had everything prepared. He had a tray with shrimp cocktails, cheese, crackers, strawberries, and Alizé wine to wash everything down with. When the time was right he was going to slip the ring on her finger and ask her to be his wife.

"James, I wasn't expecting this."

"Well, you know I'd do anything for you," he replied kissing her on the lips. He hadn't tasted her in a long time; he parted her lips to enter for more.

"James, wait, I can't do this," she said pulling away.

"Why?"

"Because I'm seeing someone else," Mirah uttered, glad it was out in the open. She was tired of thinking he could have her whenever he wanted. Sex with no ties wouldn't be in the picture any more, she thought to herself.

"Is it something serious?" James asked, surprised by her reaction. From what he was told she had just started seeing someone else. Not even dating, hardly enough time to just drop him to the curve. Besides, he could still see the flame in her eyes. She was still in love with him, so he wanted to know the deal.

"Yes, it's serious."

"And how long have you been dating?" James asked, starting to become irritated. She was definitely spoiling the mood.

"What's with all the questions?"

"I'm just asking a simple question," James told her. "Why are you being so evasive?"

"I'm not. It's just a little personal talking to you about this. I'm sure you don't tell me about every woman that flocks around you."

"All right, fine. I know the answer anyway. You couldn't possibly be serious about someone you've met just a week ago."

Mirah couldn't believe what she was hearing. How in the world did he know her personal business? It had to be Callie, she thought, biting down on her lower lip in anger.

"For your information I'm in love with him," she retaliated. That wasn't how she planned for it to come out, but right now he deserved it. Who in the hell did he think he was spying on? And she couldn't wait to give Callie a piece of her mind. She thought they were best friends, but she obviously couldn't trust her either.

"In love! What? You're trying to be vengeful or something?"

"Vengeful. No, I'm just simply stating the truth."

"So what, he fucked you or is it the money or both?" James yelled. "Tell me."

"That's none of your business," Mirah screamed back.

He surprised her when he grabbed her and threw her on the bed. "What, you're fucking somebody in a week span now?"

"James, you're hurting me. Let me go," Mirah demanded. "I'm not some kind of whore," she vented, wiggling, trying to get free.

"You're certainly acting like one. Now get out," he told her while she scrambled to her feet. "I hope the money is good but that shit won't make you happy forever," he yelled, as Mirah smacked the shit out of him. Tears were rolling down her face; she stormed out the room. When he slammed the door, he broke down and released his own tears. A part of him wanted to run after her. This wasn't supposed to happen. He had wanted to ask her to be his wife but he would not beg any woman. Tired, James slipped into the hot tub and downed the Aliźe that was chilled and refreshing. He definitely needed that, after what had just happened.

****

"Mirah, what's wrong," Callie asked, pulling out of the parking lot.

"How could you tell James my personal business?" Mirah asked. Tears started to flood down her face again.

"Girl, what are you talking about?"

"Come on, don't play games with me," Mirah replied cutting her friend the evil eye.

"First of all, I don't play games with no one," Callie replied, on the defensive. "And, second of all, I didn't go gossiping your business to James."

"Well I don't see how he just all of a sudden knew about Bryce. I've only told you, Marcy, and my parents, and it certainly couldn't be them."

"Knowing your mother she'd probably love to tell James, since she hates him so much. Somehow, James must have pried the information out of Tyron, and believe me I didn't tell him anything personal. He asked about you and I told him. I'm not about to start lying to my boyfriend, so you need to get over this silly drama," Callie spurted out in an angry tone.

"Why did you have to go there and talk about my parents? At least I have a mother," Mirah attacked, with her third cold blow of the day. It seemed like she was getting into an argument with everyone she was running in to today.

"That's low, especially coming from you," Callie said. She dodged out of traffic pulling abruptly over to the curb. "Now get out and have a nice life," she said angrily.

Mirah couldn't believe this. She got out and began walking briskly down Broadway Street. The cold air froze the tears on her face and her body grew stiff from the frigid air. She managed to find a quiet spot on the freezing bench while her trembling fingers dialed the number to Bryce.

"Hello."

"Bryce, I've had the most awful day," Mirah cried out through the phone.

"Sweetie, calm down," Bryce told her while she rattled off everything that went wrong. He could hardly catch her words, her phone faded in and out. He grew alarmed when she told him that her best friend Callie had thrown her out in the middle of the street because of an argument they had.

"Mirah, you need to get home," Bryce told her. "I don't want you out there upset and vulnerable," he said, asking where she was. "Can you catch the bus or a cab home?"

"No," Mirah cried. "I don't have a dime to my name and my credit cards are all up to the limit," she replied, crying even more. The last thing she wanted was to call her mother after she made such a big stink over being treated like a child. She was grown and an adult would surely know how to find a way to get home. She cried, rocking back and forth.

"Hold on," Bryce said clicking to a free line. He dialed the number to information before tying Mirah in on the line.

"This is information, how can I help you?" a lady's voice rang through the receiver.

"Yes, I would like the number to the nearest cab company on Broadway Street," Bryce told her. He jotted down all the information and then thanked the operator. He then dialed the number to the cab company to pick Mirah up.

"All right, they should be there in a few minutes," Bryce told her.

"Thanks so much. I wish you were here with me right now. I really don't feel like going home."

"I wish I could come up but there's an important meeting on my calendar for tomorrow. Do you want me to arrange for you to stay at a hotel for the night."

"No, you've done enough," Mirah said, thanking him again. "It's just really good to hear your voice," she told him.

"You don't have to keep thanking me. Be expecting a credit card in the next few days. I don't ever want you out there without money in your pockets."

"That's not necessary," Mirah said, calling out for the cab coming down the street.

"Don't argue with me on this one," Bryce responded. "Now call me when you get home."

"Yes sirrr!" Mirah replied, smiling for the first time this evening. "I love you," she told him before hanging up. Mirah sat back in the cab and relaxed on the drive home. She was glad her mother wasn't home and her father didn't question her as she slipped up stairs to her room and into her bed. This was sure one helluva night, she thought to herself.

Chapter 10

Mirah was so disappointed on Christmas morning. Her whole time home had been one big fiasco. Normally, she did her holiday shopping with Callie, but she hadn't spoken with her since the day Callie kicked her out of the car over a week ago. And to make matters worse, she had not spoken to Bryce much either. He had to leave town on an emergency business trip and the few times they spoke were brief.

Mirah eased her way into the hot shower, spending an extra half-hour enjoying the warmth of the soothing water. Her skin was dry to the bone; she toweled off and slipped into some clothes after rubbing lotion on her ashy body. She smelled the aroma of bacon escaping through the air and hurried down the stairs to enjoy her mother's food. At least they had made up, and Mirah was even closer to her mother now. They had a new understanding for each other, she thought, making her way in the kitchen.

"Merry Christmas," Mirah told her mother, giving her a kiss on the cheek.

"Same to you dear," Mattie said while she continued stirring the grits.

"Can I help with anything?"

"Nope, everything is almost ready. I've even set the breakfast table," she smiled. "Now you go and relax and let Mamma serve you today."

Mirah couldn't help but cheer up after seeing her mother in such good spirits. "Are you sure you don't need any help?"

"I'm positive, now you just go on and relax. You're going to be busy enough opening all those gifts under the tree."

"All what gifts? Mamma, I thought we all agreed to one gift exchange this year."

"I thought so too, but you really surprised us this time. Sorry I ruined your surprise but there was a whole package of gifts delivered this morning. I took the liberty of putting them all under the tree."

Mirah stood there puzzled while her mother continued preparing breakfast. It had to be Bryce, she thought, hurrying to the living room. *Oh my goodness,* Mirah gasped, looking at all the beautiful boxes under the tree. Each present was wrapped in the most beautiful paper she had ever seen. The green, gold, red, and purple wrapping illuminated the living room as Mirah took a peek at the nametags attached. All of her gifts were marked with a red heart; her heart bubbled with excitement. Bryce had even bought gifts for her parents and labeled them from her. She sat back in her chair taking everything in.

Oh Bryce, I wish you were here with me, Mirah thought to herself. He said he didn't think he would be able to make it since he was stopping home in Cleveland on the way back. She couldn't blame his family for wanting to spend the day with him. She hoped she would at least hear from him. Her thoughts were interrupted when her mother called out that breakfast was ready.

"Everything looks delicious," Mirah said, sitting to the table. "Where is Daddy at?"

"He's coming," Mattie said. She took a seat herself. "You know it takes him some extra time now that he has to put his teeth in."

Mirah couldn't do nothing but laugh thinking back to when she first saw her father without any teeth. He looked like a totally different person and Mirah had to restrain herself from staring so much.

"Merry Christmas Daddy," Mirah said as he walked into the room. He gave her a big kiss on the cheek before kissing her stubborn mother, who waved him off embarrassingly. They still act like a young couple in love, Mirah laughed to herself.

"Breakfast sure enough smells good."

"Thank you, honey. I enjoy cooking. We could have been rich by now if we had gone into the food business," Mattie replied, filling everyone's glass with orange juice.

"Now you know you don't like anyone messing up your food and you couldn't run a restaurant by yourself. Besides, money isn't everything, and I certainly don't need to put on any extra pounds," he said, rubbing his stomach. "Now let's say grace so we can throw down. I'm starved," Willie added before giving blessings.

"Amen," Mattie pronounced loudly. Everyone dove into their food.

Mirah thought about James while she watched her father stack his plate full. They always ate enough for two, but you couldn't tell by the way James kept his physique in perfect condition. Her father, on the other hand, needed to slow down. She had even tried to get him on a health regimen. *"Why eat turkey meat when you have the good taste of pork."* He said *"I've been eating like this all my life and I'm not about to change now."* Mirah tried everything from shopping to secretly substituting food for the healthier kind. He always noticed. He finally broke down and promised that he would cut back but that he was going to continue enjoying his food until the day he died. Mirah gave him a continuous stare; he reluctantly put back the extra sausage patty he was going to add to his plate.

Mirah smiled; he finally took her feelings into consideration. If only James could have done the same. She couldn't believe the way things had ended, and she even broke down and sent him a Christmas card with a letter attached. When she didn't hear a response from him she pretty much knew things were over between them. They would never be able to continue being friends but she loved him nevertheless. James was her first love.

****

Mirah felt like a little child while she sat around the tree opening gifts. She let her parents open their gifts first, looking on in anticipation. She wondered what surprises they would dig out.

"Would you look a here," Willie said, unwrapping a set of golf clubs. "Mirah, how in the world could you afford these top of the line clubs?"

"Bryce and I picked them out," Mirah lied. She found herself doing a lot of this lately. She explained how she worked extra hours to help with the gift.

"Well these are certainly the best clubs I've ever owned," Willie said, swinging one back and forth. "Baby girl, you certainly didn't have to go all out to buy these. I would have been happy with far less expensive ones. Next time keep that in mind," he told his daughter.

"Willie, now you know you is going to enjoy those clubs. I can see the look in your eyes," Mattie told him. "Just enjoy this day without all the worries. Remember we have to let Mirah be an adult. I'm sure she has better sense than going into debt buying Christmas gifts."

"Okay," Mirah said, motioning her mother to open her gift. "Don't worry, you know I always can find the best sales."

"Yes ma'am," Mattie replied. "Mamma show have taught you well," she said, ripping the paper off her box.

"Mattie, I swear you act just like a child," Willie said, shaking his head. "My big baby," he added, giving her a wink.

"Not in front of Mirah," Mattie said blushing. After thirty years of marriage he still had that effect on her while she opened the box.

"Oh my goodness!" Mattie gasped. She pulled out a stunning ivory church hat. It was difficult to describe but it was just perfect for her. Mattie ran her fingers along the gold trim. She knew just the suit she would wear this with, she thought, putting the hat on her head. "Now wait 'til I walk into church with this on," Mattie said, modeling around the room with a huge grin on her face. "Thank you honey, I love it," she told Mirah, giving her a hug.

"I'm glad you do," Mirah said, handing her the gift she had purchased for them herself. "This is for you and dad."

"Mirah this is too much," she said ripping the envelope open. "Tickets to a Broadway show in New York. Oh, this is perfect," Mattie said excitedly. "Maybe I'll wear this hat. You know we have to be looking sharp amongst all those rich folks."

Mirah just laughed while her father continued shaking his head. "I've also reserved a hotel room for when you come up to New York. Maybe we can go out to dinner before you head to the show. Just let me know so I can make reservations in advance."

"That sounds like a wonderful idea. Honey, you should go with us to the theatre."

"Nope. This is your night out on the town," Mirah told her. She opened her gift from them and was surprised to pull a leather coat from the neatly wrapped box. It went perfect with the black suit Bryce had bought her from Bloomingdale's. He even matched a Coach handbag to go along with a note to retrieve what was inside when she was alone.

"Well, this really has been a wonderful Christmas," Mirah said. She pitched in to clean up and came across one last envelope for her mother from Bryce.

"Look mom, here's one last gift," she said handing it over.

Mattie took the envelope and ripped it open. "Oh 'Lawdy'...'Lawd' have mercy," she screamed jumping out the seat.

"What is it?" Willie asked as he watched his insane wife.

"Sketches of our new house. Look a here, look a here," Mattie waved, almost hitting Willie in the face.

Mirah looked on until the phone rang. She rushed out of the room hoping Bryce would be on the other end.

"Merry Christmas," Mirah answered.

"Merry Christmas to you, sweetheart."

"Bryce, I'm so glad you called. We just finished opening our gifts. I can't believe what you did, thanks for everything. I thought Mamma was going to pass out when she saw the designs for the house."

"Well I'm glad everyone enjoyed them," Bryce said.

"We did, but you really should not have gone all out like this. I'll just be happy to have you in my arms again. So when are you coming home?"

"Well, my family is trying to get me to stay until after New Year's Day."

"Oh, I was hoping to see you before then but I'm sure your family must be thrilled that you were able to make it home for the holidays."

"They are, in fact they're really looking forward to meeting you," Bryce told her.

"Really, I didn't know you told your parents about us," Mirah replied, blushing. Bryce must have really loved her if he told his parents about their relationship.

"Sure did," Bryce said. "I have to go, everyone is waiting for me so they can bless the food. I love you," Bryce told her before hanging up.

****

    Mirah was glad to be back home. She sunk into the sofa to relax. She had gone over her relative's house for dinner who had prepared enough food for the whole city. She rubbed her aching stomach to sooth it, Mirah was never one to over eat but she outdid herself this time. She would have to do some serious exercise; she vowed to go to the gym to work it off.

    Mirah was actually glad to have the house to herself for some peace and quiet. She literally begged her parents to bring her home, not wanting to go over her father's best friend's house. Tony Keaton was always trying to fix her up with their youngest son Rico, short for Ricardo. Ricardo was fine but always had his ass in trouble. His parents were so naïve. He sold drugs right underneath their own nose. If her mother only knew the real side of Rico, she would have been begging James to marry Mirah a long time ago. Mirah never could understand why they couldn't stand him so much. In fact, James had done pretty well for himself considering the circumstances of his childhood. Rico, on the other hand, was raised by good parents and turned out to be the bad apple of the family. You know, everyone has at least one who is either selling or is strung out on drugs. And Rico has at least two kids out there that he hasn't claimed as his own. That son-of-a-bitch think cause he slings a few dollars their way that he's taking care of his responsibility. Well, that won't cut it, Mirah thought to herself in disgust. Never once had his parents met their grandchildren. He's too ashamed to bring them home since they have different mammas and all. Just lying up with anyone and everyone. He should have thought about all that but the selfish bastard only thinks of numero uno, himself! And his poor mother would probably have a heart attack considering they're so religious and all. What a shame, somebody needed to knock some sense into that boy head. Why should the children suffer, Mirah thought shaking her head? Her thoughts were interrupted by the echo of the doorbell.

"Bryce, what are you doing here?" Mirah asked surprised.

"Well, you said you wanted to see me," Bryce replied. "Are you going to make me stand out here in the cold?" he laughed, shivering. It was freezing cold out here. He brushed the snow off before entering.

"Come in silly. I'm just shocked to see you standing here," Mirah said, taking his coat.

"To be honest, I wanted to see you just as bad," Bryce told her. "Where are your parents?"

"They're gone over to their best friends, the Keaton's, house."

"Good, because I've wanted to do this for weeks," Bryce said, bringing Mirah into his arms. His body temperature instantly rose a few degrees as he traced his lips over hers.

"You've been on my mind so much," Bryce whispered, parting her lips. The sweetness of her tongue brushing up against his gave him an instant erection. "See, look what you've done to me," he told her. He guided her hand down to the bulge in between his pants.

"Naughty me. I have just the cure," Mirah said, disappearing from the room. She quickly returned waving the sweet gifts she had stashed in the purse he had given her for Christmas. "Now, which flavor should I use," Mirah teased, giving him some more kisses. She then unbuckled his pants and let them fall free. Inching his briefs off, she gave Bryce Whitaker the time of his life, his screams of pleasure echoed throughout the house. Afterwards, he returned the favor as her own moans rippled throughout. His tongue worked magic as she grabbed tightly on her thighs. Damn, he was good; her whole body began trembling. Afterwards, he removed the dental dam and made passionate love to her right on the floor. Things became so heated; he touched every inch of her. Bryce teased her firm breast with his hands and then suckled her nipples one by one. He stroked her on top, from behind, and then ended up on the stairs. She rode him like a wild stallion. When it was over he just held her in his arms. They sat there for a long time before putting their clothes back on.

Bryce wrapped all the condoms up and took the trash out while Mirah aired the room from their love making. If her parents had walked in on them they would probably have tried to kill him, he thought to himself. But he couldn't resist when Mirah dropped down on her knees. She sure knew how to satisfy her man, he thought, making his way back inside with more gifts for her.

"What is this?" Mirah asked.

"Just open them."

"Bryce, you've already done so much. I can't continue to accept all these gifts."

"Why not. I enjoy doing things for you," he said brushing his lips over hers again.

"You better stop teasing me with those kisses before I have you on the floor again."

"That's not a bad idea but if we get started again it definitely would be hard for me to stop," Bryce told her. "I wouldn't want your mamma walking in…she might kill us both," he laughed.

"I wouldn't doubt that," Mirah replied, imitating her mother: 'Lawdy, 'Lawdy,' 'Lawdy'…the devil is in my house tonight. Oh, Willie look at this here disrespectful gal. Oh, my 'Lawd,' I thought we done raised her better than this. Please save her, please dear 'Lawd' I beg of you," Mirah called out throwing her hands up in the air.

"Mirah, you are a mess," Bryce laughed.

"Well I know my mother like the back of my hand," she replied. "I love her to death but she can be overbearing at times."

"That's what parents are supposed to do. If they didn't we would have even more social problems than we do now. Some parents just don't give a damn and their children carry that same attitude," Bryce said. He began to suckle on the nape of her neck. "Umm, you taste so good."

"I agree," Mirah purred to the touch of his lips. "I'm the first to admit that I'm not perfect but I try to do good by everyone."

"No one is perfect. Now finish opening your gifts," Bryce told her.

"All right," Mirah replied. She ripped the package open; there was a cell phone and a VISA credit card held together by a gold ribbon.

"Bryce…"

"Don't start fussing," he said before she could complete her sentence. Bryce pulled her in his arms and relaxed for the next few hours. He then called a cab to take him to the airport so he could rent a car to drive home to New York. He was relieved he left before her parents came home. He was not in the mood to be bothered with Mattie Jones.

Chapter 11

Mirah couldn't believe Bryce had invited her to come along to Cleveland, Ohio with him for New Year's Day. She packed the last of her bags and set them by the door. Mirah took one last run through the house to make sure everything was in order. Everything was off, the house was clean, and she was ready to go. She was glad that she wasn't going to bring in the new year alone. Her parents, at the last minute, decided to go down South to Alabama with the Keaton's. Her mother didn't want to pass up the chance to visit her brother so they packed up and left. Mirah was surprised, not that they left, but because they didn't even ask if she wanted to go. They probably knew the answer and besides her mother was making every effort to treat her like an adult. She would make sure she called her mother later to tell them of her plans. Right now she had to get herself together, wondering what Bryce parents would think about her.

Mirah tried to sit and relax but she was too nervous. What if his parents hated her? What if his sister felt the same? She was traveling a long way with a man she barely knew. Sure they had been intimate with each other, but other than the basic facts she knew very little about him. He had not filled her in on personal details about his life. Maybe this was his way of doing this or maybe he was just taking her along because he felt sorry for her and didn't want to leave her alone. Maybe he had no intentions of even introducing her to his family. All kinds of questions began racing through her mind as she heard a horn blow outside. By the time she made it to the door, Bryce was already heading up the steps.

"I'm all packed and ready to go."

"Great. Let me just use your facilities and I'll be ready to go," Bryce said, kissing her on the lips.

Mirah took one more run through the house to make sure everything was in order. It was just a habit. She locked up and helped Bryce load her luggage into the car.

"I'm surprised we didn't catch a plane," Mirah said, while they backed out of the driveway.

"I've been up in the air so much this year, I'm actually looking forward to driving," Bryce replied.

"So how far is the drive to Cleveland?"

"It's a little over seven hours. And don't worry, I'll make stops on the way," he told her.

Mirah smiled, releasing a sigh of relief. She hated when she rode with someone who liked to drive straight through…didn't even like to stop for a bathroom break. She was thinking of James, in particular, who threw a fit when she asked him to stop so they could get something to eat. He said stopping would break his momentum. He had every thing timed out to the tee and didn't like to get off course, especially if it wasn't an emergency. Sometimes Mirah didn't drink anything when she traveled with him just so she wouldn't have to hear his complaining. She wondered how his holidays were. For some reason he kept coming back into her thoughts. Mirah didn't like the way things ended. She never wanted their relationship to end on a sour note; they shared too many good years together, Mirah thought quietly to herself.

"You're mighty quiet over there. What are you thinking about?" Bryce asked, turning on to I-495.

"Nothing. I'm just glad to be with you," Mirah replied.

"Same here. You've been the one bright spot in my life," he smiled.

From I-495, Bryce continued on the New Jersey turnpike I-95. He had just made it past I-280 before Mirah drifted off to sleep. Just like a baby, Bryce smiled to himself. She looked so beautiful sitting over there. Everything about her was so pure and innocent. She had never been with a real man before and he hardly considered her high school boyfriend as one. He had so much more he could offer her, and in the little amount of time they had been together she had captured his heart. She knew how to make him laugh; she knew how to sooth his worries with those magical hands of hers. Mirah gave herself completely without ever asking for anything in return. Never once had she said 'buy me this, pay me that, or can I borrow this,' especially considering she grew up in a poor household. When he tried to shower her with gifts, he nearly had to beg her to take them. She was so genuine, a woman he respected enough to bring home to his mother. Mirah had opened her arms and invited him into her family. As crazy as her mother was she welcomed him in nevertheless. Her actions meant a lot to Bryce and he only hoped his parents would reciprocate the same feelings. That would be too easy, Bryce thought to himself. Somehow he prepared himself for his mother's reaction, after all Mirah was the same age as his younger sister.

Bryce decided not to let his thoughts worry him. Heck, he wasn't that much older than his sister, he thought, slipping in his 'Body and Soul" CD to relax to the comforting sounds of the old school greatest hits. He rode for hours along I-80, a never ending highway that was filled with traffic.

"Mirah, honey, wake up," Bryce said tapping her lightly on the shoulder.

"Where are we?"

"We're almost in Ohio, about two hours from Cleveland," he told her. "I'm going to fill up the gas tank and then we can stop and get something to eat."

"I can't believe you let me sleep for so long. Sorry for not being much company," Mirah told him.

"Don't apologize. I'm just glad you're with me," Bryce replied with a kiss. "Come on let's restock on some junk food," he said, opening the door.

Mirah couldn't believe all the snacks they had grabbed. The attendant rang up their order and packed their bag full to the capacity with everything from potato chips down to chocolate peanut butter cups. The only decent thing she grabbed were a handful of Nutri-grain bars. Mirah was actually glad they had stopped at a restaurant for a wholesome meal. She had some of the best french toast she ever tasted, with sausage patties and cheese eggs to go along.

Mirah made sure she stayed up the remainder of the ride. The two hours spun by and before she knew it Bryce was exiting off I-271. He reserved them a room at a hotel right off the freeway in Beachwood, which was only about ten minutes from his parents' house in Shaker Heights. Mirah was really nervous about meeting his family. She wished they could have relaxed for the rest of the evening but they quickly showered, changed and headed back out.

Mirah took a few deep breaths before they pulled around the driveway to his parents' home. No, it was an estate. Their home looked like a hotel itself. Bryce opened the door. What was a poor girl like her getting into? Bryce gave her a firm squeeze on the hand for reassurance. He could read her mind, but it didn't help. A knot formed at the bottom of her stomach.

"Are you going to be okay?" Bryce asked.

"Yes, I'm just a little nervous," Mirah, replied.

"You'll be fine," Bryce assured her with a kiss on the cheek. "Now let's hurry up and get inside before we freeze."

Bryce's sister opened the door; he picked her up swinging her around in greeting.

"Boy, put me down!" she said slapping him playfully on the shoulder.

"All right," Bryce replied, before introducing her to Mirah.

"It's good to meet you," Briana said. She gave her a friendly hug before turning her attention back to her brother.

"Bryce, how did you get such an attractive woman to fall for your ugly butt," she said laughing.

"Don't forget we came from the same gene pool," Bryce told her. "And you can't deny that I have the better looks," Bryce teased. "Damn, I'm just too fine."

"Boy, please. Don't let that big head of yours swell before I pull out your baby pictures."

"I'd like to see those," Mirah added to the conversation.

"Bri, don't you dare. You're trying to embarrass me already," Bryce said. His parents came into the foyer to see what all the commotion was about.

"You two are always quarreling about something. Just like old times," his mother smiled.

"Mother, I swear Bri is an alien," Bryce said giving his mother a hug. "This is my girlfriend, Mirah Jones," he said, formally introducing her to his parents.

"It's nice to finally meet you," Diane said, shaking Mirah's hand. "Bryce has really said some wonderful things about you but he's never mentioned how young you are. How old are you, dear?"

"Diane, a woman never tells her age," Isek said, giving his wife a stern look.

"Mirah, I hope I'm not offending you. It's just that you seem to be around the same age as Briana."

"Mother, don't embarrass me," Bryce told her. "If there's going to be a problem we can just leave," he told her.

"There's no need to do that," Diane told her son. "And don't you speak to me in that tone, I'm still your mother no matter how grown you are."

"Come on Mirah," let's go in the kitchen where we can talk more privately," Diane insisted, taking her by the hand.

Mirah couldn't refuse. She followed behind her quickened footsteps. The last thing she wanted was to cause a scene, especially now since this was her first time meeting them. Mirah took a few deep breaths to sooth her nerves.

"Mother, behave," Bryce called out as they continued down the hall. He wasn't too worried because he knew Bri would not let things get out of control.

In the kitchen Diane was like a Drill Sergeant. She wanted to know Mirah's whole life story in a two-minute sound bite. Her main and only objective was to find out if Mirah was after her son's money, and the answer was: Hell yes! What woman wouldn't want all of this, especially growing up poor! It wasn't like she had gone looking for Bryce, but now that she had it, there was no way in the world she was about to give it up. Not even his mamma was going to stop her.

Mirah just simply went along with the flow after Briana argued with her mother back and forth. What a bitch, Mirah thought to herself. If only her mother was here, two of a kind. Mattie Jones, poor and all, would kick Mrs. Whitaker's snobby little ass. She could hear her mother saying, 'Well tell me about your son and how he can make my little girl happy. You know the 'Lawd' was a humble man; you can't buy your way into the heavenly gates. Amen, praise be God,' Mattie would say looking her dead in the eye. Mirah did the same. She wasn't about to let Diane intimidate her...money and all Mirah had dignity and respect.

"Mrs. Whitaker, I'll be more than happy to discuss the details of my life but right now I'm really exhausted. Maybe before I leave we can spend some time to really get to know one another," Mirah told her.

"Mother, your behavior is inappropriate," Briana said, embarrassed. "If you keep this up I'll leave as well."

"Oh Briana, I swear you and Bryce act just alike. Mirah it is not my intent to be rude," Diane said, shaking her head. "I'm just simply trying to get to know my…"

"Okay mother," Briana said, cutting her off abruptly. "We get the point." She grabbed a tray filled with fancy hors d'oeuvre. "You all must be starved," she said to Mirah.

"I'm sure they are," Diane added, picking up a few trays herself. "Rosa is preparing a fabulous meal for us. She had to run to the store," she added. Diane then turned around and sashayed her behind right out of the room.

Mirah picked up a few trays and followed.

"You'll have to forgive my mother," Briana apologized, embarrassed.

"Don't worry my mother is just the same," Mirah smiled. "I'm definitely used to the unexpected when it comes to my parents."

"Wow, two of a kind," Briana laughed. "Then you certainly can understand why I was so happy to leave home."

"Sure do," Mirah replied. "Total freedom…I love it."

"I think we're going to get along great. Mother will warm up to you, just give her a little time," Briana smiled. "She gives everyone a hard time," she added, before they joined the others in the dining room.

Mirah grinned as Bryce gave her a *'are you okay'* look. She just continued smiling. He immediately cut his eyes over to his sister for the real truth. She automatically began shaking her head. Briana went over to converse with her brother while Mirah helped Diane set up the food trays.

"You really have a lovely home," Mirah complimented, trying to make small talk. The dining room was elegant with mahogany wood tables and chairs to match. The cushion of the seats was a rich ivory color, which matched the table runner trimmed in artsy fabric. The dining room table was long enough to seat an army and the whole décor was meticulous. The gold trim linen, with a hue of burgundy and green went well with the holiday colors.

"Well thank you," Diane replied. "My husband built this home with his own bare hands," she boasted proudly.

"That must make it even more rewarding."

"Yes it does. We worked very hard to get where we are," she said sternly. What she really wanted to say was *'so don't your poor little ass think you can come up here and take it all away,'* she smiled.

Mirah just stared while this viscous dog continued with her attack. She felt just like prey and wouldn't be surprised if Diane started barking, she thought to herself. Well, she could do whatever she wanted, but Mirah definitely wasn't about to let his mother intimidate her or send her running. She gave her a hard stare of her own to let her know she wasn't the one who could be easily run over.

Diane looked like she wanted to say something but Bryce came over and wrapped his arms around Mirah.

"So, how is Mother behaving?" Bryce asked in a serious tone.

Diane nearly choked on one of the quiche hors' d oeuvres. She tried to clear her throat so she could speak.

"Are you okay? Mirah asked. She wanted to bust out laughing. It served that old goat right, she thought, handing her a napkin.

"Thank you."

"You're welcome," Mirah replied, assuring Bryce that everything was fine. She knew just how to handle their kind. Feed them with compliments and let them think they are right and they'll be eating out the palm of your hand. Diane took all the bait...Mirah's journalism skills kicked in just in the knick of time. She knew how to stand up with the best of them. Mattie Jones taught her that and she thanked God for her mother's wisdom, even though she had not understood it back then.

"Dinner will be served shortly," Diane said. She excused herself for a few moments and gave instructions to Rosa.

Mirah observed how friendly Diane interacted with their hired help. She was actually surprised, considering how rude she had been to her. Maybe Briana was right that her mother would warm up to her in time. The last thing she wanted was to be in conflict with his mother, because when it all boiled down she would always be the first woman in his life. Women can come and go but family is forever, Mirah thought quietly to herself. That much she knew as they sat at the dinner table.

Everything was so beautifully decorated, like in the movies. It must have taken Rosa hours to set up this lavish arrangement. The white porcelain china was immaculate with each piece trimmed in gold. Mirah breathed a sigh of relief that she knew proper table etiquette. She vividly remembered cursing her mother for sending her to all those stupid training sessions for girls. The classes that teach you everything from how to have the perfect posture to eating. 'Thank you mother,' Mirah whispered silently to herself.

Isek blessed the food before everyone started to eat. Mirah was becoming really annoyed at Diane who watched her like a hawk. Just because she was poor didn't mean she had poor table etiquette...for all she knew Mirah could be wealthy, she thought angrily to herself. It wouldn't surprise her one bit if Diane had already done an investigation background check on her. It was just her type, but instead of worrying about her she need to be checking her husband and their hired hand Rosa. Mirah could tell by their eye contact and body language that they had something going on. She could spot shit like that a mile away. She smiled cunningly at Diane. She wondered how long Isek was tapping his maid's ass. Boy, if Diane only knew she would have a fit. Mirah, for the life of her, couldn't understand why she was worried about everything else. She was too stupid to realize what was going on right under her own damn nose.

"Rosa, this meal is absolutely wonderful," Mirah complimented.

"Well thank you," Rosa replied, joining them at the table.

Diane cut her off before she could say another word. She had to be in the spotlight while she boasted about Rosa's culinary skills. She damn near gave a description of her whole resume. Rosa pulled her eyes towards Isek to intervene. He just smiled and Rosa's red face became more irritated. Mirah knew exactly how she felt being under the microscope. She didn't even know Diane, but a few minutes with her was enough!

"So, I hear New York has some of the finest restaurants," Rosa said, cutting back in before she was rudely interrupted.

"Yes, some of the finest in the world," Mirah replied.

By now Diane was boiling hot; Mirah watched on intently. This was certainly the family feud for the rich and the famous she thought quietly to herself. Diane's whole charade of being nice to Rosa was all for show. Looking at them now, Mirah knew they couldn't stand one another. This room was about to explode at any moment and Mirah did not want to be here for the fireworks. The tension was so thick, it was a wonder the rest of the family was so clueless to see what was going on. Maybe Diane did know what her husband was doing behind closed doors, but she wasn't going to give up all her richness just so the hired maid could step in her place. She'd probably rather rot in hell. Mirah actually felt sorry for Diane. If it were on the other shoe, Mirah would not take that shit. She would go right up and confront Rosa, and then kick her ass straight to the curb. Surely Isek wouldn't be foolish enough to give all this up for the hired help. Diane was the kind to suck a person dry…right down to the china they were eating off of. If Mirah intuition was correct, she wondered how long Diane would put up with her husband's behavior. This type of thing could drive a woman crazy, and Mirah would not wish that on her worst enemy, she thought quietly to herself.

Chapter 12

"Mirah answer the door," Bryce called out from the shower. "I ordered us some room service."

Mirah rolled from under the covers completely naked. The cold air hit her instantly; she grabbed a robe and headed towards the door.

"Good morning, room service," the lady announced. She rolled the cart into their room.

Mirah smiled in greeting and handed the lady some money Bryce had left on the table. "Keep the change," Mirah told her before she left.

"Thank you," the lady smiled. "Just leave your cart outside the door when you're done or you can give us a call."

"Will do," Mirah replied shutting the door. The aroma of the food smelled delicious. She took a quick peep at what was underneath the lid. There were plates filled with fresh omelets, bacon, fresh fruit, and a muffin. They had orange juice and milk to wash everything down with. Mirah picked up a copy of the Cleveland newspaper, 'The Cleveland Plain Dealer,' and glanced at the headlines. She would have to catch up on the news in Cleveland over breakfast, she thought, while she slipped out of her robe. Right now she wanted to join her man in the shower.

"May I come in?" Mirah asked. She was intrigued, staring at the water while it gently slid down Bryce's perfect physique. He was looking good enough to eat, she thought, as he invited her in. His manhood definitely peaked the instant she touched him.

"See what you do to me," Bryce said. He stroked his wet fingers across her lips.

"That's a good thing," Mirah replied, tracing her tongue over the tip of his finger. They started kissing passionately; he embraced her firmly in his arms.

"We'd better stop before it's too late to turn back," Bryce told her.

"Why? I want to feel you inside me," she whispered softly in his ear.

"You're a greedy woman," Bryce teased playfully. "Didn't you get enough of me last night?"

"Yes, but I want more," she replied getting down on her knees.

"Wait, let me run and get some protection."

"No need," Mirah responded. She opened her hands. "I think I'll try strawberry this time." She ripped open the package and did her thing.

Bryce went crazy as he held on to the metal rails for support. Mirah was sucking him down so good that he thought he would slip and fall. "Damn, baby, you love this big brown chocolate bar," Bryce said. He gently grabbed her head and helped guide her while she went back and forth. So smooth…so good, oh this woman was driving him insane.

"Yes, ooh…this feel's so good," Bryce moaned. She intensified to his response and his legs began to shake as his fluid rushed to the top and then exploded out. Afterwards he changed condoms and made love to her. They were soaking wet, the steam from the shower heated the room. That heat combined with their own created enough warmth like a hot summer day. Bryce couldn't get enough of her while he washed and toweled her dry.

Mirah quickly blow-dried her hair and then heated their breakfast up in the microwave. She never did get a chance to read the paper. After they ate, they headed out the door; Bryce wanted to give her a tour of the city. They headed downtown to

Tower City where they shopped at the mall and then visited some of Cleveland's hottest attractions. They stopped by the Rock & Roll Hall of Fame Museum, followed by the Great Lakes Science Center. By this time, Mirah was exhausted and was glad they headed down to the Flats to eat some lunch. The Flats reminded her of small city within itself. It was a whole strip of clubs and restaurants were people came to relax and for entertainment. Bryce showed her where the Cleveland Browns Stadium was. When they drove along Ontario Street he pointed out Jacobs Field, where the Cleveland Indians played. Right next to that was The Quicken Loans Arena, the home for the Cleveland Cavaliers basketball team.

Bryce wanted to show her more, but Mirah was too tired and convinced him to head back to their hotel. All she wanted to do was sit back and relax for the rest of the evening. They had just beaten the rush hour traffic and were headed up Fairhill Road when his phone rang.

"Hello," Bryce answered, quickly switching gears. This hill was treacherous in the winter as people inched their way up the slippery road. He told his best friend Kanai that he would call him back. Bryce had to swerve in the next lane; a lady almost spun into his Mercedes. Normally he would have cursed but he remained calmed. He took control of the car; even the best drivers had trouble in this awful weather.

"I see why people pack up and go to the warmer climates for the winter," Mirah said.

"Well if you want we can take off and head down to Florida," Bryce told her. "The family has a nice condo down there," he said, wishing he could catch a few sunrays. This cold was just too much.

The offer was so tempting Mirah thought to herself. She never imagined that she would be with a man this wealthy. To just pick up and leave when you wanted to was a dream everybody wished for. Mirah wouldn't mind a bit spending a few weeks basking in the sun with her man, especially since it was brutally cold up here. "Bryce, I wish we could but school will be starting back in a few weeks and so will my college co-op job."

"Well, maybe next year," Bryce said. They continued to drive another fifteen minutes before reaching the hotel.

The first thing Mirah did when they reached their suite was heat up some water for some hot cocoa. She definitely needed to take off the chill after being out in this weather for so long. Mirah sprawled out over the bed and flipped the television on. Bryce returned his best friend's phone call. She was upset to hear that Bryce had decided to go out. All the fellows were getting together while she was stuck here in the hotel room alone.

"Honey, you sure you're okay with this?" Bryce asked. He came out of the shower dripping wet.

'Hell no,' she wanted to tell him. It seemed like he would have told his friend no since he had brought her along on the trip. Sometime men just didn't think. She forced a phony smile on her face to hide her jealousy.

"No, you go ahead," Mirah told him. "I'm sure you all want to catch up on things," she managed to say convincingly. The last thing she wanted was for him to think she was some control freak. Men didn't like to feel hooked on a leash and their relationship was too new for her to say anything.

"Why don't you call my sister and see what's she's up to," Bryce said, kissing her on the forehead. He hated for her to be alone but he was excited about going out with his fellows. Everyone was hooking up: Kanai, Reese and Tyrone. They hadn't all been together in years. Bryce slipped into his clothes and dabbed a little cologne on.

"No, I'll just stay here and catch a movie on television. You sure you're just going out with the fellows?" Mirah asked while he stood in the mirror. If she hadn't known any better, she would think he was getting ready for a date as he beautified himself to perfection.

"Honey, you know I have to represent," Bryce turned around and told her. "It's not in my character to half step." Just when Mirah was about to respond, a knock echoed through the door.

"Just a minute," Bryce called out. "Mirah, you sure you're cool with this?" he asked one last time. The last thing he wanted was any surprises because he hated to be embarrassed. He's ex-girlfriend Candy was good at that shit. She was so damn jealous of everything.

"Bryce, I'm fine," Mirah told him. "Now let your friend in so I can meet him," she said getting up. She went over to the mirror to make sure she was in order. Mirah was sure Kanai would be the one to describe her to the rest of the crew. She had to be on point as she ran her fingers through her hair. Perfect, maybe I should have been a model, she thought to herself. She had the curves in all the right places. Kanai couldn't say anything bad about her, she thought, joining the two of them.

"Kanai, this is my girl, Mirah," Bryce said introducing the two.

"Hello," Mirah said shaking his hand. He couldn't take his eyes off of her, which was a major plus. Approval from his best friend would only solidify that he made the right choice. Pleased, she offered him something to drink.

Kanai eagerly gulped down a cup of hot chocolate in record time. They made small talk and after they left Mirah sprawled out on the bed again. Just when the movie on television was getting to the good part, the phone began to ring.

"Hello."

"Hi, Mirah, this is Briana. I hope my knucklehead brother has been showing you a good time."

"Yes, we've been out all day site seeing. Bryce just left back out, you missed him by a few seconds," Mirah told her.

"Where did he go?"

"Out with his best friend Kanai," she replied.

"He just left you there by yourself? He could have called me," Briana said with a snap in her voice.

"Well it was something that came up at the last minute. He told me to call you but I didn't want to bother you on such short notice."

"It's no bother, you can call me any time you want," Briana responded. "Now slip on some dress clothes because we're about to go club hopping," Briana said. "You think you can be ready in about a half-hour? I have to swing by and get a few friends."

"I'll be ready," Mirah said.

"Great. I'm glad I called. Bryce should have had better sense," she said.

"Well, you know men."

"Yeah I do. You can't live with them and you can't live without them," she laughed. "I'll see you shortly."

Mirah jumped in and out of the shower. She slipped into a solid black cashmere sweater and skirt to match. "Bryce is not the only one," Mirah laughed to herself. She curled her hair with the hot irons for a fresh look. When she was done she applied some makeup and then dabbed a little perfume on. She look good, smelled good. Damn, the fellows would be on her tonight, she thought, slipping into her black leather riding boots. Mirah stood in front of the mirror a few more seconds making sure she was on point. She would have to be on her best behavior tonight because his sister would watch everything she did. Mirah slipped on her leather coat and headed down to the lobby.

"Briana, perfect timing," Mirah waved as she walked into the entrance.

"You ready to party?" Briana called out excitedly.

"Sure am," Mirah replied. The cold air smacked her dead in the face when they walked outside. She was glad to step into the warmth of Briana's Cadillac Escalade. This truck was much too big for her to handle, but Briana drove it with such ease, like she had been driving this thing her whole life.

"Mirah these are my friends, Rochelle, Kym, and Tracey," Briana said with the formal introductions. "Tracey and I grew up together although she's living on the other half of the United States now. These other two big heads are my college friends."

"It's nice to meet you all," Mirah replied.

"Same here and call me Chelley, with a 'C'," Rochelle responded.

"Girl, you are so crazy," Briana said. "This is the lunatic of the bunch," Briana laughed while she turned the music up. They headed down to the flats to get their party on.

The first stop was to get something to eat. Mirah was glad; her stomach had begun to rumble with hunger pains. Everyone was really cool except for Tracey. Something about her didn't sit well with Mirah. Every time she looked up, Tracey was staring her in the face. What was wrong with her? Was she gay or something? Under any other circumstances, Mirah would have checked her but she didn't want to cause a scene, so she remained cool.

"How is it up there in New York?" Kym asked.

"I love it," Mirah replied. "You should come up and visit sometime."

"I'm going to hold you to that. Everything up there is so darn expensive," Kym said.

"Tell me about it," Mirah agreed. "I'm from Jersey and know how to make a dollar work," she added while they gave each other a high five.

"Enough about that. I hear you and Mr. Bryce are madly in love," Chelley said. "Do tell," she added, waiting for the juicy gossip.

"Girl, mind your own business," Briana told her cutting in. "You make it sound like I've been telling all my brother's 411," she said waving her finger.

"Bri, you know I'm nosy," Chelley laughed.

"Too damn nosy," Tracey replied. "Obviously Bryce must be in love to bring her home to his family," she said with a sting in her voice.

"Oooch!" Chelley motioned over dramatically. "Somebody certainly woke up on the wrong side of the bed."

Mirah just looked on collectively trying to gather her thoughts. What the hell was wrong with Tracey? And who the fuck was she referring to as 'HER.' I have a name and she'd better start using it, Mirah thought to herself. She hoped her temper wasn't beginning to flare. She excused herself to go to the rest room. Briana said something to Tracey and then hurried to catch up with Mirah. She apologized for her friend's rude behavior and explained that the past few years had been extremely difficult for Tracey, although she didn't have a clue to what her problem was. When they returned back to the table Tracey was gone. Good, Mirah thought to herself. One person don't stop no show, they went partying for the rest of the night.

Mirah had so much fun she didn't even stop to call Bryce. His sister dropped her back off at the hotel, it was a going on three-thirty and Mirah was surprised to see that Bryce still had not returned.

Chapter 13

Mirah rolled over when she heard Bryce come through the door. The clock read 5:45. He slipped out of his clothes and joined her in the bed.

"Honey, you awake?" Bryce asked, slightly nudging her on the shoulder.

"No, it's almost six 'o clock in the morning," Mirah reminded him in a angry tone. "You could have at least called," she mumbled rolling to the other side. Right now she was in no mood to argue with him.

"Honey, don't be mad. I called you once," Bryce responded. "I just assumed you would be staying overnight with Bri since you were out partying and all. I wasn't eager to hurry back to an empty bed," he added stroking the back of her hair.

"You shouldn't assume things," Mirah said turning back over to face him. "You know the clubs up here close around two o' clock. Would it have killed you to make a one minute call to let me know your plans?"

"I'm sorry. It won't happen again," Bryce told her with a makeup kiss. "So, did you enjoy yourself?"

"Yes, everyone was nice except for your sister's friend Tracey. She had a straight up attitude," Mirah told him.

"Tracey."

"Yeah, some childhood friend of your sister. You must know her?" Mirah asked.

"Sure do," Bryce stated quickly changing the subject. He yawned and told her they would talk later in the morning; he closed his eyes and pretended to be asleep.

Bryce couldn't believe that Tracey was back in town. She was the mother of his first child who had died shortly after birth. What was she doing back in town? She had promised to stay away from his family after the money he had set her up with. He paid for her college and even bought her a house on the West Coast to keep her silent. If she recanted on her deal then she would have to pay him back for everything he had given her. It was part of the contract, something he had to make her sign so he wouldn't be burned later. At the time he had felt bad about doing that, but business was business and he was not glad that she had resurfaced. Bryce wondered what ulterior motive was roaming in her head. He became restless; it was hard for him to think right now, his eyes weighed heavily from sleep deprivation. Whatever had happened tonight, Mirah could not know since she did not mention anything to him. Information like that just wasn't something you swept under the rug. He debated whether to call his sister to see what she knew. Bryce decided that wasn't such a good idea, it would only draw attention to the matter. It would have to wait until later today he thought, thinking back to how he got into this big fiasco with Tracey in the first place.

    It all happened a few years back when he decided to come home to visit on short notice. On his arrival he found that everyone had packed up and gone out of town. Bri was on some college orientation tour and their parents had headed down to their family condo in Florida for a few weeks. It was around nine o' clock at night when Tracey had come over looking for his sister. You could tell that she had been crying and was upset from something that was bothering her. Bryce invited her in and soothed her tears; she revealed to him how upset she had been for not being able to afford college. One kiss led to a night he wished he could have taken back. Her young virgin body was too irresistible; he slid in and stole her virtue away. He should have had better sense but he was thinking with the wrong head. One month later she called to inform him that he would be a father in eight months. Neither of them had planned on having a baby together so he came up with the ultimate plan. Money sure could buy his way out of a lot of trouble, so he shipped her off to college to have the baby. When the baby was born they would put him or her up for adoption and then they could try to put their mistake behind them.

Their plan sounded so cold but later everything seemed to change. The miracle of a child growing inside Tracey's body brought them closer together. The few trips Bryce made out there had given him a new perspective, especially the moment he heard the baby's first heartbeat. The little life inside her was part of him and there was no way he was going to ship him off to be raised by someone else's family. They agreed to get to know each other over the next few months and he had planned on marrying her before the baby was born. Bryce was heartbroken when the baby was born prematurely and died three days later. This was the lowest part in his life. He and Tracey went their separate ways afterwards since he wasn't in love with her anyway.

Bryce couldn't get Tracey out of his mind. He wondered what happened between them tonight since Mirah said she had a major attitude. Would she be able to put two and two together? He had confessed to her that his son died but never mentioned the mother's name. Should he tell her? All this happened before he even met Mirah and once one person knew your business it didn't take long for it to spiral out to the rest of the world. This secret of his was so personal, a time of his life he even kept from his own family. Why was this all coming up now? Bryce's eyes stung intensely; those were his last thoughts before he drifted off for some much needed sleep.

Bryce spent the next few days spoiling Mirah. He pampered and devoted all his time to her. They virtually remained locked up in their hotel room, and on the morning of

News Year's Eve he got down on his knees and proposed marriage to her.

Mirah looked at the large carat rock in disbelief.

"Will you be my wife?" Bryce asked her again.

"Yes. Yes, I'll marry you," Mirah cried. She dangled her hand in front of Bryce so he could slide the ring on.

"Great," Bryce said kissing her gently.

"I still can't believe this," Mirah stated looking at the huge two carat rock on her finger.

"Why me, Bryce? I'm sure you could have had your pick of any woman."

"Because it just feels right," Bryce responded. "No one has ever made me feel the way you do. I want to make you mine forever," he said tracing his finger over her lips. "I love you," Bryce told her as he eased his tongue in to taste the sweetness of her.

Mirah was still in a state of shock. She sat on the corner of the bed while Bryce made a phone call. She couldn't believe she would ever be engaged, least of all to a man like Bryce. Mirah felt like a million bucks as she twisted her hand from side to side. Her diamond was radiant, its reflection lit up the whole room.

"I'm glad you like the ring," Bryce said, hanging up the phone.

"It's gorgeous. Did you pick this out yourself?"

"Sure did," Bryce told her. He actually went to the jewelry shop a few months ago to pick up his grandmother's ring. His mother had shipped the ring up nearly a year ago to have some detail work done to it. She wanted to pass the ring down to his sister Briana on her 21st birthday that was coming up next month. He was so thankful to have the ring back into his possession after what Candy had done. Anyhow, while he was waiting in the shop he began looking at rings and decided right on the spot to purchase a ring for Candy. He thought they would be married but the ring he purchased for Candy, he gave to Mirah instead. Bryce wasn't getting any younger and he wanted a family and a few kids in his life. Mirah was the perfect candidate; she was single with no kids and had high ambitions and goals set for herself. In the few weeks he had known her, Bryce couldn't get her out of his mind. She could fulfill his needs physically, emotionally and socially. Mirah was everything a man could want with no baggage to go along. And to top it off she was drop dead gorgeous.

"Well you certainly have excellent taste," Mirah told him.

"Only the best," Bryce responded. "Now, I'm going to get dressed and run a quick errand. I have some unattended business to wrap up," Bryce told her.

"Business, you have to work on New Years Eve?"

"No, it's just an old personal matter," Bryce responded. "It shouldn't take more than an hour."

"Is everything alright? I can come along if you need me."

"Its nothing you should worry about. Besides, Bri is dying to see your ring. I asked her to pick you up around noon. We're going to have a family brunch to celebrate. I'll meet you over my parents' house."

"Your family knew all along?"

"Yep."

Well that explains why Diane was acting so intrusive when they first met. Her mother would have behaved in the same way.

"Bryce, should I call my parents before you leave?"

"Honey, I would say yes but under the circumstances it's not a good idea to tell them something like this over the phone."

"I know, the same thoughts ran through my mind. I'm just so excited. Have you thought about a date?" Mirah asked.

"Actually its up to you," Bryce told her. "I think this coming February on Valentine's Day would be a good idea."

"That's less than two months away," Mirah replied. "My parents couldn't afford to pay for anything on such short notice."

"Don't worry about it. Use the credit card I gave you to make all your purchases. There's a fifty thousand dollar limit," he told her. "Besides, knowing your mother, this kind of thing seems right up her alley."

"It sure is. Mamma loves to coordinate," Mirah responded. Now she only had to come up with a way to tell her parents. Time was not on her side to have any doubts and she couldn't waste any time trying to appease her mother because February was right around the corner.

"So then, I take it February 14, 2004, will be our wedding day?"

"Yes, I can't wait," Mirah reeled in excitement. "You've made me the happiest woman on Earth," she said kissing him.

"Same goes for me. Now let me get dressed before I change my mind," he told her, disappearing into the bathroom. A cool shower was just what he needed to relieve the bulge in his pants. Right now he had to take care of business and find out what Tracey Simmons was up to.

****

Bryce stepped out his car with a worried feeling settling at the bottom of his stomach. He wondered what Tracey was up to as he headed up the walkway. He vividly remembered this house, recounting the million times he had to come over here to pick up Bri. His mother wasn't particularly happy that her daughter was making a trip down to the projects every other day. They had actually met years back in a basketball tournament around the age of ten and has been good friends ever since. Bri had been devastated when Tracey's family packed up and moved out of state. Her parents had rekindled their old flame and Tracey's mother was all too happy to get out of her mother's home and support her family on her own. Bri cried for months, flooding the phone lines with outrageous long distance calls to talk. Tracey would faithfully come back to Cleveland during the summer, but as the years went by her trips became fewer and eventually stopped altogether. Tracey probably was making her own friends in her new home and didn't feel a need to really come back. The only reason she had come back the year they made love was to help with her grandmother who had just had surgery.

Bryce wished she had never come over to his parents' house that day nearly three years ago. He rang the doorbell, not knowing what to expect.

"Bryce, it's good to see you again," Tracey said trying to kiss him on the lips.

"Tracey, you know I'm up here with somebody," he told her. The last thing he was about to do was slip up and hop in the bed like he did with Candy. He wasn't about to make that mistake twice.

"Yes, I met the Ms. Lovely Mirah. Was she a virgin too?" Tracey asked in a sarcastic tone.

"What's your problem?" Bryce asked ignoring her comment. He wasn't about to get in a heated argument with her. Bryce just wanted to know why she was here and then he would leave.

"Boy, I really wonder what your mother would think knowing her son chases after naïve little girls."

"Tracey, you were hardly naïve. You damn near dropped the panties before a brother had time to think."

"That's because I was in love with you. Do you really think I would just give up my virginity to anyone? The last thing I expected was for you to hit it and run, you arrogant bastard." Tracey was so mad she could choke him right now. Couldn't he see that she was still in love with him? After everything he had done to her, she would give it all up to be with him again. She could not believe he had the nerve to bombard his way through her grandmother's house with his nonchalant attitude.

"And don't you dare think you can come over here and insult me like that," she added snapping her fingers. "You must have forgotten that I carried your child for nine…I mean eight months. You probably was happy to see the day he died so you could rid us both out of your life," Tracey retaliated.

Bryce's hands quickly flew around her neck. He pushed her against the wall. "Tracey, I've never raised my hand to a woman before but you're pressing me," he yelled in her face. "Don't you ever question my love for the son we had…EVER," he demanded before he let go of her.

"Than why did you want it kept a secret?" Tracey hollered. Tears started flooding down her face. "You act like you were ashamed of us. What…was you scared of your mother's reaction? What would she think of her eldest son knocking up a poor little girl from the projects?"

"Tracey, don't even go there," Bryce warned her. "Do you think I'm that callous after everything I've done for you?"

"You just think your damn money can solve everything, don't you?" Tracey screamed out loud.

"Don't player hate on a brother for having the finer things in life. And I certainly didn't hear you complaining when I forked out over forty thousand for your college tuition and over two hundred thousand for the house you're living up in."

Tracey knew she would live to regret this day. If there was one thing she hated was for someone to throw up what they had done for her.

"Get the hell out of this house," Tracey yelled slapping him in the face.

"Not until you tell me why you're here."

"Look Bryce, you don't own the city of Cleveland. I have just as much right to be here as you."

"Why can't you just answer a simple question? I don't know why I even got involved with your sorry ass. Tracey you're nothing but trouble and you better stay away from my family or you will pay the consequences," Bryce told her.

"Are you threatening me? Bryce, don't think I won't play my own cards," Tracey warned him. "I wonder what your little friend would think of the scandalous man she's getting involved with?"

"Oh, my fiancée knows about my son and if you think of telling my family then so be it. Blood is thicker than water and we'll always be family no matter what. You on the other hand have everything to lose. I'm sure you haven't forgotten about the stipulations of our agreement and you will also lose Bri's friendship in the process," Bryce replied angrily.

"Get out. Bryce, get out before I call the police."

"My pleasure. I wouldn't want my Benz to be striped right from underneath my nose anyway," he retorted. "You're certainly not worth it," he said before he turned to walk away.

Bryce got no further than two steps before Tracey jumped on his back. She was swinging like a wild woman; he grabbed and pushed her up against the couch.

"You just don't know when to stop," Bryce said, forcing her hands over her head.

"Bryce, how could you be so cold?" she cried trying to wiggle her hands free. "All I ever did was love you."

"Well the feelings are not mutual. I loved my son but not you, Tracey. Believe me when I tell you that," Bryce said while he got up.

Tracey just laid there sobbing like a wounded bird. She did not move or even call out for him as he walked out of her house and life forever.

Bryce was pissed off as he sped out of the driveway. He was mad at Tracey and the fact that he never found out what she was up to. He never meant to lose control but she pushed him beyond limits he thought heading back towards his parents house. The thought of Mirah brought and instant smile to his face. He looked forward to marrying his future wife.

Chapter 14

James nearly punched a hole through the wall. He paced back and forth in anger. Mirah's engagement to this Bryce Whitaker was unbelievable, and it was definitely true since it came from her own mother's mouth. Mattie Jones damn near told the whole community that her precious little girl was marrying a doctor. "Dr. Bryce Whitaker," James imagined her saying boastfully to anyone who would stop and listen. How could this be happening? It should have been him who was marrying the love of his life. He should have done it nearly two years ago but her parents had begged him to wait until she finished college. They said, "it was the right thing to do." That all was a bunch of shit. The bottom line was they didn't like him but they didn't seem to have any problems with their daughter marrying this rich old man. They ought to be ashamed of themselves pretending to be so religious and all. He couldn't believe he let them talk him out of his plans. James was even more upset at himself for not proposing to her last week. He shouldn't have let his anger get in the way and now the most important person in his life was slipping away forever. He grabbed his coat and headed out the door.

"Operator, can you give the phone number and address for a Bryce Whitaker?"

"One moment please."

James could hear the clicking of the keyboard in the background while he waited patiently.

"I'm sorry, there's no listing for a Bryce Whitaker."

"Damn," James howled underneath his breath.

"Is there anything else I can help you with?"

"No, but thank you for trying," James told her before hanging up. He then quickly dialed the number to Callie. James knew she would have the information and he nearly had to beg

Callie, who finally broke down and divulged the information to him. Now James could see for himself this chump who was brainwashing Mirah with all his money.

His adrenaline pumped up into overload. He cranked up the volume to his favorite rap CD and sped down the street weaving in and out of traffic. James felt invisible; he was ready to take Bryce Whitaker on.

James was irritated by all the New York traffic and was glad when he made it to Manhattan. He squeezed into a parking space against the curb and quickly headed up to the elegant condos Mirah would soon call home. Well, not if I can help it, he thought, making his way towards the elevators. He was lucky the security personnel were engaged in other matters while he made his way to the top floor. James rapidly knocked on the door to confront the man who had stolen Mirah right from underneath his hands.

"Yeah, who is it?" Bryce called out irritated by the constant noise echoing throughout his home. It couldn't be Mirah who had keys. He unlocked the door so he could get rid of whoever this was; Bryce wasn't in the mood to be bothered.

"Can I help you?" Bryce asked, surprised someone was standing at his door unannounced.

"Bryce Whitaker."

"Yeah."

"Good. Yes you can help me. Let this be a warning that I am not going to get pushed to the side so you can marry my woman," James told him. "Mirah is not for sale."

"Excuse me," Bryce stated in disbelief. "Who in the hell do you think you are coming up in my place with this shit?"

"I'm your worst fucking nightmare," James responded stepping up to his face and pushing his way in. "You think you can buy your way into a marriage? You ain't nothing but a punk," James said. His fist collided with Bryce who had reacted in a bitter rage.

James quickly over powered him and slung his ass to the floor. "Old man, you ain't no match for me," James yelled. He gave him a swift kick to the mid-section and was surprised when Bryce leaped back up. They fought blow for blow.

"Oh my God, what's going on?" Mirah screamed. She ran to the phone to call for help. There was a brawl going on right in the middle of the living room. Furniture was scattered out of order with broken glass all over the place.

"James is that you?" Mirah screamed as she caught a glimpse of his face. "Get off of him," she yelled jumping on James's back.

James didn't have time to think and threw Mirah to the floor by accident. When her voice registered it was already too late. He turned by her side to see if she was okay, which gave Bryce a window of opportunity to quickly turn the tables. James went crashing to the floor with one swift blow to the head. Afterwards, Bryce let the wooden African sculpture fall to the floor while he ran over to see about Mirah.

"Honey, are you okay?" Bryce asked her.

"Yes," Mirah cried. She reached up to touch Bryce's bloody face and then turned to see James sprawled out on the floor. Her heart stopped. He just laid there, no movement at all.

"Oh my God, what did you do to him?" Mirah called out. She scurried over to him on her hands and knees and winced in pain from the shards of glass that cut across her skin.

"Call for help," she told Bryce in a panic.

"Fuck that asshole," Bryce replied before he left out the room.

Mirah hurried back to the phone and dialed 911. She was so nervous, barely able to speak clearly on the phone. It was only a matter of minutes before the police and ambulance came racing through the door. Mirah tried to push life back into James.

"Let us take over," the medical team told her. She stepped aside trembling so bad that she thought her knees were about to buckle right from beneath her.

Bryce made his way back into the room while the police officer asked Mirah a million questions. He was mad as hell being caught off guard like this. He eased his hand across his swollen face; damn I should have capped his ass he thought while the rescue team rushed to bring James vital signs back to life.

Mirah breathed a sigh of relief when the words, 'we have a pulse,' echoed throughout the room. She ran back over to his side as they prepared to rush him to the hospital.

"Bryce, are you coming with me?" Mirah asked interrupting his conversation with the police officer. He sharply cut her a look of disbelief. She didn't have time to deal with Bryce's attitude right now. Mirah grabbed her purse and followed behind the rescue team.

"Where do you think you're going?" Bryce asked grabbing her by the arm.

"To the hospital. I have to make sure he's going to be all right and to let his family know," she told him.

Bryce didn't say a word as she left out the house. She better be glad the police officer was standing in my face, he thought to himself. She would definitely hear about it later. He couldn't believe she had the nerve to run after her ex after he broke into his place and started all this shit. Now he was under the microscope, being questioned by the damn police.

****

Mirah begged Bryce not to prosecute James for breaking into his home with the intent to assault or murder him. With

Bryce's high-powered attorneys, James could easily be sitting behind bars for the rest of his life.

Bryce would only comply with her request if she promised to stay away from him. Mirah couldn't believe it when he placed the restraining order in front of her face to sign. Her signature upon the document affirmed that James was a threat to her and it was required by law for him to refrain from any and all contact. This was so ridiculous. She scribbled and dated the document before Bryce affixed his signature across the bottom. He personally left out to make sure it was properly delivered to James by the authorities.

Mirah broke down in tears when she was alone. She couldn't blame Bryce for wanting to protect her but James would never intentionally hurt her...NEVER. She was so angry that he forced her into signing those damn documents. James was in the hospital fighting for his life and she didn't even want to think of the possibility of him going to jail. Mirah was left in a situation she couldn't control. If she had refused to sign the papers then it would have been a direct insult to Bryce. It was a no win situation. She picked up her cell phone and dialed the number to the hospital.

"Yes, I'm calling to check on James Gibson," Mirah said politely over the phone.

"One moment, let me find his attending nurse," the receptionist responded, putting her on hold.

"Hello, this is Candy. How can I help you?"

"Yes, my name is Mirah and I'm calling to check on James Gibson."

"He's improving. As a matter of fact, he just came to a few hours ago and has been asking to speak with you."

"Oh," Mirah thought biting down on her lower lip. "Tell him I'll be there as soon as possible," Mirah told her before hanging up the phone. She made arrangements to borrow Marcy's car and headed straight for the hospital.

****

James was relieved to see Mirah walk through the door. She embraced him with love; he held tightly to her and began kissing the softness of her lips. When she didn't pull back he slowly eased his tongue to join hers. Mirah was so sweet, just like he had remembered.

"James..."

"Mirah, I'm so sorry for everything," James said cutting her sentence off. "I just had to see for myself who this man was who asked for your hand in marriage," he told her with a tired yawn. The medication was beginning to kick in; his eyelids closed then opened again.

"James, you should have just asked me," Mirah told him. She ran her fingers across the bandages wrapped around his forehead.

"I couldn't live with myself if anything bad ever happened to you and that's why I wanted to speak with you."

"Only after you kiss me," he said.

"James, I'm engaged."

"That didn't stop you a few minutes ago," he told her. "Engagement or not, you still are in love with me. You should be mine," he said easing his arms around her again. It hurt him to see tears rolling down her face. She was so beautiful, he thought, tracing his fingers along her silky brown face. Those were his last thoughts of her before he drifted off into a deep sleep.

Mirah stayed there awhile despite the fact that he was asleep. This would be the last time she would be able to spend with him. She knew the initial break would be hard but he would be fine without her. This was a sacrifice she had to make for the both of them by signing the restraining order. Mirah loved him enough to let him go, so he wouldn't wind up in the legal system that already had too many brothers locked up behind bars. Mirah said her good-byes and kissed his forehead before heading out the room. She was glad she ran into his nurse Candy before leaving out the hospital and his life forever.

"Will James make a full recovery?" Mirah asked.

"Yes. All his lab work and x-rays came back fine," Candy said starring at her. She couldn't believe she was talking to the same woman involved with her ex boyfriend, Bryce. She would never forget that girl's face because she had thought about confronting her on the night when she had went to pick up the rest of her things at Bryce's home. Candy was even more surprised to see the huge rock on her finger. That couldn't be from Bryce she thought quietly to herself.

"What a lovely engagement ring," Candy said probing for information.

"Thank you," Mirah replied.

"Well I'm sure glad your fiancé is going to make a full recovery. I know you must have been terrified."

"Actually he's not my fiancé. James is a old friend of mine and I'm just so thankful that he's going to be okay."

"Oh," Candy responded confirming her suspicions.

"I left James a letter on his dresser. Can you make sure that he reads it?" Mirah asked.

"I certainly will," Candy told her before she left the room. She waited a few moments until Mirah was out of sight and then slid the neatly addressed letter to James into her pocket. Candy sashayed out the room like she had won a million bucks. She went to read the contents of the letter.

Chapter 15

Mirah spent the next month planning for her wedding. Her mother virtually moved into the guest quarters of Bryce's home so she could be involved in every aspect of the planning. She was the world's greatest coordinator and what normally took people a year had taken her mother less than a month, thanks in part to the credit card Bryce had given her.

In a few weeks they had charged more than thirty thousand dollars. The biggest expense was the reception and the two-hundred dollar dinner plate that would be served. Mirah's father nearly flipped out at the huge bill. Deep down she knew he wasn't pleased with this speedy wedding. He told her that they just met and should take their time to get to know one another. He also said, if Bryce really loved her he wouldn't mind waiting until she finished school. Mirah was a little saddened to watch her father take a side corner on one of the most important days of her life. She tried her best to get him involved but he never came up with her mother who was flying all over the city in preparation for their day, which was only a few weeks away. Mirah would have thought the reverse and was actually stunned by her mother's acceptance of this marriage. Mirah laughed knowing her mother enjoyed spending all this money on the whim of a hat. She held her head up high saying, "Yes, we'll take that," when those uppity white folks thought we were to poor to even be in the shop. Mattie Jones enjoyed when they swiped that credit card across, giving them a 'how dare you insult me' look.

****

Mirah's stomach twirled in anticipation while she paced back and forth in the kitchen. She glanced over the meal prepared for tonight's events one last time. Everything had to be perfect. This was the first time that their two families would meet and Mirah prayed that everything would go smoothly. Her heart fell to the bottom of her stomach at the sound of the doorbell.

"I'll get it," Mirah called out. She gathered her composure and ran to the door.

"Mrs. Whitaker, I'm so glad you could make it," Mirah said giving her a hug. "Please come right in."

"Briana and Isek are just grabbing a few things from the cab," Diane told her.

"Do they need any help?" Bryce asked, joining the two.

"No, they should be fine. Now give me a hug," Diane quipped at her son.

"Mother, it's always a pleasure to see you," Bryce said with a kiss on her cheek. "Now, I expect for you to be on your best behavior," he reminded her, right in front of Mirah.

"Bryce, why would you say something like that to your mother, especially in front of Mirah."

"Mother, Mirah is going to be my wife. Anything I say to you is open to her."

"Mirah, can you believe this?" Diane asked. "You wouldn't dare say such a thing to your mother, would you?"

Mirah's mouth fell open; she was at a loss of words. Honestly, yes she would tell her mother that but thought it inappropriate to say to Diane.

"Mother, now I didn't say this to be rude," Bryce interrupted. "This is a special night and I just want everything to be perfect."

Mirah was relieved Bryce cut in. She definitely did not want to engage in a dispute with Diane, not now especially. She had a hard enough time with her own parents and hoped tonight would not turn into a disaster. Mirah glanced back over at Diane who was staring her son directly in the eyes. If she didn't know any better; it looked like she wanted to go to war.

"I ought to turn you over my knee and spank you," Diane told her son. "You're never too old, and as long as I have breath in this body, I will be your mother," she snapped with a wave of her finger.

"Mother, please don't be upset. You know how over bearing you can be sometimes," Bryce responded, wrapping his arms around her. "You're my mother, if I can't be honest with you, then who else can I be honest with?"

"Okay, you've made your point. I'll make every effort to be on my best behavior."

"Good, now come on in and get settled," Bryce told her. "I'm going to run down to make sure Dad and Briana are okay," he said before leaving.

Mirah was surprised to see her parents come up with Bryce's dad and sister.

"Mother, I see you've already met most of Bryce family," Mirah smiled. She wished that she had a moment to speak with her parents like Bryce had just a few minutes ago. Mirah wasn't worried about her father but her mother was a different story.

"Well, I see everyone has arrived," Diane said sashaying back into the foyer.

"Yes," Mirah responded while Bryce made the formal introductions.

"Mr. and Mrs. Jones, it's a pleasure to finally meet you in person," Diane smiled.

"Please call me Mattie...and this here is my husband Willie," Mattie boasted, patting him on the shoulder.

"Well, same here...since we're all going to be family now. Call me Diane and of course you've already met my husband, Isek, and our daughter, Briana."

"Yes, I sure did," Mattie, replied. "Briana, you and Mirah seem to be around the same age. Is that correct dear?"

"Mother, why don't I take your coat," Mirah interrupted with a 'how dare you,' look. She hadn't been in here for five minutes and was already starting mess.

"Mirah, now don't be rude and interrupt your mother," Mattie said. "I done show raised her better than that," she smiled, handing her coat to her daughter.

"I believe they are around the same age," Diane answered putting the question to rest. "Normally, I would have been concerned like you but your daughter here is something special. She's really mature for her age and a perfect fit for my son. We're going to have some lovely grandchildren, Mattie."

"Well thank you," Mattie replied. "And yes, soon as Mirah finishes her studies, I look forward to a house full of grandchildren. Isn't that right Willie?"

Willie just nodded in approval while he circled his arm around his daughter back. He gave her a gentle squeeze on the shoulder, assuring her that everything would be all right.

Mirah was surprised at how well both families got along. She thought her mother would go to battle with Diane but they were talking to one another like best friends. Come to think about it, they were alike in many ways; they only differed in economic status.

"Mirah, you sure prepared a feast," Briana said helping her finish set up the table. "I'm just so glad it's some good old black folk cooking. Mother drives me crazy with all that fancy stuff that you can't even pronounce."

"Well I'm glad you approve of the selection. I was a bit worried," Mirah told her. "I also have to be honest…my mother came up earlier today to help."

"That's better than what I would have done. Mother spoiled us so much that all I know is how to prepare box food. You know, Rosa prepared all our meals. I'm just surprised she picked up and left after all those years."

"Not to be offensive, but you and Bryce are grown, and if your mother is anything like mines, she would have been left," Mirah laughed.

"Oh, I didn't even think of it that way but you're absolutely right. I was so glad of the day when I turned eighteen; it was so good to leave that castle and have a peace a mind."

"I understand," Mirah said, with a high five. If only she knew the real reason why Rosa left, Mirah thought to herself. It definitely wasn't because of her mother, Diane. As difficult as she may be, this was all on her father Isek. What a dirty dog...Mirah sure hoped that saying, *like father, like son,* wasn't true.

"Well, everything looks magnificent," Diane interrupted helping bring the last of the food items to the table.

Everyone was seated and ready to throw down on the honey baked ham, roasted chicken, collard greens, black-eyed peas, macaroni and cheese, cornbread, rolls, cakes, cookies...enough food for a feast.

"Mattie, will you please do the honor of blessing the food?" Bryce asked.

Mirah thought her mother was about to fall out of her chair. She stood up and smiled with the biggest grin on her face.

"It would be my honor," Mattie smiled showing her pearly white teeth. "May we bow?" Once everyone complied with her request the blessing was given. That was the longest ten-minute prayer; Mattie said anything and everything that came to mind.

"Amen," everyone said in unison, glad to sit down.

The conversation over dinner went pleasantly well and Mirah sighed a breath of relief when it was over. Now she prayed everything would go well through the night. All the men gathered their things and left out. They would be staying in one of New York's high priced hotels until after their marriage tomorrow.

The women all stayed at the house finalizing last minute details.

"Well, Mattie, I sure thank you for letting me partake in the plans," Diane said before she sipped on a glass of red wine. If they hadn't she sure would have protested since it was her son's money they were spending.

"Not a problem at all, though we really should thank Mirah. I had no idea the things you can do on a computer," Mattie said. "It actually felt like you were right here with us."

"Yes, thank heavens for technology. I guess we should thank both our daughters. Before this wedding, I didn't know how to turn a darn computer on, but now I'm a natural pro. I've even signed up for classes, there's so much I need to know," Diane said, fascinated that she found a new hobby.

"Well, I'm getting tired and have to be up early," Mirah yarned clearing the table. With everyone's help, the house was cleaned in no time.

Mirah and Briana stayed up late talking 'girl' talk. It felt good to have a sister, she thought before drifting off to sleep.

Chapter 16

Mirah woke up all bright eyed and excited. Normally she would have been bothered by the brutal cold weather but today she didn't care because it was her wedding day. She slipped into the shower and hurried to get dressed. Her first appointment was to get her hair done. After that she was headed straight to the Salon to get her make-up and nails done. Once she was complete with that, Mirah would be heading to the church to become Mrs. Bryce Whitaker.

At the church Mattie enjoyed helping her daughter dress in her wedding garments. She looked so beautiful in the full-length silk embroided gown that flared out like Cinderella's ball gown.

"Mirah, I must say how pleased I am to witness this day. Honey, you look so radiant. You make your old mother so proud."

"Thank you, Mom," Mirah said with tears welling up in the corner of her eyes.

"Now don't you mess up that make-up and start crying," her mother said.

She thought it best to give her daughter a few moments alone while she went to make sure everything was in order. It was a good thing she did. Her heart nearly dropped to the floor. "James, what on God's green earth are you doing here?" Mattie hissed, pulling him into a side room.

"I need to speak with Mirah."

"Oh, no you're not. Oh 'Lawd,' why did you send the devil in your sanctuary?" she called out throwing her hands in the air.

"Mattie, what is going on?" Willie asked, peeking in the room. When he saw James, he immediately knew the answer. He quickly came in and shut the door.

"Look, I didn't come here to fight with you. I just need to speak with Mirah before she goes through with this wedding."

"Over my dead body," Mattie shrieked, coming face to face with him.

"Willie, get over to that phone and call the police," she snapped without taking her eyes off James.

"I'll be darned if you think you're going to ruin my daughter's wedding day. And thank heavens it's not you. My little girl is marrying *Dr.* Bryce Whitaker," she spat, putting her hands on her hips.

"Mattie, you are such a witch!" James called her right in front of her husband.

"You call me a devil, but you should look in the mirror and see the devil horns growing out from your ears."

"James, I will not let you speak to my wife that way," Willie intervened.

"Whatever," James snapped back. He had to get out of here before the police came. The restraining order was still in place and he wasn't about to go to jail trying to fight with her crazy parents. There was no way they would let him get anywhere near her, so it was in his best interest to high tail it right out of there. James shoved his way past them and then turned to stare their evil behinds in the face one last time before he left.

"You're letting Mirah make the biggest mistake of her life. You know she loves me. She always has and always will. I'm just sorry I'm not a rich man; otherwise I would have had no problems getting your approval. Isn't that right, Mattie?"

"James, you better leave now," Willie warned.

"I will, but one last thing needs to be said. You all call yourselves Christian but you need to really turn to the Lord for the sins you placed before Mirah and me. Mark my words, this marriage is going to fall apart before it even begins."

With that being said, James flew out of the church and just missed the police who had pulled up to the curb. He saw Willie racing down to talk to them because 'Lawd,' knows Mattie couldn't be embarrassed with explaining this whole ordeal. He knew if they did have to explain, Mirah might, no, definitely would change her mind about walking down the aisle to become Mrs. Bryce Whitaker. She loved James that much, but there was not a damn thing he could do about it. James knew it wouldn't do Mirah or him any good if he were sitting behind bars, so he just sucked it up and decided to be patient. Once the richness spell dried up, their marriage would crumble and James would be there to pick up the pieces.

****

Mirah stood behind the closed doors of the church and looked in to see the crowd of guests who had come to witness this marriage. As happy as Mirah was, she could not get James Gibson out of her mind. Even though she was marrying Bryce, she always imagined they would be together raising a family. It brought tears to her eyes thinking how their encounter at the hotel had ended. James damn near called her a whore when she tried to explain her relationship with Bryce. It wasn't even serious then and she would have gone back to him in a heartbeat if only he had asked; but Mirah was just tired of thinking he could dangle her by the rope and have her when it was convenient for him.

Her relationship with James went downhill after that, especially when he confronted Bryce and attacked him. With the signed restraining order to keep him away, Mirah knew he was out of her life forever. It was selfish of her but she wished she had the chance to see James one last time before her life changed forever with her marriage to Bryce. Deep down, maybe she wanted James to rescue her. He had always been there for her before. Although she loved Bryce, there was no love that could ever replace or compare to the love she shared with James Gibson. Mirah would always hold a special bond in her heart for him, but today she had to move on. It was her wedding day; she had to let go of the past and get on with her future.

The sound of the wedding march began while the ushers opened the back doors of the church. Mirah situated her bouquet of red roses in her hand, took a deep breath, and then journeyed down that aisle to become Mrs. Bryce Whitaker.

Chapter 17

Mirah's life was turned completely upside down as she tried to get adjusted to her new marriage. The honeymoon was over and she had a hard time coping with the events that had happened just over the past few months. The first mistake she made was giving up her job at the newspaper. Her passion for writing and the promise of a job upon graduation slipped from her hands while she began to work tedious hours to help Bryce jump start his own business.

The second and worst mistake of all was dropping out of school. In just a few months her grades had dropped drastically. It was bad enough that she would lose her scholarship, but she didn't want her GPA to go down too. Mirah had no other choice but to withdraw from her classes. Bryce agreed that this was the best thing to do and he would pay for the remainder of her education if she started back up in the fall.

This change of events created the first spark of resentment Mirah had towards Bryce, aside from severing her relationship with James. She believed deep down he was just being selfish to satisfy his own needs. All of her time now was totally being consumed with this new business venture. Not only was she his wife, but she also became his secretary, coordinator, and consultant. If that wasn't bad enough she had to attend these so-called *high social functions*. Bryce literally demanded she go to every one. She was the pretty face on his shoulder. He said networking, was the most important factor in making sure his business became a success. After a while a conversion took place and the black mask overshadowed the person she used to be. Mirah stood in front of a mirror and looked at herself. The person starring back at her was an identical replica on the exterior, but inside was a different story. All the questions she should have asked before getting married was consuming her mind. Deep down Mirah wasn't happy; her true feelings became masked and bottled up from the rest of the world. Her feelings for Bryce even changed and she began to question the validity of their marriage.

****

"Where are you going?" Bryce asked Mirah, as she came down the stairs in a form fitting black dress.

"I'm going out with Marcy and a few friends," Mirah said. "Remember, I told you about it last week."

"No, I don't remember. I've already made plans for us tonight, so go change into something a little bit more tasteful," he told her.

"Bryce, you didn't mention we had any plans for tonight. Do you think it's fair for me to just cancel what I was going to do?"

"Look Mirah, you're married now and your commitment is to me," he told her in an annoyed tone. "This business dinner tonight is very important."

"Bryce, you say that about all your business engagements," Mirah replied. "Look, I'm tired. Can't I just relax for one night? For the past few months I've been so wrapped up in helping you with your business that I haven't seen much of my friends or family to be exact."

Bryce couldn't believe her nasty damn attitude. "Look, don't you ever take that tone with me," he yelled back at her. "Do you think you can have all of this shit for free?" Bryce asked, waving his hand around at all the luxuries that some women would kill for.

"For free. Don't you think I've sacrificed enough," Mirah told him. "I gave up my job and even had to drop out of school for the semester to help you start your business. Now you're asking me to give up my family and friends too? What's next?" Mirah asked as tears started to flow down her cheeks.

"Not a thing," Bryce replied angrily. "You know I never forced you to leave your job or school for that matter. You came willingly and it's not my fault your grades slipped. Mirah, you could have come to me for help," Bryce said. "From now on you can do what you please. I'll hire an associate," he told her before walking out the door.

After their argument, Mirah didn't feel much like going out so she cancelled her plans for the night. She slipped out of her black dress and crawled up under the covers and cried her heart out.

It was a quarter to four when Mirah woke up. The other half of the bed was still empty. She got up to see if Bryce was sleeping in any of the other rooms, but they were all empty. Mirah made her way down to the kitchen to get something to drink. Now what could he be doing at four in the morning, Mirah thought to herself? No business deal lasted that long, she thought, pouring herself a tall glass of orange juice. Mirah returned to bed angry. She flicked on the television set and watched a whole movie before she heard Bryce come in and disarm the alarm system. She listened as he made his way up the stairs. Mirah was ready to go to battle.

"So where have you been?" Mirah asked as he slipped out of his clothes.

"Don't worry about it," Bryce responded. "If you really wanted to know you should have came along with me," he added, before going into the bathroom to take a shower.

"Bryce, what are you taking a shower for?" Mirah yelled, grabbing the glass door open. She definitely knew the signs of a cheating man while she stood there waiting for his response. Like father like son she thought, thinking about his father's affair that Bryce had no clue about.

"Oh, so now I can't take a shower without your permission? What's next?" he asked mirroring the same smart ass question she had asked earlier today.

Mirah's anger blew out of control. She tried to slap Bryce across the face but he caught her by the hand and forced her into the shower with him. Her silk gown clung tightly to her body as he pushed her against the shower wall.

"Bryce, let me go," Mirah screamed. The water continued to bounce off her body and her hair became soaking wet while she tried to wiggle free.

"Hell no," Bryce responded in a muffled voice. He pressed his lips tight against hers. "Are you worried about this?" he asked pulling the straps down.

"Bryce..."

"Look, Mirah, I went on a business cruise. There was a boat full of people mingling and networking so to speak. This was a very high profile affair and you should have been beside me."

"I'm sorry."

"Apology accepted. Now, I'm sorry that you feel the way you do. I had a lot of time to think and decided, like I told you before, to hire an associate and a small staff. The salaries will have to come directly out of my pocket for now so things will be tight for a while," Bryce said wiping the tears from her eyes.

Mirah couldn't say anything as the water from the shower continued to drizzle down her naked body. Her conscience was getting the best of her, even though she hadn't done anything wrong. She just wanted to relax with her friends for tonight, but their argument had prevented that and now she felt worse that Bryce made the decision to hire staff without her input. Well, how could she argue against that? He had made his decision based upon her feelings and now she began to regret the fact that she did not go.

"Are you going to be okay?" Bryce asked. He continued to watch the tears flow down her face.

Mirah could hardly muffle up any words; she just stood there and nodded yes.

Bryce wiped the tears from her eyes and held her tightly, feeling her body tremble against his. He covered her lips and eased his tongue in. He relished the sweet taste of her as he slid his tongue down to brand the softness of her neck. Next, he made it to her hardened nipples where he slowly suckled her tender breasts. Bryce didn't stop there; he eased down to the shower floor to sample the juices from her running river. He couldn't get enough of her as her body trembled now from pleasure. Bryce eased her around while she held on tightly to the metal shower rails. From behind he held on tightly to her, he entered in and made passionate love to her. The whole shower was steamed as they created their own heat.

"I love you, baby," Bryce told her before he released. Afterwards he lathered and washed every inch of her body again before carrying her off to bed.

Bryce went to sleep in no time as Mirah caressed the top of his shoulders. He turned over on his back and eased her close to him; she nestled her head on his chest.

"I love you, Bryce," Mirah whispered before closing her own eyes. She continued to listen to the sound of his heartbeat before finally drifting off to sleep.

****

"Are we going to church today?" Mirah asked, watching Bryce retrieve one of his suits from the closet.

"Not today, Honey, I have to interview a candidate for the associate position."

"On a Sunday? I had no idea you already had someone in mind."

"Yes, and this was the only time that could be arranged. I was very impressed with the potential candidate I met last night and don't want to delay the process."

"You sure don't waste no time," Mirah told him, easing out of bed.

"Well, you know how I am once I make my mind up," Bryce responded.

Actually no, Mirah thought to herself, but she was sure finding out quickly. Maybe she should have known considering how fast they were to walk down the aisle to get married. She wondered if Bryce used the same rationale when he asked her to be his wife? She never once stopped to think why the hurry. Any sane person would have considered the motives before making such a monumental decision. Maybe this was why her father stressed that they should get to know one another first. Had he seen something she had not? Mirah found herself questioning her marriage over the last few weeks. She prayed she made the right decision, and if Bryce really loved her the way he had expressed, than she would try her best not to let things he did upset her so much.

"So, do you want me to come along for the interview?" Mirah asked.

"Technically, I have already decided to hire her," Bryce replied. "Her name is Pamela Johnson and she's perfect for the position. Our meeting today is just to complete the formalities, but you can come along if you would like to meet her."

You're damn right, Mirah thought to herself. "Let me run through the shower right quick. I'll be ready in no time," she said, hurrying into the bathroom. How could Bryce make such an important decision without her? It was his business and all but she worked her butt off helping him jumpstart his business. The thousands of forms she had to fill out: tax forms, registering the company name, ordering equipment, and the million other things she had to do all seemed to have been unappreciated. Just like that he had pushed her out and brought somebody else in. She gave up her job, school, family, friends, not to mention the life she used to live. Was she supposed to take a back seat now? Hell no. Mirah knew she didn't have any skills as an architect but she sure wasn't about to be a side show and let some woman come up in here. Her presence would surely be known. She would make sure of that. Mirah quickly lathered some soap on her body before rinsing off and dressing.

"I'm ready," Mirah called out, making her way down stairs. Bryce sat at the kitchen table reading the morning paper, sipping on some hot coffee and eating a cinnamon raisin bagel.

"Would you like a cup of coffee?"

"No thank you," Mirah replied. There was no way she was about to mess up her make-up; she had to look perfect. She brushed her fingers across the bottom of her gray business suit. The minute you let a woman know your weakness is the minute you lose your man. Mirah had seen it too much as she retrieved her light jacket out the closet. Although it was May, the wind was still cool. They headed out the door and to his office to meet Pamela Johnson.

At the office Mirah paced around while Bryce turned his computer on to check his email. There was a slight tap on the door and Mirah waited a few seconds before she went to answer it.

"Yes, my name is Pamela Johnson and I'm here for an interview with Bryce Whitaker."

"Yes, we've been expecting you," Mirah said, extending her hand in greeting. "I'm Mrs. Whitaker," Mirah added in a professional tone.

"Well I'm glad you're feeling better," Pamela smiled. "Sorry you missed the cruise last night. We all had such a wonderful time," she added taking a seat.

Mirah was sorry she had missed the cruise, too. She looked Pamela Johnson up and down and noticed there was no wedding ring on her finger. She probably was hanging all over my husband last night, Mirah thought to herself with a jealous streak. Pamela was good looking, petite, well groomed with a gorgeous smile. Her short hair was cut to perfection and complimented her face structure. Her caramel skin was smooth, not one blemish. Pamela couldn't be no older than thirty-five and although Mirah had youth on her side, Pamela looked like the smart and experienced type.

"Do you have a resume?" Mirah asked, as polite as she could be.

"Actually, I gave Bryce my last copy when he interviewed me last night over a late night/early breakfast," Pamela replied, while she fumbled through her briefcase. "Would you mind printing a few off this CD?" she asked handing it to Mirah.

"Sure," Mirah said taking the CD. She printed out a few copies in no time and handed Pamela her disk back.

"Thank you."

"You're welcome, Ms. Johnson. Dr. Whitaker will be with you shortly," she emphasized. Her blood began to boil. Mirah went right in to let her husband know that his appointment was here. Who the hell does Pamela think she is referring to her husband on a first name basis? She didn't even know him personally and even if he had told her to call him Bryce, you would think she would have had enough sense to address him professionally in her presence. Maybe she did know him, Mirah thought, as a thousand questions began racing through her mind. Right now she was just plain jealous, an evil streak rushed through her body. How could Bryce come home and make love to her the way he did and forget to mention all the details about this new associate he decided to hire last night over an early breakfast?

"Ms. Johnson is here," Mirah told him in a snappy tone. "Would you like me to sit in on the interview?" she asked daring him to say no.

"Sure. I think that would be a good idea."

"Well, here is a copy of her resume," Mirah said laying it right in front of his face. From what was written on her resume, Pamela Johnson went to the best schools and worked at the top jobs in this industry. She wondered why she was even interested in this position.

"Oh, you keep that one. I already have a copy," Bryce said retrieving a copy from his folder. "We already had an informal interview," he added.

"Yes, over breakfast I hear," Mirah replied, rolling her eyes. "I imagine that's why you were so late coming home last night," she stated before leaving the room to get Ms. Johnson.

Chapter 18

Mirah grew angrier and angrier as Ms. Pamela Johnson transitioned into her new job. Anything to make Mirah's life a living hell, she did. Quite honestly, Mirah began to think she enjoyed working her last nerve. It started out with her always hovering around her husband. They were working around the clock night and day trying to bring new clients in. This would have been okay if that bitch wasn't trying to seduce her husband. That hussy started wearing her skirts shorter and tighter, hardly anything appropriate for work. When she mentioned this to Bryce he just brushed it off as a jealousy thing. Of course he had no problems looking at her double "D" breasts and the cleavage she just had to show all day and all night for that matter.

Mirah knew this was going to be a roller coaster ride when he started taking her on every business extravaganza. It wasn't that she should not have been there, since she was an employee, but Bryce seemed to replace her role entirely with this new associate. Mirah was so pissed at how he would introduce Pamela to his so called networking friends? The gleam in his face was the same he did with her. He paraded her around like she was his prize showcase piece. To make it worse, Pamela loved every minute of it, something Mirah had grown tired and disgusted with over the past few months. She had grown accustomed to putting on her black mask and pretending to be happy. Now that the spotlight was off of her she was still unhappy. It just seemed like her husband was substituting her entirely, so Mirah stopped going to the functions all together. She thought Bryce would beg her to change her mind but when he didn't, the gap in their relationship became even greater.

Their lovemaking even wasn't the same anymore. The flame that he once had for her seemed to dissipate. He always had some excuse, 'I'm tired. It's been an exhausting day or what have you.' When they were intimate he was in and out like an inexperienced person…a virgin.

Mirah would never forget the explosion that took place on the summer night of July 29. She had gone to visit with her mother for a few days to get a clear perspective on her life. She told Bryce she needed to help her mother with a few things, and she told her parents that she wanted to spend some time with them while Bryce was away on a business trip. Mirah couldn't believe how easy it was for her to lie. She had actually enjoyed being away from Bryce, but when her father began to catch on she decided to head back to avoid explaining how miserable her life was. When she got back she couldn't believe Pamela was trying to take over her house. They were having too much fun swimming in the pool, something she and Bryce used to do.

For the first time Mirah did something foolish without thinking. She ran to her bedroom in record time and hurried back to their little party. They were so into themselves that they never noticed her appearance. Just a little too intimate, as Bryce chased her around finally capturing and encircling his arms around her. Mirah just stood there watching while her temperature began to boil. She knew what was coming next and sure enough Pamela took things into her own hand and playfully kissed Bryce on the lips. He fell right for the bait and Mirah just waited there to see her husband's response. When Pamela realized he didn't resist, their embrace became even tighter and they started kissing passionately. Mirah nearly gasped while she watched her husband slide his tongue in her mouth.

Mirah waited a few moments as she watched angrily. She wanted to make sure his ass couldn't back out of this one, and it was the perfect excuse for firing Pamela Johnson. Finally, Mirah had the control.

"Well, well, well. What do we have here?" Mirah asked walking in on the two. She folded her hands as they spun around surprised. "I see you two are taking this business arrangement real personal," she added in disgust. For some reason Mirah was calm. She had always suspected this and now it was confirmed.

"Mirah, this isn't…"

"Shut up, Bryce," Mirah snapped cutting his sentence off. "I've seen enough. Now you get this whore out of our house before I do something I will regret," Mirah told him. She eased her hand over his automatic revolver; yes she knew right where to get his piece. Pamela's eyes nearly popped out her head at the sight of the gun.

"Mirah, honey, please put the gun away," Bryce said, while he eased his way out of the pool.

"There's no negotiating. Either you get her out of here or this pool will be filled with her tainted blood," Mirah said, pointing the gun directly towards Pamela's head. Mirah never had any intention of using the gun but she loved to see them both squirm. Pamela quickly rose out of the pool afraid.

"Oh, hell no. You let that bitch put on one of my swim suits," Mirah yelled in disbelief. "You bought that for me, how could you let her wear it?" Mirah asked angrily.

"Mirah, just calm down," Bryce said walking towards her.

"Calm down! No you didn't just tell me to calm down," Mirah screamed. She was so pissed off that she unclipped the safety lock off the gun.

"Now take my suit off," she demanded hysterically. That was the bottom line, while she watched Pamela scurry at her request. It took her only a matter of seconds as she stood there completely nude.

"Now get a good look," Mirah told her husband. "Isn't that what you wanted to see?" she asked waving the gun. Tears began flooding down her eyes out of nowhere.

"Mirah, please."

"Look at her, or have you already seen her?" she asked. Her hands began to shake out of control.

Mirah had never seen anyone run so quickly. Pamela grabbed her belongings and darted out the house butt naked. Bryce took the gun from her hand and unclipped the ammunition, which was already empty. Mirah never had any intentions of using it. When he returned, Mirah had collapsed and was floating at the bottom of the pool.

"Oh, my goodness," Bryce called out. He jumped into the pool after her. She was unresponsive while he felt for a pulse. He started to pump and blow air into her before water gushed from the corner of her mouth. He immediately turned her to the side and was relieved to hear her gasp for air.

"Honey, are you alright?" Bryce asked trying to reach over to the cordless phone. He quickly called for help and explained what happened. It was only a matter of minutes before the EMS technicians came rushing through the door.

"What happened?" one of the emergency crew asked, kneeling down to the floor besides Mirah. He took over while Bryce stepped to the side.

"I'm not sure what happened," Bryce replied. "We were just out here talking and I left out for one minute. When I returned, my wife was at the bottom of the pool."

"I slipped and fell," Mirah managed to get out. "My head hurts," she said before closing her eyes.

"We need to get her to the hospital right away," the EMS said.

"Is she going to be all right?" Bryce asked with a worried look on his face.

"Her vital signs seems to be okay but we have to make sure she doesn't have a concussion."

"I'll follow right behind you," Bryce said, hurrying to slip into some clothes. He damn near fell himself as he grabbed his car keys and headed out the door.

Bryce couldn't believe he let things slip out of control. Things really weren't what they seemed, he thought, racing behind the ambulance. He and Pamela normally worked at the office but today of all days their office air conditioning had broken so they went to his house to work in comfort. They had really been putting in some hard hours and their little break at the pool was just for fun, nothing more. The kiss was something that just happened unexpectedly. It wasn't planned but to be truthful he was enjoying the attention, which he wasn't getting from his wife lately.

The past few weeks had been difficult for him. Mirah was constantly putting pressure on him, always complaining about something that would usually end in an argument. Why couldn't she just understand his desire to get his own company started? First the problems started with quitting her job and dropping out of school. He had no idea that her grades had slipped and she should have definitely said something before it was too late. He felt terrible that she blamed him for this so he decided to hire Pamela, thinking this would relieve some of the stress. When he did that Mirah seemed to even be jealous of that. She automatically assumed that he would jump into the sack with the next beautiful thing that walked his way. All of a sudden she felt the need to want sex at every waking opportunity. She didn't even want to hear how tired he was, so when he didn't perform up to her expectations she started to complain about that. It made him feel like an old man, wondering if he should have considered her age before marrying her. The bottom line was, it seemed like he never had any peace and quiet around her. No matter how hard he tried, Mirah was never truly satisfied. Bryce didn't know why things were happening this way as he pulled up into the hospital parking lot. He parked his car and ran in just before they wheeled Mirah through the emergency door.

"Candy…Candy, where are they taking my wife?" Bryce called out frantically.

"Bryce, calm down," Candy told him. She gently began to knead the palm of her hand across his back to comfort him.

"They're taking Mirah to get a scan of her head to make sure everything is okay. That's a routine procedure for someone with a possible head injury," she assured him.

"Do you think everything is going to be fine?"

"We'll know more when they complete all the testing," Candy replied. "Come on. I'll wait with you until Mirah gets through. Would you like a cup of coffee?"

"No, thank you. My adrenaline is already up. I don't think coffee will help at this point."

"All right, I'll get you a cup of water instead. It will do you some good."

Bryce didn't argue and gladly sipped down the water while he told Candy his account of what happened, with the exception of Pamela. She didn't need to know that information. In fact, nobody did. Bryce found it amazing how much Candy had changed over the last few months. She seemed to have her life back on track, something he wished for himself right now. Maybe he should have stuck around to see if he could have rekindled his relationship with Candy; after all, the wedding ring he gave Mirah was the one he had purchased for Candy in the first place.

"Bryce, you can see your wife now," the attending nurse came in and told him.

Bryce gave Candy a hug and headed off to be with his wife. How could he doubt his decision of marrying Mirah? He felt guilty for thinking these thoughts, especially at a time like this. He really did love her. Bryce went in her room and sat by her side thinking of their wedding vows, *'in sickness and in health.'*

****

The next few days were completely relaxing for Mirah. Bryce attended to her every need. He was certainly going out of his way to be nice, Mirah thought quietly to herself. Well, if her husband thinks she would have second thoughts about keeping Pamela on the job, he had another thing coming. She wanted that woman out of their life for good. Who the hell did she think she was going after Mirah's man. Her bony little ass didn't have nothing on me, she thought, wondering why Bryce thought the need to turn the other eye. Why do men have to do this? They're never satisfied, and they wonder why it's so hard to find a good woman.

Mirah laughed thinking back to the incident at the pool. Pamela was shaking in her boots as she ran out the house butt naked. She could see the reaction on Pamela's face if she was able to air her dirty deeds out. She wondered what her rich daddy would think to see how devilish his daughter behaved. He would probably disown her if he so much as thought their name would be smeared across the headlines of the daily news. Mr. Johnson was a good respectable man and it surprised Mirah how different his daughter was behaving, since she was raised with a decent background and all.

Mirah was livid to hear that Bryce wanted to keep Pamela on. After everything that had happened she should have been fired. There was no question about the issue and

Mirah couldn't for the life of her understand why he was coming to her defense.

"Honey, I know what you saw was upsetting but I swear nothing is going on between the two of us."

"Well then, why are you having such a problem letting her go?"

"You know her father has strong connections within the community. With his backing, Whitaker and Associates can be prominent within a few years. Baby, this can take some companies a lifetime but we can do it here in no time."

"Whatever," Mirah said sarcastically. "I just wonder how far you would have gone if I had not come home. Probably ten minutes longer you would have had Pamela rolling around in our bed."

"Mirah it was just a kiss, nothing more, nothing less."

"And the point? Do you think I'm supposed to feel better because it was just a kiss? Like you said, we're married and your responsibility is to me."

"Mirah, you're taking this all out of context."

"And you didn't with James. For goodness sake, you made me sign a restraining order to keep him away. Too bad I can't demand the same for Pamela."

"Now you're taking this way over board," Bryce said throwing his hands up in the air. "I can't believe you're trying to compare the two situations. Your ex-boyfriend broke into this house and tried to attack me."

"Look, I'm not going to argue with you," Mirah cried. "The point is, I let James go even though I know in my heart he would never hurt me or someone close to me. Things just got out of control that day, the same as the situation here. Why can't you do the same? Bryce you can make your business prosper on your own merit. You don't have to kiss up to anyone, not even to the daughter of the man who can help you."

For the first time in his life Bryce was speechless. He just stood there in thought, unsure of how to respond to his wife's request.

"I just don't know how to please you," Bryce finally said breaking the long silence.

"What do you mean by that?" Mirah asked, tears started to form in the corner of her eyes. Those were the last words she expected to hear coming from her husband's mouth. She knew the last few weeks had been rough but this was totally unexpected.

"Well, first you told me that you didn't want to be so heavily involved with the business, so when I hired an associate, the last thing I expected was for you to be angry about that."

"Bryce, you two were kissing in each other arms. How do you expect me to feel?"

"Come on, Mirah, you had a problem with Pamela from the first day she started."

"Okay, lets just lay all the cards out on the table," Mirah said. "Yes, I was mad but not because you hired Pamela. It was the way you handled the whole situation. That night when you asked me to attend another business function, I was just exhausted. I had already made plans to go out and you knew about it. My feelings were just hurt that you didn't care about what was going to make me happy. The past few months have been all about the business and I just needed a break from it all."

"Honey, why do you think I hired Pamela in the first place?"

"Please let me finish," Mirah said trying to keep all her thoughts together. "Anyway, that day you made me feel so low.

First you implied that I looked like a whore from the outfit I was wearing and secondly you never mentioned anything about this so called business cruise, especially since it was supposed to be such an important event. When you walked out and said you would hire an associate, I never imagined you would have done it in the same night. Sometimes I feel like you can just snap your fingers and get what you want because you have money."

"Mirah it's not even like that," Bryce told her. He had to admit that from time to time he did use his money to influence a situation but never with Mirah. That was the one thing that really attracted him to her. She never asked or expected anything from him. She gave her heart freely unlike so many of the other women he had dated in the past.

"Well it just seems like that sometimes. Anyway, I was so upset from our argument that I stayed home. When you came home so late that made me even angrier, especially when you told me the next day of your decision of interviewing an applicant so quickly. To make matters worse you left out the fact that you had already had an informal interview over a late night-early breakfast. We made love that night…it just seems like you could have told me everything," Mirah told him.

"Okay, Mirah. You spoke your peace so let me do the same," Bryce told her. "I believe the whole source of our problems has been miscommunication. You tell me one thing but feel differently when I change things based on your feelings. Mirah, I can't know how you're feeling so just come out and tell me. You wait until things escalate and it has driven a wedge in our relationship. That's why I told you it has become difficult to please you. It's hard to know where you're coming from."

"All I want is for you to love me," Mirah replied as tears continued to roll down her cheeks. "Sometimes I feel you don't understand me," she added wishing she had taken her father's advice.

"Are you saying we got married too quickly?"

"Maybe we did. Just look at me...I've never had an evil streak in my body and it really scared me how stupid I was to put a gun in my hand. When I saw you and Pamela kissing it just confirmed my suspicions about the two of you and also my failure as a wife."

"Mirah, you're not a failure as a wife," Bryce told her.

"Than why were you in the arms of another woman?"

"Sometimes things just happen. I'm not going to sit here and tell you a lie but my love for you has not changed," Bryce said, embracing her in his arms.

"I just want our marriage to work."

"Honey, it will," he assured her. "I'm sorry for everything that has been happening. From now on let's just be honest with each other," Bryce said.

"Okay, well I want Pamela gone. A woman like her cannot be trusted," she told her husband.

"Consider her gone," Bryce responded, tracing the tears in his wife's eyes.

"Are you serious?"

"If that's what will put our marriage back on track, then yes. Just never put me in a position like that with my family because you will lose," Bryce said kissing her lips.

"Where did that come from? I don't have any problems with your family. In fact, we get along just fine," Mirah, told him.

"Well I'm just laying the cards on the table," Bryce stated. "And while we're being honest, you need to work on getting your father to come around. I know he doesn't like me much."

"My father likes you. He's just old fashioned," Mirah replied. "He'll come around. You'll see," she promised.

"Okay, enough about everything else. Are you up to going out for some fun?"

"That sounds good to me."

"Are you sure you're feeling up to it?" Bryce asked not wanting to push her. "You know the doctor told you to take it easy for the next few days."

"I'm fine. Besides, some fresh air will do me some good."

"All right, but we'll take it easy," Bryce told her before they headed out the door.

Chapter 19

Mirah was relieved to have Pamela Johnson out of her hair. She never did like her from the start. Pamela was one of those women who seemed to have everything and would do just about anything to get what she couldn't have. Why couldn't Bryce see it? She could easily imagine a strong man like her husband succumbing to her evil ways. Pamela was a low-down dirty down snake. She could outwit the best of them, Mirah thought, while she went through her desk drawer to make sure all her things was cleared out. It seemed like she hardly did any work around here anyway with the exception of seducing Mirah's husband. Mirah made sure she backed up her computer before Bryce gave her the axe. She was hardly intelligent enough to stand with the best in this field; Pamela was living off the coattail of her parents' reputable name.

Mirah spent most of August interviewing candidates for the Associate's position. Whenever they found a potential candidate to resume Pamela's role, they ended up turning down the offer. The salary was too low and they weren't comfortable giving up a secure job to work for a new company that could literally fold overnight.

In the end Mirah convinced Bryce to hire someone fresh out of college. She told him more people would be willing to come on board once the company was established. For now this would work perfectly since the salaries were being paid out of their own pockets. Mirah even hired an intern and decided to hold off on going back to school so she could help with the administrative side of things. This was the least she could do since she demanded that Bryce fire Pamela.

Mirah felt good being back in the driver's seat. She ordered two nameplates for Sheila Hendricks and Raymond Orr to hang up on their doors before they started next week.

Mirah enjoyed doing work like this. She was proud of how she had set up the office space. Each employee had their own office with a spectacular view of the city. The computers and office furniture were all new and Mirah knew that Sheila and Raymond would appreciate having a comfortable work space. They also had two conference rooms, a beautiful lunch room with all the bells and whistles. Even though they had just started this business, Bryce had spent a lot of money getting the office space together. They were in New York business district just like the rest of the top companies. He felt that was important if he wanted to attract the top clients in the architectural engineering field. They built everything from elaborate homes to skyscraper buildings.

    Mirah took a few moments to glance over their new employee resumes again. Sheila Hendricks had graduated with honors from Howard University and had come back to her hometown to find employment. She was brilliant and even Bryce was impressed with her talents and the portfolio she presented. Mirah knew once Sheila established herself in the field, people would be knocking her door down to hire her. The woman had both talent and brains and for now the situation was ideal for both parties. Sheila was from a well-rounded family and was just recently married. Mirah could see them easily bonding as good friends since they had so much in common.

    Raymond Orr was an intern from an area college in New York. This brother was fine and had a promising future ahead of him. Raymond kind of reminded Mirah of James. He was tall, handsome, and his physique was built to perfection. His dark chocolate skin was smooth as icing, good enough to lick with your fingers. Although he was in the corporate world, he had a rugged look to him and a great personality out of this world. During the interview, Bryce immediately identified with him.

He was much like Bryce during his years in school, motivated to work and perfecting his skills. Mirah was glad Bryce had decided to bring him on board. It's not enough of us helping each other along the way, Mirah thought to herself before leaving for the day. Things seemed to be looking up and she prayed they stayed that way.

****

Even with their hectic schedules, Mirah found time to squeeze in a little fun. Her friend Callie had invited her to come along to a party, and she didn't want to refuse since they were getting their friendship back on track. She asked Bryce to come along and was surprised when he told her to go ahead alone. He had to continue preparing for this huge business deal that would bring in millions of dollars for the company. Mirah didn't feel bad in leaving since Sheila and Raymond were helping around the clock to make sure this deal was a success.

Mirah packed her bags and headed to her hometown of Jersey. She was even more shocked that Bryce gave over his keys to the Mercedes Benz. She headed to her parents' house and when she arrived things were pretty quiet. Her mother had gone out of town on a church trip and this was the first time in years that Mirah and her father were alone. She enjoyed the quality time that she spent with her father.

"I'm glad you're home," Willie told his daughter. "I'm so used to your mother fussing, that the days seem to be very long sitting here alone."

"I bet," Mirah laughed.

"So, what brings you home?" Willie asked.

"Callie invited me to the last summer party before school starts back," Mirah told him.

"Well I'm glad that the two of you are getting your friendship on good terms again. You've known each other for as far back as I can remember and I will be happy of the day to see both of my daughters walk across the stage together to receive your degree."

Mirah's heart nearly caved. She had to sit there and lie straight to her father's face. Mirah just couldn't bring herself to tell him the truth. She offered to take him out to lunch to take his mind off her school life, that wasn't happening at the moment. They had a wonderful time and even spent a long part of their conversation talking about Bryce. Mirah did break down and admit how rocky their relationship had been over the past few months. She told her father she understood how upset he was by their jumping into marriage so quickly and probably should have waited a while before getting married. Nevertheless, Mirah did not regret the decision she had made and promised her father that things were better now.

Mirah felt relieved when her father circled his arms around her in support. He promised to make an effort to get to know his son-in-law better and even had Mirah call Bryce right then to talk with him. They spoke for nearly an hour and set up a golf outing just for the two of them. It felt strange that things were going so well and Mirah promised herself she would get back in school for the upcoming spring semester so she wouldn't let her parents down. Her education was the one thing they desired for her and they deserved to see that day just as much as she did.

Night time approached quickly and Mirah started to get ready for tonight's party; she had to look absolutely radiant. She took a nice soothing shower. There was going to be people from the party that she hadn't seen in years. She was glad James would not be there, unsure she would be able to face him. Mirah couldn't believe how Candy flaunted their so called relationship in her face. Candy was all too eager to let Bryce know that she had moved on with her life, when Mirah had been taken to the emergency room a few weeks back. Candy went on and on about how James had been promoted to Director and was in California, training employees of their partner company that had just recently opened. Mirah had been a little jealous and wondered why James would even give Candy the time of day. She wondered the same for her husband, as the growing list of potential threats became branded in the forethought of her mind. Some women would do anything to get a man, and especially one who was good looking and rich too. Candy must be kicking herself everyday for letting a wonderful man like Bryce slip from her hands. Oh well, her loss and my gain, Mirah smiled, stepping out the shower. She dried herself off and lathered some oil all over her body.

Mirah was pleased; she stood in the mirror admiring how good she looked. The thin sheer burgundy sundress she had on revealed all her womanly curves. She spun around doing a few dance moves. Her hair was looking good too as she let it hang freely down her back. Mirah put on a little make-up and then dabbed some sweet scents on before heading downstairs.

"You look radiant," Willie told his daughter, when she joined him in the living room.

"Thank you, Daddy," Mirah replied kissing him on the cheek.

"I'm surprised Bryce is not here. Do you need me to come along as your chaperone?" Willie laughed.

"Dad, you are too funny," Mirah told him. "I'll be just fine and I'll be home late," she warned him.

"Just make sure you're home to fix your old man some breakfast."

"I promise," Mirah told him. "I love you daddy," she said before leaving.

"I love you, too," he called out. He watched his daughter get into the car and pull off.

The party was in full force when Mirah walked in. A few people that she recognized stopped to greet her while she made small talk. Mirah could tell some of the women were jealous as they stared her down, and the men were trying to get game even with her huge diamond ring displayed. She was glad Callie came to her rescue as she politely excused herself.

"Where have you been? I have something to tell you," Callie said, trying to talk over the loud music.

"Well, out with it," Mirah told her as she saw James enter into the room. Their eyes instantly locked and he made his way over towards them.

"That's what I was trying to tell you," Callie said. "I've been calling your cell phone and the line was disconnected. I even tried to reach you at your parents' house with no luck."

"We just got new cell phones and our numbers were changed. My father and I have been out all day," Mirah told her.

Callie seemed to be a little nervous as James continued to make his way over.

"Callie, it's okay," Mirah assured her. She took a deep breath, trying to contain her own anxiety.

"Good, because I didn't want you to think this was some kind of setup. Tyron just told me today that James was back in town."

"Well, we were bound to run into one another at some point and time. I'm just glad my husband isn't here," Mirah responded.

"Hello, ladies," James said, joining the two of them. "Long time no see," he told Callie. He embraced her in a friendly hug. "And you look lovely as ever, Mrs. Whitaker," he said, stepping back a few feet.

"Thank you," Mirah replied feeling very uneasy. 'Mrs. Whitaker,' now why did he have to be all formal like that? She couldn't blame James for having such resentment towards her after the restraining order she slapped against him, but this was so out of character. It was like they hardly even knew each other.

"So where is Tyron?" he asked, turning his attention back to Callie.

"He's in the back," Callie pointed out.

James didn't stick around long before excusing himself. Mirah just looked on as he disappeared into the crowd. She didn't take her eyes off of him, a spark of guilt swelled within her heart. A part of her still loved him. She would never forget the special ties they shared. Mirah tried to hold back the tears.

"Are you okay?" Callie asked her.

"Sure," Mirah lied. She knew this was going to be a long night. Callie diverted her attention and grabbed Mirah to join her on the dance floor to groove to the latest hip-hop music blasting from the DJ's speakers.

Mirah twirled around to two songs before a slow jam came on. She made her way over to the bar while couples embraced each other. Callie was snuggled tight in Tyron's arms and he took no time in easing his hands to her butt. James was slowly grooving with Tina Flamboyant, who had a crush on him all through high school. She tried many a day to break up their relationship and James never gave her the time of day. Now he was all over her blossomed curves. Mirah just looked on with jealousy in her eyes.

"What are you having?" the bartender asked.

"Give me a Long Island Iced Tea," Mirah told him. She was in no mood to flirt; she sent any man who walked up to her away. Her eyes stayed glued to James while he continued to bump and grind on the dance floor. Damn, he was looking good as ever, Mirah thought angrily. It hurt even worse to see Tina glued all over him.

The one thing that bothered her the most was how their relationship ended. Sometimes Mirah couldn't rest easy at night, but with all the problems she was having in her marriage, she really didn't have time to think of much else. Now that her home life was back on track, Mirah needed to smooth things over with James. She thought her letter had explained pretty much everything that night when she gave it to him at the hospital. By the way James was acting, she wondered if he had ever even received the letter. It dawned on her that she had given it to his nurse, Candy. Why hadn't she put two and two together sooner, she thought angrily to herself? God only knows what James was feeling. She walked over towards him on the dance floor; she had to settle things once and for all, and right now.

"Excuse me, James, can we talk?" Mirah asked interrupting his dance with Tina. She eyeballed Mirah up and down with disdain.

"I don't think that's such a good idea," James told her, like he was annoyed she would even ask.

"It's really important," Mirah responded. "Please just give me a few moments of your time," she added, wanting to slap Tina, who was taking pleasure in her begging.

"Can we finish this dance later?" James asked Tina.

She whispered something in his ear and he nodded with hungry eyes in approval. He then followed behind Mirah who led him outside the hall. Callie looked on as Mirah quickly told her that they would be back shortly.

Outside, people were hanging around or going in the hall to join the party. Mirah didn't want to talk here; she was surprised James agreed to go to their old spot, which was about ten minutes away. When they were in high school they used to come to the park all the time. They even made love there on more than one occasion. She wondered what was going through James's mind, the quiet lingered in his truck, with the exception of the tunes coming through the radio speakers.

"You know, I can go to jail for being within 500 feet of you."

"That's what I want to speak with you about," Mirah responded, as he put the truck in park. He got out and then came around and helped Mirah out. They went over and sat on the same picnic table that their initials were inscribed in: 'JG & MJ Forever.' Mirah brushed her hands across the wood table before sitting down.

"James, I'm sorry about the way everything ended," Mirah told him.

"Me too," James replied. "I'm surprised you would go to such lengths to keep us apart. It was like I never meant anything to you."

"That's not true," Mirah told him. "My husband put me into a hell of a situation; James, my hands were tied," Mirah said. Tears welled up in the corner of her eyes, "I hope you know that this was the last thing I'd ever do."

"When did you start letting a man decide what's best for you?" James asked.

"James, you're not the only one who has agonized over this. I've had many restless nights, but I'd do it all over again rather than see you sitting behind bars."

"What are you talking about?"

"Well, I see Candy never gave you the letter," Mirah replied, confirming her earlier suspicions.

"Wait, what letter are you talking about? And what does this have to do with Candy?"

"The night when I last saw you in the hospital, I gave the nurse a letter for you. I had no idea at the time that she was a former lover of my husband."

"What!"

"Yes, I gave her the letter and she must have taken it. It just dawned on me at the party today that you had probably never even seen the letter."

"I can't believe this shit," James said out loud. "Candy has been using our friendship all this time for her own agenda."

"So you two are involved?" Mirah asked.

"Not in a relationship," James replied. "I'll deal with her later. Let's get back to the point about this letter."

"Everything I felt was in that letter, something you never had the opportunity to see."

Mirah still couldn't believe what was going on. What was it about her men and all the deception that had been going on?

"James, my husband had brought his attorneys in to press charges against you. The last thing I wanted was to see you sitting behind bars."

"Mirah, never step in to do a man's job. I'm capable of defending myself."

"I was just trying to do what was best. Bryce was trying to get you brought up on attempted murder charges."

"What? I'm the one who almost lost my life."

"Yes, but he argued that you were the one who broke into his home. Bryce said he was just defending himself. Look, I didn't want anyone hurt or in jail over me, so when he came to me with these restraining orders I had no choice but to sign."

"Mirah, you always have a choice," James told her. "Don't you know how much I love you? I would have done anything for you."

"James, I love you too. Enough to let you go," Mirah told him. By this time tears started to stream down her face and didn't stop.

James didn't know what to say as he embraced her in his arms. He wondered where their relationship would be today if he had never gone over to confront Bryce.

"Why did you go over there anyway?" Mirah asked.

"The truth, because I was angry that you were going to marry a man you barely knew. That should have been me," James told her. He looked directly into her eyes: "I had already bought you a ring and had planned on proposing to you the night we had an argument back at the hotel. In fact, it was something I had planned on doing right after high school, but your parents talked me out of it. Now do you see why I was so angry? I let the opportunity to marry you slip by, not once but twice."

Mirah was speechless and didn't know what to say. James pulled her back in his arms and covered his lips over hers. There were so many things looming around in her mind as he slid his tongue in to taste hers. Mirah didn't know if she was trembling from the night's breeze or from the fact that she was enjoying being in his arms again.

"James, we shouldn't be doing this," Mirah told him, pulling away. "I'm married."

"Yes, you are but your heart will always belong to me. Leave Bryce and come back to me."

"James…"

"Sshh…" he said cutting her sentence off. "Don't tell me you're not enjoying this as much as I am," he whispered, gliding his tongue back in her mouth. He lavished getting reacquainted with the person he loved most. Mirah's lips were so full and vibrant and he could sit here all night with her in his arms. James eased Mirah back on the table and he stood between her legs. He let his hands linger, cupping the softness of her behind.

Mirah just sat back and enjoyed letting James run his hands across the smoothness of her body. She knew it was wrong, but the temptation was too much for her to resist. He leaned on top of her and his lips met hers again, she tasted the warmth of his breath. His hands were now in her panties, he stroked his fingers to sample the water flowing from her river. Mirah let a soft moan escape her mouth as the hunger in James's eyes grew. She couldn't believe he had plans to marry her. She knew for sure her fate would have been different if they hadn't been interrupted by outside forces. Tears welled up in her eyes knowing she should have been Mrs. Mirah Gibson. Instead her life had gone into a different direction, she was married to Bryce Whitaker and she suddenly came to her senses.

"James, we can't do this," Mirah told him; she eased him off her.

He could see the agony in her eyes and embraced her in his arms tightly.

"I love you," James whispered softly in her ear.

"James..."

"Mirah, you don't have to say it," James said cutting her sentence off. "I already know how you feel," he told her, tracing the tears from her eyes. The softness of the park lights illuminated them as they held tightly to one another. He traced his hand slowly over her heart and branded a soft kiss in the core of her being. Mirah trembled; she traced her hand over his face. The tears in the both of their eyes sealed their forever lasting love for one another.

The party was over when they returned back to the hall. James walked Mirah to her car and kissed her goodbye. Mirah drove in complete silence; her life just became much more complicated. She pulled into her parents' place in no time and eased her way up the steps. She really wanted to talk to her father right now but decided it could wait. Mirah slipped off her clothes and crawled into bed. She picked up the phone and called Bryce. For some reason she had to hear his voice, feeling guilty of what happened tonight.

Mirah could barely get any sleep; she tossed and turned all night. The clock was now reading 6:00 a.m. She swept her feet to the floor; there was no need in trying to sleep in. Besides she had promised to fix her father a delicious breakfast. He normally woke up around seven o' clock and would be surprised to see his food already prepared just as if her mother was here.

Mirah slipped into the bathroom and took a quick shower before she headed downstairs. Bryce should already be halfway to California for an emergency meeting that came up. He even took Raymond along for the experience and to help out with any extra work.

Mirah opened a package of bacon then turned the stove on. She shook her head as she put a few slices in the skillet to cook. She wished her mother had been adamant about her father's poor eating habits. Too much of this food isn't good for the body, Mirah thought to herself. She was finished cooking in no time; she prepared a plate and set it on the kitchen table. She knew her father would bicker about the two slices of bacon she had on his plate. The scrambled eggs, grits, and toast would make up for it, she thought, putting on a pot of fresh coffee. Mirah was surprised the aroma hadn't woken her father up as she headed up the stairs. She just decided to wake him up so his food wouldn't get cold. Besides, she wanted to talk to him about what happened last night. Well, not everything, Mirah thought quietly to herself. She just wanted to know why they kept James from proposing to her when they had graduated from high school. She understood that her parent's wanted her to go to college, but this should have been her decision. Maybe her life wouldn't be all this complicated if everyone would have just been open and honest. Now she was in love with two men and married to the one she barely knew. Her love for Bryce was on a different level and she didn't know how she was going to look him in the face after everything that had just happened. It was going to be difficult, especially since they finally got their marriage back on track. Mirah didn't know what to do. She tapped on her father's bedroom door. He always had sound advice and she could hardly wait to speak with him.

"Dad, are you up?" Mirah asked, calling through the door. "I have your breakfast ready as promised," she said, waiting for him to get up.

When he didn't come to the door, Mirah eased the door open to look in. Her father was still sleeping; she called out for him again. A streak of panic raced through her body when he didn't respond. Mirah rushed over to see about him. She nudged him slightly. When there was no response she started to shake him aggressively. Nothing!

"Oh, my God!" Mirah screamed. She ran over to the phone for help.

She hurried back over to her father and slid her hand over his heart…no beat.

"911."

"Oh my God…my father is not breathing. Please get some help over here," she pleaded in disbelief.

Mirah was hysterical while she tried to pump life back into her father.

"Daddy, wake up" she yelled. "Please," Mirah pleaded. She continued blowing and pumping his chest until the EMS arrived. When she heard the sirens, she flew down the steps to let them in. They followed her upstairs and took over to work on her father. Time seemed to stand still; her heart continued to pound rapidly in fear. She couldn't believe when the EMS Technician said that her father was dead.

"No," Mirah yelled out loud to everyone in the room. "You haven't even worked on him long enough," she cried scurrying back over to her father. She started her CPR again. She rapidly blew and pounded on his chest. "Daddy, wake up," Mirah shouted. "God, please make my father better," she wailed. The emergency crew pulled her away.

"I'm so sorry. Is there anyone you can call to be here with you?" the lady asked.

The question ran through Mirah's head with a pounding sensation. Oh my God, how am I going to tell mamma, she thought? Her heart dropped to the floor.

"Ma'am, you really shouldn't be here alone. Is there someone I can call for you?" she asked again.

Mirah knew her husband was halfway on the other side of the states. She blurted out James's name and phone number. Her mind went blank...she sank to the floor in tears.

"Yes, I'm trying to reach a James Gibson."

"Speaking."

"Yes, my name is Sherry of the New Jersey EMS Department. I'm here at the Jones' residence and was wondering if you could come over to help with Mr. Jone's daughter. Her father has just passed away."

"I'll be right there," James told her.

Mirah just sat there while people came in and out the house. The Coroner's office was called to take her father away as they prepared his body. Mirah tried to answer all the questions; she was glad James was standing by her side. The next door neighbors were there helping and called the pastor over to pray over her father. Picking up the phone was the hardest thing to do. She dialed her mother's cell phone number.

"Mamma," Mirah cried through the phone. A lump clouded her throat and prevented her from speaking.

"Sweetheart, just calm down and tell me what's the matter," Mattie told her nervously. Whatever her daughter had to say did not sound good. She braced herself for the worst.

"Mamma, its Daddy...he's...you just need to get home right away," Mirah cried out loud.

"Mirah, where are you and what's wrong with Willie?"

"I came up to wake daddy for breakfast, but he was dead," Mirah managed to say in a rasp muffled tone.

"Oh, Lawd," Mattie screamed dropping the phone.

Mirah could hear her mother's anguish, she closed her eyes hoping this pain would all go away.

Willie, Willie. Oh, God, not my Willie Mirah heard her mother cry out. Mirah just held the phone and she listened to her mother call out to the heavens. Mirah's heart was ripped in two for having to give this news, especially over the phone, and for not being there to circle her arms and grieve together with her mother. There was a long silence and then one of her mother's friends picked up the phone. Mirah talked a while longer, making arrangements for her mother to fly home. When she hung up the phone, James circled his protective arms tightly around her. She needed all his strength as they carried her father away. Mirah dropped her head further into his chest and told her father how much she loved him.

"He loved you, too," James said, caressing the fear that was running through her body. "Always hold that in your heart," he told her. He continued to comfort her from something he had no control of changing. James eyes filled with tears while he watched the droplets fall to the floor. No matter what he had done, Willie Jones was a good man.

Chapter 20

Bryce feelings were spinning out of control as he headed back to New York alone after the funeral services. Understandably his wife wanted to stay with her mother for a few weeks to cope with her father's death. Bryce still couldn't believe Willie was gone. They never even had a chance to make it on their golf outing. He had looked forward to getting to know his father-in-law better, but at least he had a chance to have one last conversation, which ended on good terms. It was better than nothing, and it was comforting to know he was finally at ease with him marrying his daughter.

James, on the other hand, was a different story. He couldn't believe he had the nerve to show his face at the services. That didn't bother him so much as when he came through the family line to give his condolences. Bryce wanted to choke the life out of him, when he had the audacity to kiss and embrace his wife right in front of his face. If only it was another time and place, he would have paid the consequences for disrespecting him in front of everybody like that. Bryce thought about hauling his ass to court in violation of their restraining order but his wife didn't need that right now. He hated not having control of a situation. Damn, he shouted, pounding angrily on the steering wheel.

Bryce would have never agreed to let his wife come up to this party alone if he knew James was in town. He thought James was somewhere in California. He cringed at the thought of that punk's arms wrapped around his wife.

Bryce could see James begging his wife for one last dance. He knew how men's minds worked. A simple dance could lead into a simple kiss and once you get them that far they try to go all the way until they have you in their bed. Hell,

I did that many times in my day, he thought angrily to himself. If that punk so much as touched his wife, he would be sorry.

Bryce made it back to Manhattan in no time. He searched his car from top to bottom making sure no one who wasn't supposed to be in here was. When he opened the sun visor an envelope fell to the seat. The writing scribbled across definitely didn't belong to his wife; he opened to read it contents.

My Dearest Mirah,

I'm glad we had the chance to spend some quality time alone. I know I don't say it often enough but I love you so very much. I'm so proud to be your father and you are the best daughter anyone could ever ask for. When you find this letter, you may well be back on your way home to New York. Just wanted to write you a quick note while waiting for you to come out the store. Thanks so much for lunch and I'm glad we had this chance to talk. Always know how much I want the best for you and you make me so proud, though I haven't told you enough. Don't forget to tell my son-in-law that I'm really looking forward to our golf day. He's going to be surprised what this old man can do on the greens. Love you always.

Willie

Bryce folded the letter. He was in tears as he headed towards the lobby to his penthouse. Inside, he gulped down a few shots of cognac before he made his way up the steps and crawled into bed with his clothes on. He held Mirah's pillow tightly against him thinking of her father who passed at such an early age. The thought sent a chill through his body, knowing that tomorrow is never promised. Bryce closed his eyes and rolled onto his back. "Lord, please embrace Willie into your ever lasting Kingdom," he prayed before drifting off into his own sleep.

Chapter 21

James was infuriated as he stepped on the pedal speeding down the highway. Candy had some serious explaining to do after the information he had learned from Mirah. He had planned on confronting her a few days ago but when he learned of Willie's death he put everything on hold.

James last memory of Willie hadn't been on the best of terms as his eyes clouded up with tears. In fact, things got down right nasty when Mirah married Bryce back in February. He remembered going to the church and before then to Willie's house to talk with her father. He wanted to talk man to man, about why they approved of this marriage to Bryce but flat out demanded that he wait until their daughter was through with college before he could propose marriage to her. Mattie went ballistic when she came in and overheard the conversation that was transpiring between the two.

James could vividly remember her saying, 'Lawd, get this heathen out of my house. Get him out now before I call the polices.'

James was so angry at the time that he didn't go anywhere. He wanted answers and demanded that they give them to him. James was sure that if Mattie hadn't abruptly sabotaged things they could have hammered things out man to man. All he wanted was the truth, that much he thought he deserved. Mattie was having none of that and all Willie could do was come to the defense of his nagging wife. They exchanged some heated words and James remembered telling them they were going to rot in hell for all this mess. Mattie nearly fell out, and when James started quoting scriptures from the bible, he thought her head would fly off the top. He even pulled some money from his wallet saying, money is the root of all evil...and if they thought it was going to make their daughter truly happy, they had another thing coming.

Well Mattie didn't like that one bit and Willie demanded that he get out of their house. James knew he wouldn't get anything out of them so he just threw the money in their faces and walked out. Mattie was running behind him cursing every which word in the book. He had never seen so much anger in her eyes, when he turned around. "God don't like ugly. You're not being very Christian like," he told her, and then she slammed the door in his face. James could hear her screaming, "That boy ain't nothing but the devil." James hollered back through the door, "well I'll see you both in hell then."

He heard Mattie pounding on the door in tears. He got in his truck and sped off. God, how he wished that day had never happened. He never meant for things to get out of control but Mattie just had a way of doing that. She was far different from her daughter and James wondered if all this could have been avoided if Candy had just given him the letter in the first place.

****

"James, I didn't know you were back in town," Candy said, inviting him in.

"And I didn't know you were once involved with Bryce Whitaker," James responded coldly.

The happy expression on her face quickly vanished.

"Did you think I would never find out?" James asked.

"James..."

"Before you say anything, I want the truth...the whole truth," he told her. He didn't have any time to play games...he awaited for her response.

"Yes, I was involved with Bryce, but what does that have to do with us?"

"First of all there is no us. And second of all, if there was a chance for us getting together, you just blew it."

"James, you're being kind of harsh."

"Harsh...Candy you've been playing me from the moment we met."

"That's not true," Candy replied.

"Don't play games with me," James replied heatedly. "I'm not a fool and whatever you were trying to run is over, so you better tell me the truth."

"Okay," Candy sighed as tears started to flow from her eyes. "When you were in the hospital was the day I found out that your ex-lover, Mirah, was involved with Bryce. She didn't know who I was but I'd seen her over his house before. When Mirah came to see you at the hospital she gave me a letter to give to you," she told him.

"James, I was angry so I took the letter. I was so upset that Bryce was so quick to marry someone he hardly knew. We had been together for a year, and yes I believed it should have been me walking down that aisle instead of Mirah. Why should she enjoy both worlds? If she wanted Bryce, she definitely didn't deserve you, too."

"That wasn't for you to decide," James told her.

"I realize that now, but you have to believe that I never intended on hurting you."

"It's too late for that Candy. The damage has already been done."

"Please James, don't walk out on me," Candy pleaded with him. "Don't do this to me, too. I'm sorry for everything."

"Sorry doesn't cut it. Give me one good reason why I should stay?"

"Because I'm carrying your baby."

"What!"

"I was just as shocked to learn of this news," Candy replied.

"This can't be true," James stated in disbelief. "Candy, you better not be running games on me. We were protected the few times we were intimate together."

"Don't tell me you don't remember the tear," Candy reminded him.

"Yeah, but you said not to worry because you were on the pill."

"James nothing is a hundred percent except for abstinence."

"Don't fucking get sarcastic with me," James yelled. "If you were taking the pill right there would be no problem.

"Problem. So you think your baby and I are a problem?"

"Candy..."

"James, just get out," Candy screamed. "Do you think I want to be pregnant at my age. Hell, my son is near grown and I never planned on starting over again."

James didn't know what to say. He just stood there numb. It wasn't any use in pointing blame because he was just as responsible. He bit down on his lower lip, damn, Candy had been a good friend and all but she definitely was not someone he wanted to start a family with. Even more so, when he found out about what she had been keeping from him.

"Candy, you can understand why it's hard for me to believe anything you say at this point. Hell, for all I know this could be someone else baby. You sure it's not Bryce?"

"James I can't believe you would think that."

"Well sometimes people do desperate things under pressure. Maybe Bryce didn't want anything to do with you so you're laying the responsibility on me."

"James, we've all lied or did something in our life that we're not proud of. Don't worry, we won't be a problem for you," Candy assured him.

"Look, I'm just really upset right now," James told her. "I grew up without my real parents and my child will never go through that," he told her. "No matter what happens between the two of us I will take care of my own."

Candy just stood there crying. Her life had been up, down, and in circles over this past year. First she was dumped by Bryce, the one person she loved most and now she was pregnant by the man who was still in love with Bryce's wife. Mirah would always be the love of James's life and she couldn't believe she let herself get tangled in this love triangle. Why was this happening to her? She should have never kept that letter or gotten herself involved with James who, legally, couldn't even buy beer. He was just a few years older than her own son and she should have known better. James seemed so much more mature, but when it all came down to it, their relationship was just casual sex.

"I'll be back in a minute," Candy said, leaving the room. When she came back she gave James the letter that she had kept and told him to leave.

"What in the hell is wrong with you?" James asked. "First I find out that you lied to me; then you drop this bombshell on me and tell me to get out."

"I should have just kept my mouth shut and handled my business," Candy said, walking away.

James didn't mean to hurt her as he grabbed and pushed her up against the wall. "Handle your business. Don't you dare come at me like that! I can't even believe you were thinking of getting rid of the baby in the first place. When are the lies going to stop?" James yelled angrily at her.

"You probably wouldn't mind one bit if I lied about this bombshell, as you call it."

"Candy, don't go twisting this around. Why don't you grow up and take responsibility for your actions in all this.

Things might have been different if you would have just been honest from the start."

"James, just get out," Candy cried, pulling away from him. "I don't need this from you right now."

"Too bad," he told her, embracing her in his arms. "Whether you like it or not, you're going to have to deal with me," he said.

****

James was relatively quiet on the drive home. Any chances, no matter how remote, of getting back together with Mirah was over. There was no way he could expect her to leave her husband when he had a baby on the way. He wasn't ready to be a father, at least not to the baby growing inside of Candy. However cold that may sound, it was just how he felt. James would just be turning twenty-one next month and now his whole world was turned upside down. As mad as he was about the situation, he had no one to blame but himself. He laid down like a man so he had to take the responsibilities as one.

James pulled over to the emergency side of the road to collect his thoughts. Right now he was in no condition to drive. He pulled out the letter Mirah had written him a few months ago.

James:

How do I find the words to explain something as difficult as this? The thought of even thinking about it pains me so much and the reality of what I have to do will silently kill a part of my heart that yearns for you. I love you so much, enough to do what's best for your well being. After the confrontation between you and Bryce, he asked (I feel more like demanded) me to sign a restraining order against you. James, I have no other choice but to sign these papers because Bryce has all but assured me that you would be sitting behind bars for the rest of your life for breaking into his home and trying to murder him. I know that was the last thing you would ever do so if a court battle can be avoided, then I will do what it takes because I only want the best for you, even if it means giving you up completely. James that's how much I love you and I pray that you will find it in your heart to forgive me. Although our lives will go in different directions from this point forward, always remember the love we shared for one another. I will hold on to that for the rest of my life. You were my first love. James you taught me so much during our time together. You made me happy, you gave your love freely, and you taught me how a man should treat a woman, even at our young age. The qualities you have are genuine and I hope that your heart never turns against me. I only wish the best for you.

Love always, Mirah

Tears formed in the corner of James eyes as he read the letter over again. He picked up his cell phone and dialed Mirah's number.

"Hello."

"Mirah, its James. How are you feeling?"

"I'm doing as well as can be expected. My mother, on the other hand, is not doing so well. Her brother convinced her to go back down south with them for a few months. They just left about two hours ago."

"I'm sorry to hear that. You know your parents and I were not on the best of terms but…"

"James, I know you have good intentions," Mirah said cutting his sentence off.

"I'm just sorry your family is going through this. Your father was a good man."

"Thank you," Mirah told him. "I miss him so much. I'm packing up right now to go home. I can't stay here alone right now."

"Before you leave can you stop by my place?" James asked. "I really need to talk with you."

"James, don't take this the wrong way but I don't think that's such a good idea. I haven't even had a chance to think about what you asked me. Quite honestly I'm scared. There are other people's lives at stake."

"I know," James told her. "There are some things going on in my life that you should know about. We really need to talk. Please stop by in about a half hour," James said. "Besides, I've finally read the letter that you wrote me all those months ago."

"The letter…when did you read it? Are you in New York right now?"

"Yes, I just read the letter and I'm on my way back home as we speak. Can you swing by before you head back home?"

"Sure," Mirah told him before hanging up.

Mirah really wasn't in the mood to confront James right now. She pulled out of the driveway and adjusted the mirror to her mother's Honda Accord and glanced back at her parent's house before she headed down the street. That house will never be the same again, she thought, remembering the last day she shared with her father. Mirah was so thankful she had come home and was glad of the time they shared. He was the one person she could talk with. Mirah started crying. *'I'm going to miss you dad,'* Mirah said in a faint whisper.

She never did have the chance to speak with him regarding the dilemma she was in. Mirah would have to figure this out for herself. She picked up the phone to dial Bryce.

"*Hmmm*, I wonder where he could be at this time of night," Mirah said to herself, clicking over to dial his cell phone. There was no answer, so she clicked over to dial the office number. She knew that no one would be there this late but it wasn't like Bryce to be unavailable.

"Hello, Whitaker & Associates."

"Raymond is that you?"

"Yes, how are you doing Mirah?"

"Better. I'm surprised you're at the office so late. Is my husband there with you?"

"He left about an hour ago. There was an urgent meeting that came up and I had to drop him off at the airport."

"Airport."

"Yes. I thought he would have called you by now. He's on his way back to California."

"Oh. Well maybe he left a message back at my parents' house," Mirah said. "Now you stop working so late and go home," she told him.

"Yes ma'am," Raymond responded in an enthusiastic tone.

"Raymond, before we hang up, I just wanted to thank you for all the hard work you're doing. I'm glad you came on board," Mirah told him. When she clicked off the phone she called to check her parents' voicemail. A knot formed in the pit of Mirah's stomach while she listened to her fathers recorded message.

"*You have reached the Jones residence. We're unable to take your call but please leave a message and we will get back to you as soon as possible.*" Mirah listened to the two messages that came through since she left. None were from her husband as she clicked off to dial the airport.

"Yes, can you tell me what flight my husband is on," Mirah asked. She gave the representative the information. Mirah jotted down the details and then called the hotel in California where Bryce last stayed. Knowing him, he probably made reservations at the same place, especially since it was last minute plans.

"Five Season's Hotel, may I help you?" the receptionist asked.

"Yes, I'm trying to reach a Bryce Whitaker," Mirah said, listening to her click on the keyboard in the background.

"Bryce and his party are not scheduled to arrive for another few hours."

"His party," Mirah thought to herself. Maybe he took Sheila along, she thought, asking the receptionist to confirm.

"No, that name is not listed," she replied. Mirah knew she wouldn't divulge anymore information so she took matters into her own hand. "Oh, it must be Pamela Johnson," Mirah stated. "I work for them at Whitaker & Associates and I need to email their presentation for their business meeting tomorrow morning."

"Yes, let me give you our corporate business line," the receptionist, said. "You can route any information to this office."

"Wonderful," Mirah said. "Could you also put me through to Ms. Johnson's line. I would like to leave her a message," Mirah said trying to contain her anger.

"Well there's only one room reserved. I can put you through, one moment please."

"Thank you," Mirah replied, biting down on her lower lip. She started to leave a message but just hung up instead. *"How could you Bryce...how in the hell are you going to play me like a fool?"* Mirah screamed at the top of her lungs. He knew how she felt about the situation. She pulled up into James's apartment complex and before she had time to think, he swung his truck in the space next to her.

Mirah tried to compose herself as James helped her from the car. They were both relatively quiet while they made their way up to his apartment.

"So, Mirah, I'm not going to waste your time," James told her. "I'll get right to the point," he said after offering her something to drink.

Mirah quickly gulped down the refreshing water and took a seat on the couch. James had come a long way, she thought, scanning over his place like she was visiting for the first time.

"Mirah, I read the letter," James said pulling it out of his coat jacket.

"Well I hope you understand why I did what I did."

"Yeah, I can see your perspective on things, but I can't help but wonder how things would have turned out if I had this letter from the beginning."

"James, we can't take back time," Mirah told him.

"I know. There are so many things going on in my life right now. Considering that I asked you to leave your husband for me, you have every right to know what those things are."

"What, Candy is pregnant isn't she?"

"How did you know?" James asked.

"I know you like the back of my hand. You sounded so upset when you called me on the phone and there's only a few things that could put you in this type of mood," Mirah said, tears clouding her eyes. Sadness seemed to be the story of her life lately.

"Mirah, I'm sorry…"

"James, we're not together. I really don't like the idea of Candy carrying your baby, but how can I be upset or angry with you? I have no right," Mirah told him in a raspy voice. Contrary to what she was telling him, her whole world was falling apart. Her father was gone; her husband had gone off to the other side of the country with the enemy, and now this. What else could go wrong, she thought. Tears in her eyes welled up even more, it was only a matter of seconds before she completely broke down, crying like a little baby. Her whole body was trembling. James pulled her into his arms.

"Mirah, tell me what's going on." James said . "Maybe I shouldn't have put this on you with everything that is going on with your family."

For the next hour, Mirah poured her heart out to him. She left out nothing, recounting all the events that had occurred in her life since her marriage to Bryce.

"Mirah, I'm so sorry," James said. He gently kneaded the palm of his hand against her back to comfort her.

He hated to see Mirah suffering. This was a time in her life when she should be having fun. Instead, she was bogged down with a bunch of problems and a husband whose main concern was starting his own business.

"I'm just tired of everything," Mirah said. "Everyone's always looking from the outside in. They think everything is perfect. I've been wearing this black mask for months now. No one has noticed but it's slowly killing me inside."

"Mirah, something has to give. I'm just sorry I complicated your life even more. I love you too much and right now your only concern should be getting yourself together."

"How? I'm not sure where to start," Mirah said. After what she learned today, there was only one thing she wanted to do. Mirah decided to go home, pack her things and leave her husband. She wanted to separate herself from him so she could decide where her life would go from here.

"Mirah, as much as I want to be with you, this is a decision you'll have to make on your own. My last intention was to put more pressure on you. I only want for your happiness, and if you feel your life is with your husband then I'll respect that."

Mirah just held on tight to James and cried. Why couldn't she be married to him? She didn't realize it before but

James was the one person who could make her happy. He loved her unconditionally, something Mirah had taken for granted. His love was worth more than all the money, the fancy penthouse, the cars, and luxuries Bryce could ever afford her. What it all came down to was Bryce could never love her the way James did.

"James, I love you," Mirah cried softly in his ear.

"I love you, too," James said, kissing her on the lips. "Now, I want you to stop crying," he said tracing his finger over her tears. "Everything will work out fine, you'll see."

"You always know how to make me feel better," Mirah replied.

"That's because I know you like the back of my hand."

"I know," Mirah said taking his hands in hers. "Why didn't I listen to you or my father?" she said kissing his fingers one by one.

"Your dad?"

"Yes. He was against my getting married so soon. He told me if Bryce truly loved me then he should wait until we got to know one another better. My father saw something I could not and now I'm paying for it."

A spark of guilt rushed through James body, thinking back to the same conversation he had with Willie. If only her mother Mattie hadn't barged in on their conversation. Whether Willie liked him or not, he was a fair man. That's why James had gone over to talk with him in the first place.

"My father thought Bryce was trying to influence me with all his money. I guess when I really think about it, he was right," Mirah said. All the gifts and the status quo of being with a man in a prominent position had really intrigued her. It was just surprising that a man in Bryce's position would even be interested in her she, thought to herself, recounting why her life went in a different direction than she had planned.

"You know money is the root of all evil," James told her. "Look, I'm not trying to preach to you or anything but you don't have to be rich to have class. The richness comes from your heart; your beauty shines both inside and out. You're a good person and I can't sit here and hate Bryce for asking you to be his wife. I should have done it long ago and it kills me every day knowing you're in the arms of another man."

"Well to be honest, seeing Tina in your arms the other night at the party drove me nuts and knowing Candy is carrying your child doesn't sit well either. James how did we get to this point?"

"I don't know. There are just so many things that I would do differently if I had the chance to do it all over again. No matter what happens you will always be the love of my life. Mirah, I know that my life is complicated now but know that I'll accept you in my life and make you happy if you decide to come back with me. No pressure, I just wanted you to know that."

Mirah was overcome by his words; she snuggled tighter in his arms. James truly loved her, more than she could say for her husband who was sharing a room with Pamela Johnson, who he promised was out of their life for good. What hurt the most was she thought their life was back on track but instead he lied to her face and carried on as if she didn't mean anything to him.

Chapter 22

Bryce was exhausted as he settled into his hotel room. He stretched across the bed and flipped on the radio to sooth his nerves. In just a few hours he would know whether Newman Corporation, a company who's revenue ranked in the hundred-million dollar range would accept his proposal and put Whitaker & Associates on the map.

"Bryce, you seem out of it," Pamela said, joining him.

"Yeah, things have just been so hectic this past month," he said, slipping the towel off her wet body. He gently eased her naked body next to his and started kissing on her belly button. He slid his tongue up and nibbled on each breast while she moaned in excitement. Pamela was so impatient, she handed him a condom to slip on. It was just as well; he slipped in and gave her what she wanted. With every stroke he hated her more and more and was glad this deal had finally come. Once he secured this account, Pamela would be dismissed and he could finally end this one sided affair. Yes, this was one sided and he definitely wouldn't be making love, no having sex, with this two bit whore if it wasn't for his main agenda.

Why couldn't he just have listened to his wife? She had every ounce of faith that he could make Whitaker and Associates a prominent business without Pamela's influence. It would have taken longer but Bryce was too impatient to wait, so he set his eyes on the short-run and did what he had to do to push his business over the top. He knew this wasn't the right thing to do but it was too late to back out.

Pamela whined for more and he increased the intensity of his thrusting. He just smiled in vain while she dragged her claws deeper into his skin. Once Pamela reached her pinnacle, he instantly released and removed himself from her hold. This was something he didn't want and she knew it. It didn't matter that he told her he was in love with his wife. Pamela just wanted what she couldn't have and would do anything to get what she wanted. She was like a drug making you do things that you normally wouldn't do with a clear head. Bryce was glad he could kick this bad habit after today. He headed to the shower to clean himself from her dirty grime.

Bryce felt so bad that he didn't even have the courage to call his wife to let her know of his business calendar. He felt even worse for using Raymond, thinking back to when they were here just a few weeks ago. Yes, he should have brought Raymond along for the experience but it was just a cover up to hide his fling with Pamela. He knew his wife wouldn't question his sudden travels if he came along and it scared him that everything went along so smoothly. He hated to see how Pamela enjoyed sneaking into his bed knowing one of his employees was just in the room next door. It was too easy, since they shared joining rooms. Today he made this trip alone and hoped Mirah wouldn't call, reminding himself to check his voice mail on his home, cell, and office phone. Even if she had contacted Raymond or Sheila, they knew his agenda and he would just tell her he didn't want to worry her more since she was taking care of her mother and all. His lies were building up one after the other; he let the warm water sooth the tension building in his mind. It was so thick it could be cut with a cord as a streak of shame rushed over his body. How could he do this to his wife? He should have dropped everything to be with her, especially after her father died.

Instead he focused his priorities before her, promising to get things right upon his return. What bothered him the most was all the deception, especially since they talked things out and promised to be open and honest with one another?

Bryce eased out the shower and just relaxed in the bathroom for a while to gather all his thoughts. Pamela was so consuming and he enjoyed this time to take a few deep breaths and gather his composure.

"Bryce, are you all right in there?"

"Yeah," Bryce replied in an irritated tone. He felt sorry for the man she would go after next. What looked good on the outside was terrible in the inside. Just like sour grapes…they look so delicious but soon as you bite down on one your mouth instantly tunes up in displeasure.

"I'm going to get a few hours of rest," Bryce said, before he checked his message. *Good*, there was none from his wife. He slipped into bed and closed his eyes. He sighed a breath of relief before drifting off to sleep.

Chapter 23

Mirah was furious as she headed home. Not one word from Bryce, she thought, steering the car ahead. She hated driving in the dark but right now she had only one thing on her mind, leaving Bryce. If that bastard thought he could get away with cheating on her, he had another thing coming. He can't have his cake and eat it too. That was out of the question, Mirah thought angrily to herself.

"From now on let's be open and honest," Mirah remembered him saying when they had supposedly gotten their marriage back on track. Her jaws tightened knowing he lied straight to her face. How could he? How could Bryce be so cold, especially now when she needed him most. Mirah pulled in the driveway and rushed in the house to pack her bags. Before she left, she tore through all of Bryce's things before finding a set of unfamiliar keys.

"How much do you want to bet these belong to Pamela's place," Mirah said sliding the keys into her pocket. She grabbed some paper and quickly expressed her feelings before she sealed the envelope and laid it on their bed. Mirah wondered if that no good snake had been in this bed as tears formed in the corner of her eyes.

Mirah high tailed it right out of there without looking back. If Bryce thought he could dangle money to keep their marriage together, he had another thing coming. He would pay dearly but first she had to deal with Pamela; she headed over to her place. Her penthouse wasn't far from here, she thought, thankful she had a key. She wouldn't have to worry about going through security. She parked and caught the elevator up to the top floor with no interruptions.

Her apartment was decked out with the finest of everything, but Mirah was not here to care about that. All rich people lived the same...the best of everything. If you've seen one, you've seen them all, the only difference in moderation and style from a woman's touch. Mirah was so grateful she came down a few notches. People think being rich can solve all your problems but she had to learn the hard way. Yeah, it's nice having money and all but it damn sure couldn't buy her happiness, especially with all this drama her life had gone through over the past few months. Come to think about it, Mirah was happier when she was poor. People would swear she was crazy for leaving all of this but she had to put her feelings first, because apparently her husband didn't care one way or another.

Mirah made sure here gloves were secure and combed through the place like a fine tooth comb. There was nothing out of the ordinary so Mirah just decided to leave. She would have to find something really worthwhile to get Pamela back. Something she couldn't pay her way out of. Just when Mirah was about to leave, the computer sitting on the table caught her attention. She clicked it on and was thankful she didn't have password protection on it.

She quickly jotted down the files she had saved in her document queue so she could make sure those same files were there when she left. People knew what they had been working on and Mirah didn't want to leave any traces behind. She wasn't about to get in trouble for breaking in but, come to think of it, she hadn't because she had a key.

Mirah found a lot of business files and downloaded them to a CD. What she came across next made her nerves jump. There was a folder named "PAYBACK," and each of the files was locked. What bothered her the most was all the files were entitled with men's names, Bryce being one of them. Mirah typed in over fifty possible codes that she thought might work. Frustrated she searched around the room again for possible clues. A thought finally came crashing to her as she ran back over to the computer. What did Pamela hold over people's head? "Money," she thought, typing it in quickly. She was disappointed when the wrong password prompt kept flashing in her face. With no luck she just decided to type it in backwards. *"Bingo,"* Mirah screamed hitting the jackpot. She instantly clicked to open the file with Bryce's name and nearly gasped while she watched her husband having sex with this woman. Mirah head began twirling a mile a minute as the vulgar images played clearly across the screen. She found herself vomiting all across the marbled floor as the sounds of their moans echoed through her ears.

Mirah wanted to tear the place to shreds but instead she cleaned up her mess then downloaded all fifty of her PAYBACK files to a CD. It wasn't any sense in acting all crazing when she knew this was happening anyway. She wondered what her husband would think knowing his sex acts were being recorded? The images still made her sick to her stomach as they replayed in her mind. As hard as it was, this was her ticket; it was her "ace" card out. Sometimes life is like playing poker; she would hold on to her feelings of hatred and play this ace card when she needed it most.

Mirah made sure everything was in order before she tiptoed quietly out of Pamela's place. She was amazed at how she was reacting, far better than the time at the pool. In just a few months Mirah had grown so much. Besides, she would get Pamela where it hurt the most…her pockets.

She wiped the tears from her eyes and headed back to Jersey. The half-hour trip went by quick, and she dreaded going back to her parent's house alone. There were too many memories there that she just wasn't ready to deal with yet. Somehow Mirah found herself pulling in James's driveway. It was 3:00 in the morning but she had nowhere else to go. She closed the car door and headed towards his apartment complex.

Mirah took a deep breath before she rang his apartment doorbell. She had no right coming over here unannounced and hoped James would be alone.

"Who is it?" James called out drowsy.

"It's Mirah," she whispered, her body began to tremble. Before he had a chance to unlock the door her face was in a pool full of tears.

"What's wrong?" James asked. She could hardly get any words out; he hurried to get her a glass of water.

Mirah could hardly hold the glass steady; she gulped a few sips of water down. "I left Bryce," she managed to say handing him back the glass.

"What happened? Did you two argue over the phone?"

"No. As a matter of fact I haven't even talked to him," she said filling him in on what she had found out.

James didn't know what to say embracing her in his arms. The only thing he cared about was protecting her and he would not stand by and watch her life fall apart.

"Come on, you need to get some rest," he told Mirah, carrying her to his room. He put some fresh sheets down before helping her remove her clothes. It took every ounce of energy to tuck her in but right now she needed a friend.

"James, don't leave me," Mirah whispered pulling him close. "I don't want to be alone tonight," she said kissing him softly on the lips.

A rush of energy rushed through James body; he lavished at the softness of her lips. After the day he had been through he was dead tired but Mirah's touched revived him instantly. He parted her lips to taste the sweetness she had to offer. James wanted to relish every moment as their tongue interlocked passionately. He loved her, he loved this feeling, something he had taken for granted until it was gone.

"James, make love to me," Mirah told him in a soft tone.

Did he just hear her right? His body was all ready to fulfill her request but his conscience was telling him something different.

"Mirah, as much as I want to, you're upset right now and I don't want you to wake up and regret this when you have a clear mind."

"Please, don't turn me away right now," Mirah pleaded with him. "I need you. I need you to fill me with love," she cried.

"Baby, don't cry," James said tracing the tears that flowed from her eyes. He traced his hand down to her heart; it had been torn, fragmented into tiny pieces, and she begged for him to put them back together.

"Mirah, I have so many of my own problems, something I don't want you to have to deal with, especially now."

"James, we can work through any problems. We always have. The moment I forgot that is the day my life fell apart. Help me put the pieces back together. Make love to me. I need you," Mirah told him kissing to reaffirm her feelings.

James nearly lost control; his heart pounded a mile a minute. He had dreamed of this day so many times, to have Mirah in his arms again. James inched the covers off Mirah's body. She was so beautiful; he just stared at her for a few moments taking everything in. Her cinnamon chocolate nude body was illuminated by the shadows of the moonlight. She was perfect in form and his hands melted the instant he touched her body. James's heart exploded with emotions. He never thought he would be with Mirah again.

Starting from the top, James caressed every part of her body. He pressed his lips against hers, tracing his tongue over the edges of her full lips before parting them. Mirah tasted so good…she made every hair on his body stand in anticipation of what was to come. James had to take things slow; he wanted to indulge every moment of making love to her again.

"Mirah, you don't know how much you mean to me," James whispered softly in her ear. He brushed his tongue gently over her earlobe and suckled on the diamond stud earring she had clipped to her ear. Mirah's moan only intensified his state while he continued to journey down to brand her body with his kisses. He playfully toiled with each of her breasts. Her nipples hardened instantly to his touch. James traced his tongue around and around the brown buds until he engulfed the entire nipple in his mouth, suckling on them like a newborn baby. His dabbling didn't stop there; his tongue was to busy at work while he glided down and brushed over her belly button. Mirah's moans never stopped. She enjoyed his body being against hers again. She cried out in pleasure while James kissed the inner softness of her thighs, waiting in anticipation of his tongue stroking against the wetness of her womanhood. Her hands grabbed tightly around his shoulders. Her body was moving out of control and when she reached the height of her pinnacle James started again, this time sliding his hard shaft inside the moist opening that awaited him. At first his thrusts were slow and then he increased the rhythm to her pleasure. They went at it for over an hour as the heat enveloped the room from their passion. When it was over, James circled his arms around Mirah. He never wanted to let her go. He was there just like he said he would be to pick up the pieces of her shattered marriage.

****

Mirah kissed James goodbye and gathered her belongings together.

"I'm going to miss you," James said, pulling her back into his arms.

"Will you? Well I'm only ten minutes away," she smiled kissing him again.

"Call me if you need me," he told her before she left.

"I will," she replied. Mirah started walking down the hallway, when she glanced back he was still watching her. Mirah dropped her bag and ran back into his arms.

"James, I'm scared," Mirah cried.

"I'll handle everything for you then," James said.

"No, no I don't want you anywhere near Bryce. Please, I don't want anyone hurt," she pleaded. Her heart pounded a mile a minute. "I have to handle this alone. Everything will be okay," she tried to convince herself.

"Whatever you think is best," James told her. Right now that was probably as well because he didn't know what he was capable of if he ran into that fool again. "Just call me everyday at 7:00," James told her pointing at his watch. "If not, I'll come looking after you."

"Yes, sir!" Mirah laughed out loud. Something so simple as laughing felt good. She kissed James one last time before heading out. "Thank you for everything," she told him. She picked up her bags and vanished from his apartment complex.

Mirah headed to her parents' house promising to get herself together. She had to face her father's death as well as the ending of her marriage. There was no way she could be with Bryce after seeing that video image of him making love to Pamela. Her heart didn't truly belong to him anyway. Mirah parked her car and unloaded her bags before heading to the house she grew up in, a place that would be so different without the presence of her father.

Chapter 24

Bryce was glad to be back home as he pulled in the driveway. The business had gone better than expected and his firm had just signed on a major account that would take Whitaker & Associates over the top.

Now that this business was past him, he was ready to get his personal life back on track. Come tomorrow, Pamela would be history, but right now he wanted to be with his wife. He started to call her but decided he'd rather see her in person. It was only 7:00, still early enough to shower and get to Jersey. Bryce left his bags at the door and darted up the stairs to get ready. He threw his clothes on the bed and was surprised to see a letter neatly sitting on his pillow. Had Mirah been home? Bryce tore the letter open to read its contents.

'If you think you can sleep around with Pamela and have me too, you're dead wrong," the first sentence of the letter read. Bryce sat heavily on the bed. He continued to read on.

'I gave my heart to you and somehow you've managed to tear it in two. I'm sitting here still wondering why you're trying to play me for a fool? I gave up so much to be with you and the one thing I asked of you...well lets just say I know where you stand. Bryce, I'm leaving you. As much as I tried to make this succeed, it takes two to make a marriage work.'

Bryce ran to the closet. All Mirah's clothes were gone. He pulled out the dresser drawers, they clattered to the floor. Everything was moved out.

"No," Bryce screamed picking up the phone.

"Hello."

"Mirah, baby its me," Bryce said hoping she wouldn't hang up the phone.

"So how was your trip with Pamela in Los Angeles?"

"Mirah, I was on last minute business…"

"Well all work and no play isn't fun," Mirah said cutting his sentence off. "I'm sure Pamela had a play-filled agenda for you. Let me guess, swimming nude in the pool."

"Mirah, this isn't funny. I was not with…"

"No, it isn't amusing," Mirah cut in. "And don't lie to me. I know you were in Los Angeles with Pamela. You just couldn't let her go, could you?"

"Yes, baby I can let her go. We were just wrapping up this one business deal she had been working on, but now it's done."

"Well, we're done too. I hope it was worth it."

"Baby, no. I'm sorry I lied to you but please don't throw our marriage away over this. I promise Pamela is history."

"Don't you dare put this on me. You threw our marriage away sleeping around with Ms. Johnson. I hope she was worth it."

"No…"

"Don't lie to me," Mirah screamed. "Just turn on your computer."

"What!"

"Just turn on your computer," Mirah demanded.

Pamela was going to pay if she had emailed his wife news of their affair. She must be crazier than he thought; he tried to think of a way to wiggle out of this lie.

"All right, you should have the email any moment now," Mirah said. Silence took over the phone.

Bryce's legs were shaking while he read more spiteful words from his wife. What really shook him was the letters, 'PAYBACK' from your secret lover Pamela Johnson. Bryce clicked on the file and nearly fell out when a video appeared on the screen of him and Pamela making out.

"The cat got your tongue?"

There was no response; the phone went crashing to the floor. Mirah held the receiver and listened as a thud echoed through the phone. She held on a few moments before she heard a dial tone.

He threw things around, as he fumbled around to find his keys. He quickly made it to his car and sped toward Jersey.

****

Bryce slammed the car door and ran up the steps. "Mirah, open the door," Bryce called out, ringing the doorbell. With her mother away she was liable to make him stand out here all night.

Mirah opened the door to let Bryce in. "You know, you really should not have come over here," she told him in an angry tone.

"Honey, our marriage is on the line…"

"Well, whose fault is that? Bryce, nothing you say is going to change things. It's over."

"Mirah, I know you're angry right now but can't we talk about it? Please."

"Bryce, it's too late," Mirah, cried. "Where were you when I needed you the most? I'll tell you…you were in Pamela's bed. How could you, Bryce? Why did you even marry me in the first place if you didn't love me?"

"Baby, I do love you."

"Just stop. I don't want to hear any more," Mirah yelled, slapping him across the face. "You did this to us," she continued, pounding on his chest.

"Baby, I'm not going to let you go," Bryce said. He embraced her tightly in his arms; "Let it out," he told her as she continued to act out.

Mirah's head began spinning. She hung on to Bryce who helped her to the couch. This was just too much; she laid her head back in tears.

"Mirah, talk to me," Bryce said, wondering what was going through her mind.

"I'm tired, Bryce. I don't want to argue with you anymore."

"Mirah, I'll do anything you want. We can get some counseling or whatever, but please don't leave me. I'm sorry for hurting you."

"Then why did you do it?"

"Baby, that's not important right now. We need to focus on us, and only us."

"Us," Mirah laughed between tears. "There's never been 'us,' just you and Whitaker & Associates. I hope it was all worth it. Bryce, I really tried to love you but you made it impossible."

Bryce couldn't say anything; his tears streamed down his cheeks.

"I'm sorry, Bryce," Mirah told him kissing the top of his forehead. "I never imagined we would have ended up this way," she told him before leaving the room to try to get some much-needed sleep.

****

Mirah was surprised to find Bryce sleeping on the couch.

"Bryce, wake up," Mirah said, giving him a slight nudge.

Bryce couldn't resist, he pulled her on top of him. "Good morning," he said, kissing her on the lips. "Please tell me everything that has been happening was a bad nightmare."

"No, it wasn't," Mirah, replied. "Do you want some breakfast?" she asked him.

"Yes, I'm starved," Bryce, told her. "I'll go freshen up then come down to help you."

Mirah just nodded her head and went into the kitchen. The last time she made breakfast in here was for her father. All the memories came flooding back; she sunk into the kitchen chair in tears. Mirah just sat there in a daze, she felt Bryce's hand softly messaging the back of her neck.

"Do you want to talk about it?"

"I miss my father," Mirah said, filling him in on their last day together.

"I know. He really loved you. I'm so glad you had the chance to take him out and spend some quality time on his last day here."

"How did you know?" Mirah asked. She hadn't remembered discussing any details of the last day she spent with her father. The memories were too much and she focused all her attention on helping her mother, who was a reckless mess.

"This is for you," Bryce said pulling out the envelope from his pocket.

Mirah could barely focus while she read her father's last words to her. She read it over and over again, bringing the letter to her heart.

Bryce embraced his wife in his arms, while she broke down and cried.

"Where did you get this letter?"

"Your father left it in the car," Bryce told her. "He loved you so much. Always remember that," he said, trying to soothe her pain.

"I don't know how to move on without him. I'm trying to face my fears, but this is just too much."

"I know. Baby, come back home to New York with me. You shouldn't be here alone."

"Bryce, I can't," Mirah told him. Their marital problems came crashing back to her forethoughts. Her life was falling apart from every angle. Here father was gone, her marriage was hanging on by a thin thread, and she was still in love with

James, who was going to become a father to another woman's child.

"Baby, I'll give you all the space you want. Just come home with me."

"Bryce, I need some time to put my life into perspective. I've decided to go down South with my mother for a while."

"Mirah…"

"Bryce, my mind is already made up," she told him.

"When are you leaving?"

"In the next few days. I need to take care of a few things for my mother here before leaving."

"Do you want me to stay with you?"

"I'll be fine," Mirah told him. "I'll make sure to stop by before leaving. Will you take me to the airport?" she asked, trying not to brush him off totally in a disrespectful way.

"Sure, but I wish you would change your mind and stay home. We need to work through this together," Bryce told her. He didn't want her going off alone. Too much time to think and a distant separation could make the transition of her leaving him easier. He wanted to prove to her that he loved and needed her. That would be really difficult if she was miles away.

"Mirah, I know you're angry with me, but I love you so much," Bryce told her. Tears formed in the corner of his eyes. "I'll do anything to make things up to you," he said, covering his lips over hers. She tried to pull away but Bryce was firm in trying to reassure her. He wasn't going to give her up so easily. She rested in his arms and accepted the sincerity of his kisses.

The morning went by quickly and Bryce left reluctantly as his wife prepared to leave the state. He headed back to New York and his first stop was to see Pamela. He couldn't believe his lies had caught up to him, and there wasn't a damn thing he could do about it. He couldn't buy his way out of this situation like he had done so many times before. His wife didn't care about his money, all she wanted was to be loved. How could he mess that up?

The half-hour trip went by quickly to his surprise and he made it up to Pamela's penthouse. He rapidly rang the doorbell; his blood pressure continued to rise. By now Bryce was pounding on the door as he heard her yell *'just one minute.'* As soon as she opened the door he lost control and grabbed her around the neck.

"Bryce, let go of me," Pamela yelled as she broke free. "What the hell is wrong with you?"

"What's wrong with me! YOU," Bryce shouted angrily at her. "You have been nothing but trouble to me ever since the first day we met."

"How dare you come in my house and put your hands on me?" Pamela shouted in disbelief. "I've done nothing but help you. If it wasn't for me, Whitaker & Associates would never have had the chance of getting the Newman account."

"Oh really."

"You're damn straight," Pamela replied. "Don't you forget I have high rank in this business," she reminded him. "All it takes is one phone call," she said threatening him.

"Oh, am I supposed to be shaking in my boots?" Bryce replied dramatically. "You done gone and messed with the wrong person," he told her.

"Please, I ought to have your ass arrested for breaking in here and attacking me," she responded heatedly.

"Go ahead," Bryce yelled. "Let's see what the police say since I have a key," he said, dangling it in her face. "As far as putting my hands on you…well you certainly seem to take pleasure in that, don't you?"

Pamela was fuming; she tried to grab her house keys back.

"You're nothing but a two-bit ho. You don't have no clout in this business," Bryce smirked. "You're just living off your daddy's name or sleeping your way to the top. Probably the latter seeing that's the only way anybody will pay attention to you."

"Bryce, don't push me," Pamela said, slapping him in the face. "I can ruin you in more ways then one."

"Really. What do you have that I don't already?" Bryce said pushing her up against the wall. "What, you're going to tell my wife?" he asked pointing in her face. "She already knows," he said digging in his pockets to retrieve the CD.

"My wife already knows about this 'PAYBACK'," he yelled, flicking the CD in her face. "Now, what are you going to do?" Bryce challenged. She looked on surprised.

"I wonder what your daddy would think seeing his precious little daughter all knocked up with his top clients. Better yet, maybe I'll let them in on your dirty little secret, too!"

"Bryce, don't you dare," Pamela shouted swinging her arms at him like a mad woman.

Bryce just laughed as he caught both her hands and forced her back up against the wall. If she weren't a woman her sorry ass would be laid out on the floor.

"You ain't nothing but a sorry excuse," Bryce said, looking her dead in the eye. He should have knocked the shit out of her for spitting in his face, but he just pushed her aside and walked out the door.

"Who has the Payback now?" he turned and laughed before leaving. As much as he hated for his wife to have seen that CD, he now had the upper hand, he thought, walking down the hallway glad to be rid of her.

Bryce couldn't even get to his car before his cell phone started to ring.

"What does she want," he yelled. Pamela's number popped up on his caller ID screen.

"Yeah, what is it?" Bryce answered in an annoyed tone.

"How did you get a hold of my files?" Pamela asked in a worried tone.

"Don't worry about that," Bryce told her. "You ought to be more concerned about what may happen if this gets into the wrong hands. You've really gone too far," Bryce told her. The images of their encounters rushed back to his mind. It nearly made him sick knowing that Mirah got a hold of this. To know he was having an affair was one thing but for her to actually see those images was something beyond explanation. He couldn't lie or talk his way out of this. Bryce had absolutely no control of the situation, which was the one thing he hated the most.

"Bryce, can we talk? Why don't you come back over," Pamela begged him. She had to know what was going through his mind. He could ruin her if those files were to get into the wrong hands. The tables were turned on her, worst of all with her own files that she had intended on using as leverage if need be.

"Pamela, there is nothing else I want to talk with you about. My only concern is mending fences with my wife," he told her.

All of a sudden Pamela head clicked. She put two and two together. "Mirah, did this," Pamela spoke out loud into the phone. "Bryce, she broke into my place and stole from me."

"No, she did not," Bryce, replied.

"Bryce, it can't be hard to prove. All I have to do is go down to security and ask for the tape."

"Do whatever you please," Bryce told her, laughing. "What is it about you and these tapes? Oh, I forget, it's your way of getting payback. Well it won't work and my wife didn't break into your house, she had a key. And don't think you can get us on that crap...it won't even stand up and besides don't forget we have a copy of your dirty little deeds," Bryce told her before hanging up.

He rode the rest of the way home trying to think how he was going to win his wife back. He had to stop her from going out of town or their marriage would be as good as gone.

Chapter 25

James was just about to head out the door as the phone rang. Normally he would have just let it roll over to the answering machine but he was hoping to hear from Mirah. He ran across the room to pick up the phone.

"Hello."

"James, it's me."

"Candy. I was just on my way to work," he told her so he could hurry her off the phone.

"Well I'm glad I caught you," she replied in a panicking tone. "I need you to come up here right away."

"Candy, I can't just take off my job at the drop of a dime," he told her. "Is everything all right with the baby?" he asked concerned.

"No. Everything is not all right," Candy cried hysterically.

"I'm on my way," James told her before hanging up. He rushed out the door, wondering what could be going on. James weaved in and out of lanes in a hurry. The drive to New York was a nightmare as he made his way through the bustling traffic. When he stepped out of his truck, he was surprised to see that Candy had already opened the door and was waiting for him; she raced into his arms.

"What's wrong?" James asked, trying to calm her down.

"We're going to lose our baby," she cried before she shut the door.

"What do you mean? When did you find this out?" James asked helping her to a seat.

"I started spotting a few days, so I went in to see my doctor early this morning. He said the baby did not develop and that we would miscarry," Candy managed to say in a raspy tone.

"I don't understand. Why didn't you call me when this first started happening?"

"James, I didn't want to worry you," Candy told him.

James just sat there clueless as to what to say next. No matter how he felt about Candy, he still loved the baby that he thought was growing inside of her. He just rocked her in his arms and prayed that they could get through this together.

Chapter 26

Mirah was surprised to learn she was pregnant. With her life in such chaos, this was the last thing she expected. Images of her lovemaking with James came rushing back to her fore thoughts. She wondered who the father of this baby could be? Was there a possibility that this could be James's baby? She eased off the examination table to get dressed; her heart began to race a mile a minute in fear.

"Well I'm sure your husband will enjoy the good news," Dr. Lowe said, interrupting her thoughts.

"I'm sure he will, too," Mirah replied uneasily. "I'm just a little surprised," she told him. A million questions raced through her mind. She had actually come here to pick up a prescription for her mother and this was the last thing she expected to hear.

"Well considering you didn't come here for yourself, I'm sure you were quite surprised. I'm glad the nurse convinced you to get a check-up since we had a last minute cancellation. We need to get you started on some prenatal vitamins."

"Sure, anything that will help the baby. Can you tell me how far along I am?"

"I'm not sure since you couldn't tell me exactly when your last menstrual cycle was."

"I just can't remember with everything that has been going on. I'll have to check my calendar at home," Mirah said, biting down on her lower lip. Damn, why couldn't she think, she thought angrily to herself?

"Well, give me a call if you find your calendar, otherwise we will know more in a day or two when your blood work comes back. Again congratulations," Dr. Lowe told her before leaving.

Mirah gathered her things and left. With the news of her pregnancy, Mirah was glad she was going to be traveling down South. If she told Bryce he would definitely oppose; considering the situation, that was the last thing she could possibly do right now. And what about James? He already had a baby on the way.

Mirah's mind kept going in circles while she headed on the freeway back to New York. She had to get there quickly, so she could take a look at her monthly calendar. This wasn't just about her anymore. How could she have been so stupid as to make love with James without protection? At the time she knew she was leaving her husband but still there was no excuse for her recklessness, especially considering he had a baby on the way by another woman. Mirah didn't know what to do. If this baby was her husband's then her child deserved the best even if it meant sacrificing her own happiness. Mirah thought about all the single parents out there struggling, just to make ends meet. If this baby were James's then all hell would break loose. Bryce would go crazy if he knew she was carrying another man's child.

"Whoa," Mirah said, wiping the sweat off her forehead. How did her life become so complicated? She was too young to be going through all this drama. Why did she have to sleep with James? As much as she needed him that night, she should have taken his advice. After all two wrongs don't make a right and she was still a married woman. Should she be honest and tell Bryce of her affair and the dilemma she was in?

"No," right now was not the best time to add fuel to the fire. She still had some time to make up her mind before she started showing. Mirah had to find the right way to deal with her husband.

"Dag, who is this calling me?" Mirah said as her thoughts were interrupted. She dug through her purse to find her cell phone and quickly answered.

"Hello."

"How could you break into my house and steal my belongings?"

"Pamela, is this you?" Mirah asked. A bitter chill ran down her spine.

"Yeah, it's me," Pamela replied. If she couldn't get what she wanted from Bryce then she would go straight to the horse's mouth.

"I don't think it's a good idea for me to talk with you."

"Wait. Don't hang up. I think you should know what your husband just did, and believe me he's lucky I didn't haul his ass off to jail."

"I'm listening," Mirah said in an irritated tone. Tears started flooding from her eyes, wondering what else could go wrong.

"Well, I know you learned what happened between your husband and me. Bryce just came over here in a fury and literally attacked me."

"And you expect me to believe that?" Mirah asked.

"You think he wouldn't? I guess you really don't know your husband then. He'll do anything to get what he wants…anything. He really scared me and it wasn't pretty. He acted like a lion chasing his prey."

"Not that I'm agreeing with you, but people do things they normally wouldn't do when pushed in a corner. You did everything you could to ruin our marriage. Why Pamela?"

"What do you mean?"

"It's not a difficult question," Mirah said angrily. "Why Bryce? Is it because you saw how happy he was with me. If you can't be happy then nobody else can be either?" Mirah asked.

"What's done is done," Pamela responded. "I'm just calling you to see where Bryce's head is. I don't want to press charges against either of you but I need to know…"

"About the videos," Mirah said cutting her off. "You ain't nothing but a selfish bitch. All you care about is yourself," Mirah shouted.

"Look, like you said people do desperate things when they are pushed up in a corner. I have to protect myself because no one else will," Pamela told her in a nasty tone.

"So what do you want from me? You have some nerve calling for my help after what you did."

"We're both women…"

"Don't come at me with that," Mirah told her. "If you was a real woman, you would have kept your legs closed. You knew Bryce was a married man; you're nothing more than a two-bit whore."

"Why does it have to be all like that?" Pamela asked enraged. "Your husband came to my bed with open arms," she said, trying to upset Mirah. "And he was very good by the way, oh but I forgot you saw it. Never send a girl to do a woman's job," Pamela growled, adding fuel to the fire.

"Well I hope Bryce was worth it," Mirah responded calmly. As mad as she was, she was not going to give Pamela the satisfaction. "I wonder what your daddy would think of his precious little daughter's dirty deeds," Mirah said. This time her tears were hot in anger while they scrolled steadily down her cheeks. "Your father took years to establish a respectable relationship with his top clients. How long did it take you? Two…maybe three days. I can ruin your ass with the click of a button, and as for my husband' well we're still together. He used you like you were trying to use him but who has the last laugh," Mirah said before clicking her off the line.

She was so distracted from the phone call with Pamela that she did not pay attention to the truck merging into her lane. She laid on the horn and tried to speed up but it was too late. The truck collided into her mother's Honda Accord and pushed her against a cement wall.

****

"Ma'am are you okay," the EMS worker called out, as they approached the accident scene. There was no response; they quickly began to pry the door open.

"She has a faint pulse," the rescuer yelled, while they worked rapidly to pull her from the car. Scattered all over the seats was baby literature for mothers-to-be.

"I believe she's pregnant," he added. His pace quickened even more. They worked on her bloody body and tried to get her vital signs back to normal.

"Let's get her to the hospital now," the rescuer called out. They lifted her in the ambulance, flipped on the sirens, and raced to the nearest hospital near Manhattan.

****

Bryce was furious; he paced back and forth across the kitchen floor. He could have strangled Pamela for the mess she involved him in. Angry, he took a few sips of cognac before the phone began to ring.

"What," Bryce yelled out as he picked up the phone. Pamela better not be calling him at home. She was already hanging on a thin rope and the only thing that was saving her neck was the fact that she was a woman.

"Hello," Bryce answered dryly.

"Is this Mr. Whitaker?"

"Yes, who am I'm speaking with?" Bryce asked pacing back and forth. He was in no mood to be dealing with any telemarketers or someone trying to solicit money.

"This is Cathy calling from Manhattan General Hospital. Are you the husband of Mirah Whitaker?"

"Yes, what's wrong?" Bryce asked, as a chill ran down his spine.

"Your wife has been involved in an accident. You should get to the hospital right away."

"Accident, what type of accident? Is she okay?"

"I'm sorry, I can't release any information over the phone. You need to speak with the attending physician. Would you like me to make arrangements to have you picked up?"

"No, I have a way. I'll be right there," Bryce said before hanging up.

He didn't know whether his wife was dead or alive. He raced out to his car, backed out the parking garage and slammed the gear in drive, speeding down the street through the congested New York traffic. It didn't take him long as he ran through the emergency room door to find his wife.

"My wife was rushed to the emergency room," Bryce called out frantically. He cut right to the beginning of the line.

"Sir, I can help you over here," a nurse told him, while everyone looked on. "What is your wife's name?"

"Mirah Whitaker," Bryce said, the adrenaline rushing straight to his head.

"Yes, follow me right this way, sir," the nurse responded, leading him down the hallway.

"Is she okay?" Bryce asked nervously, trying to prepare himself for the worst.

"I'm not the attending nurse," she responded softly. "I'll have the physician come speak with you right away." She led him into the room with Mirah.

"Oh my goodness," Bryce yelled out, running over to her bedside.

"Mr. Whitaker, she's sleeping right now," the nurse told him, placing a gentle hand on his shoulder. "Will you be all right for a moment while I get the physician?"

"Yes," Bryce replied. He took a seat next to his wife. Her cinnamon brown face was all bruised and swollen. Tears instantly swelled in his eyes. He ran his fingers along all the bumps and scraps on her face.

"Mirah, it's Bryce, honey…I'm here," he told her, hoping she would wake up. All the tubes plugged in her body scared him to death; he kissed the top of her forehead.

"Mr. Whitaker, this is Dr. Stanton," the nurse announced, coming into the room.

Bryce stood up and extended his hand in greeting. He wanted answers, what in the world happened to his wife? Who was responsible?

"Mr. Whitaker, I'm sure you would like to know what's going on with your wife." Dr. Stanton motioned Bryce to sit down.

"Yes, I would like to know," Bryce replied, annoyed that he had to wait. "No one has been able to tell me anything."

"Mirah was involved in a car accident. Apparently from the police reports a truck ran into her lane and forced her car against a cement wall."

"Oh, my goodness," Bryce gasped; he stood up again in disbelief. It killed him that he was unable to protect his wife.

"Your wife is very blessed to be alive considering the magnitude of the impact. Her safety belt and air bag really helped to save her life. The baby is fine, too, but we need to keep a good eye on Mirah," Dr. Stanton stated.

"Baby, my wife is pregnant?"

"Yes, I assumed you knew."

"No, I didn't," Bryce replied in a state of shock. Mirah has been in New Jersey for the last month helping her mother since her father's death."

"Oh, I'm sorry to hear that," Dr. Stanton said. "With the exception of these bumps and bruises, Mirah should be fine. We would, however, like to monitor the baby."

"How far along is she?"

"About 8 weeks. Would you like to hear the baby's heart beat?" Dr. Stanton asked, hoping to offer some comfort to him.

"Yes," Bryce replied. He spoke with the nurse to arrange everything. After a few moments the hospital staff left out the room and Bryce went back to sit by his wife's side.

"Honey, we're going to have a baby," Bryce cried. "I'm sorry for putting you through all of this," he said, kissing her on the forehead again.

Bryce was relieved when Mirah opened her eyes. "Mirah, I'm here," he told her as he picked up her hand.

"Bryce, I'm glad you're here," Mirah cried. Her husband embraced her gently in his arms and she accepted his affection. It felt good even if it was for the time being. "I was on my way home when this all happened. I wanted to tell you something."

"Don't worry about a thing," Bryce said soothing her back. "The baby is doing just fine," he assured his wife.

Mirah nearly choked on her own salvia in fear at the sound of those words.

"Bryce, how did you find out about the baby?"

"The doctor just told me. Is that what you were coming home to tell me?"

"Yes," Mirah lied. A guilty streak shot through her body. Now that he knew, there was no way she was going to tell him that this baby may not be his. "So did the doctor say the baby would be fine?"

"Yes. They're going to bring in the machine so we can hear the baby's heartbeat," Bryce smiled. "Our little gem is eight weeks. So when did you find out?"

"Today," Mirah replied. "I went to pick up a prescription for my mother and the nurse convinced me to have a check up since I hadn't been there in so long. I was just as surprised to learn that I was pregnant."

"Baby, I know this hasn't been the best of times for us but this little gem growing inside of you will bring us so much joy," Bryce smiled. This news was exactly what he needed to put his marriage back on track.

"Mirah, I love you so much," Bryce said, kissing her on the lips.

"Ouch!" Mirah whimpered from the soreness of her face. "Bryce, bring me that mirror over there," she asked, feeling her face.

"Baby, you're fine."

"Bryce, please just give me the mirror," Mirah repeated impatiently. When he handed her the mirror, tears instantly started to flow from her eyes.

"Look at my face," Mirah called out as she continued to cry. "This is all Pamela's fault."

"What," Bryce said. "What does Pamela have to do with this?"

"She called harassing me on my cell phone. I told her I didn't want to talk with her, but she kept going on and on making me lose my concentration. I was so distracted and upset, by the time I hung up the phone it was too late for me to maneuver around the truck that was coming into my lane."

"I'm sorry this happened," Bryce cried. He held his wife in his arms, "I'm going to kill her," he muffled angrily. His blood boiled straight to the top of his head, until Bryce was ready to explode. Pamela Johnson is going to pay.

"Bryce, you stay away from Pamela," Mirah told him. "She already said you came over and attacked her. Promise me you'll stay away from her," she pleaded.

"All right I promise. Now you sit back and get some rest. I don't want you to worry about anything," Bryce said, taking the mirror away.

"Yes sir," Mirah smiled giving him a military salute. Her face was so sore; she sat back and took her husband's advice to relax. There was no need worrying about Pamela or the cuts and bruises on her face. What's done was done and Mirah was just happy to be alive and grateful her baby was doing well.

"So are we ready to see the baby?" Dr. Stanton asked, while the nurse brought the ultrasound machine in and stationed it on the side of Mirah's bed.

"We sure are," Bryce replied. He held his wife's hand in anticipation, under the circumstance of being here; this was the one bright spot in their life right now.

Mirah just squeezed his hand. Sweat formed on the top of her head. She was definitely worried. How did she allow her life to become such a mess? This should have been the happiest day of her life, but instead she was trying to figure out who the father of this baby was.

"I just need you to sit up a little," the nurse told her before she turned the machine on. She clicked a series of buttons and then covered the device with a latex condom and some lubricant.

"This may be a little cold," she told Mirah before inserting and moving it around to locate the baby. "Okay, here we are," the nurse stated. She turned the monitor to the parents-to-be.

Mirah nearly gasped as she saw her baby's heart beat.

"Beautiful," Bryce said looking on equally amazed. Everything terrible that was going on right now was frozen in time. They were happy while they looked at their new little bundle of joy growing inside of her. For those few moments everything seemed perfect. If only it could stay that way. Their attention never left the monitor while they focused on the baby.

Chapter 27

James didn't know what to say as he drove Candy to the hospital. In less than a few hours their baby would no longer exist. Silence lingered between the two of them.

"Candy, I'm really sorry," James finally said.

"It's probably just as well," Candy replied in a somber voice. "You didn't want to have a baby with me anyway."

James nearly lost control of the car; he swirled to get back into his lane. "Candy, how can you be so cold? I can't believe you would even say that."

"Look, I'm sorry. I just needed to vent," Candy replied.

"Candy, no matter what you may think I would never wish anything like this to happen."

"James…"

"Wait, let me finish," he said, cutting her sentence off. "I was going to give you this later but I think now is as good a time as ever," he said handing her the box.

Candy was surprised. She opened the box and there was a hand carved crystal plaque of the both of them.

"I was going to have the baby engraved in with us after he was born."

"Or she," Candy smiled. "James, please forgive me for taking out my frustrations on you."

"Don't worry about it," James told her with a gentle squeeze to her hand. "We're going to get through this together."

"I know," Candy responded before they pulled into the hospital entrance.

"Do you want to take a few minutes?" James asked. He parked the car then turned off the ignition.

"No, I'm ready," Candy replied. James helped her out of the car and they headed to the hospital door. Her mind raced back to the day she first found out she was pregnant. She had been surprised by the news and really had doubts about having the baby in the first place. Look at her life...she was older, her only child was almost grown himself, and her personal life was in disorder. Messing around with a young man like James was refreshing but she had no intentions of this ever happening. For goodness sake, she was on the rebound from her relationship with Bryce. When she found out he was getting married, especially to a young girl that was James's ex, Candy desperately needed someone to comfort her.

"Are you okay?" James asked, breaking the long silence.

"Yes," Candy lied. Right now a rush of guilt was shooting through her body for having doubts about having this baby. Candy had a difficult time coping with the fact that there would be no baby. In just a few hours her body would be empty as if the pregnancy had never happened.

"Are you sure you want to go through this today?" James asked. "Maybe we should see if there is any counseling available."

"James, I just want to get this over with as quickly as possible," Candy told him. "I'll be fine...I'm a nurse and deal with this sort of thing everyday."

"It doesn't matter," James responded. "You're human too and it's only natural for you to grieve. If you don't it will build up and only hurt worse in the end."

"I know. Will you be here for me?" Candy cried.

"You don't even worry yourself about that," James told her. He embraced her in his arms and she hung on tightly to him a few moments before they headed into the hospital.

Candy was not used to being on the patient end. She sat anxiously, trying to mentally prepare herself for the inevitable.

"What is taking Dr. Stanton so long?" Candy asked her colleague.

"He won't be long, he's over in ER?"

"ER," Candy replied.

"Yes. A patient was in a bad accident with a truck."

"She was pregnant?"

"Yes, but luckily the baby and mother is doing fine. Dr. Stanton is over talking with her husband, Mr. Whitaker. Isn't that someone you know? The name sure sounds familiar."

"Mr. Whitaker?" James repeated cutting in on their discussion.

The nurse didn't reply; she cut her eyes over towards Candy.

"It's okay," Candy told her friend. "Are you referring to Bryce and Mirah Whitaker?"

"Yes," she replied before the phone rang.

Candy knew she was glad to be interrupted to avoid further questioning from James. Patient information was strictly confidential and she explained that to James.

"I understand," James told her. "I just need to see with my own eyes that she's okay," he said without thinking.

"Well let me find out which room she is in," Candy said. She went over to the computer station, clicked a few buttons and gave him the information he wanted.

"Candy, I'm sorry," James said. "I don't want you to think that I'm going to run off and leave you here alone. I was just surprised when your co-worker mentioned that Mirah had been in a bad accident."

"James, I know you're still in love with Mirah. Go see about her. Just be here when I get out from having this procedure done."

"Candy…"

"James, just go," Candy told him. "I'm fine with it, besides I owe you that much," she told him thinking back to how she even met him.

"Okay, but only when the doctor calls you in." He helped her get ready; this was the hardest thing they ever had to do. As much as he wanted to see Mirah right now, his priorities were with Candy who was preparing to have any traces of their baby surgically removed.

****

Bryce couldn't believe he was seeing his baby's heartbeat. "Honey, we're going to be parents," he said proudly, kissing her on the forehead.

"Are you certain the baby is fine?" Mirah asked, worried.

"So far the test are looking positive but we would like to monitor the baby closely over the next few months to make certain he or she is progressing normally."

"So you can say for sure that this accident didn't hurt the baby?"

"Mrs. Jones, no pregnancy is 100% guaranteed. From the tests we've done, everything looks normal," Dr Stanton told her.

"Honey, you have to think positive," Bryce said reassuring her.

"I agree. I have to go now," Dr. Stanton said looking at his watch. "I'm running a little behind for my next appointment, but if you have any questions, please feel free to set up an appointment where we can have more time."

"We will," Bryce said shaking his hand. "Thank you for taking time out of your schedule to see us."

"Not a problem. Mrs. Jones, the nurse, will talk with you about everything," he said before leaving.

Mirah just shook her head, closed her eyes and prayed that this baby would stay in her womb for nine months.

"Honey, are you okay?" Bryce asked.

"Yes," Mirah replied. "I just want to make sure the baby will be all right. I can't take losing anyone else. I should have never been driving and talking on the phone," she added.

"Don't beat yourself up over this. It's not your fault. I'm just glad you and the baby are okay," he said kissing her on the forehead again. "Now you get some rest. I have to take care of some things," he told her.

"Bryce, you stay away from Pamela," Mirah said squeezing his hand tight. "She's caused us enough trouble."

That's for sure, Bryce thought angrily to himself. "Don't worry," he lied to his wife for the last time. There was no need in upsetting his wife but Pamela was about to pay dearly, he thought, angry that she was the cause of his wife and baby being in the hospital.

"Bryce, what ever problems we've been having I don't want anything bad to happen to you," Mirah told him reading his mind. She knew her husband all to well and knew Pamela was in a world of trouble.

"Mirah, I love you," he said kissing her again. "I love our baby, too." He bent down and kissed her stomach before leaving out.

After he left, Mirah just closed her eyes and cried. Her life was in such shambles and now she had a baby on the way.

"Are you okay?"

"James, what are you doing here?" Mirah asked surprised to see him.

"I just wanted to see for my own eyes that you are okay."

"With the exception of these awful bumps and bruises, I'll be fine."

"And the baby?"

Mirah looked at him in shock. She was at a loss for words. "James how did you know I was here and about the baby?"

"I'm here with Candy. We just lost our baby," James told her.

"Oh, I'm so sorry to hear that," Mirah told him.

"Me too. So you didn't answer my question. Is your baby okay?"

"Yes," Mirah replied.

"Is there a possibility that this is our baby?"

"James, how could you even ask me this, especially now."

"Mirah, I didn't come here to upset you," James told her. Besides, her reaction could tell a thousand words. This wasn't the time to press her about this issue but he knew her all to well. James knew the baby she was carrying inside her could possibly be his.

"James…"

"Mirah, I want you to get some rest," he said cutting her sentence off. "We'll have plenty of time to talk later. I just want you to concentrate on getting well," he said kissing her on the lips.

"Thank you," Mirah replied caressing his hand. The last thing she needed right now was to explain things. She was confused herself but somehow she had to think of a way to get her life back together.

"Mirah, you know I love you and would never do anything to hurt you. Always remember that," James told her. "Your happiness is important as well. Always remember that too."

After James left, Mirah closed her eyes. What in the world was she going to do if this baby was James's? How could she even find a way to tell her husband if this was the case? There was no way she could keep this secret for too long. As much as James loved her he would never let another man raise his child.

Chapter 28

Bryce was livid as he quickly made his way home. Every time he thought about his wife lying in that hospital bed, it made his blood boil beyond measure. Mirah had planned on coming home to tell him the wonderful news about their baby and the thought that he could have lost them both was beyond belief. All this chaos in their lives over the past year was all because of Pamela Johnson. Well she is going to pay Bryce thought, biting down on his lower lip. He pulled quickly in the parking garage, slammed the door and rushed to his place. Bryce headed straight for the computer and turned it on. He prepared an interesting email attaching all Pamela's dirty deeds with the exception of his own. Chuckling at what he was about to do, Bryce picked up the phone to make a phone call.

"Hello."

"Pamela, this is Bryce," he said in an arrogant tone.

"Bryce."

"Yes, its me. I'm really disturbed by your constant harassment. It's bad enough you bother me but to go after my wife is totally unacceptable."

"Bryce, I was just trying…"

"Shut up damn it! My wife is in the hospital because of your ass," he snapped angrily. "I told you to leave well enough alone but you couldn't even do that. You're so concerned about yourself that damned be everyone else. Well for once I'm going to truly enjoy making your life hell," Bryce said before he pressed the 'send' button on his email.

"I think you better check your email," Bryce laughed. "I'm sure you'll be getting a bunch of phone calls, and definitely one from your father." He hung up the phone.

"Now deal with that," he smirked quietly to himself. This payback was definitely sweet, he thought, imagining

Pamela's embarrassment right about now. He wished he could be a fly on the wall when all her victims opened their email. Not only did he send them her dirty tapes but he also emailed every last one of them to her father. He had really tried to avoid doing this but Pamela had pushed him over the limit. It was about time someone put a stop to her rampage and who better than her own father, the man that raised her. Knowing him, he would probably ban her from the family. Mr. Johnson was a respectable man and even his own daughter would pay dearly for such behavior. To think of Pamela without a pot to piss in brought a smile to his face. Satisfied, he turned his computer off. Bryce normally didn't like to back anyone into a hole but she deserved it. With his business taken care of, he picked up his jacket and headed back to the hospital to be with his wife.

****

James was relatively quiet while he drove Candy home from the hospital. He couldn't believe he had lost his first child and could possibly have another one on the way with Mirah. How did he let his life get tangled into such a mess? As much as he loved Mirah, she was a married woman. He should have never had sex with her when she was so vulnerable. Matter of fact, he should have never had sex with Candy either. His actions had created pain in both their lives and James promised to get himself back together.

"So how is she?" Candy asked breaking the long silence.

"What are you talking about?" James replied.

"Mirah. How are she and the baby doing?"

"They're fine," James replied.

"I'm glad to hear that," Candy told them. As much as she disliked Mirah for being with her ex, she would never want any woman to experience the pain she just went through.

"So I take it you didn't run into Bryce?"

"No. I didn't want to cause a scene," James replied. "Mirah don't need any extra stress in her life right now," he said thinking back when he went to her room to see how she was doing. It about killed him to see Bryce hovering over her in there. The smiles on their faces while they looked excitedly at the ultrasound machine struck every nerve in his body. What if that was his baby? Didn't he have the right to be in there? If that child was his he knew he couldn't let another man raise him or her. Would Mirah tell him the truth? She knew him so well and the implications this could cause would certainly have an effect on the decision she would have to make. He didn't press her for now but she was going to have to tell her husband of her infidelity at some point, because there was no way in hell he was going to take a back seat. Nope, not with his child, James thought, pulling into the driveway.

"How about I take a few days off," James told Candy. He came around and helped her out the car.

"Don't do that," Candy replied. "I just really need to be alone right now."

"Alone. Candy, you shouldn't be alone right now."

"James, please don't argue with me. Just walk me to the door," she told him.

James didn't want to argue with her, so he did what she asked. "Call if you need me," he said kissing her on the cheek.

"I will," Candy lied. She watched him walk back to his car. She knew she had to get her life back on track and that was definitely without James. His heart belonged to another woman, Mirah Whitaker.

Candy closed her door and slid to the floor in tears. They came flooding down even harder as she rubbed her empty stomach. Every thing in her life was gone. Why did bad things have to happen to her, she thought, rocking back and forth in fear? That was the one thing she feared the most, being alone.

Candy knew she had to face it in order to get her life back. She had to do it for herself. She pulled herself up and made her way to the bedroom.

Chapter 29

Mirah felt guilty at all the attention Bryce was giving her. She was glad she convinced him not to tell her mother right now. She didn't want to worry her with anything else; besides she wasn't ready for anyone to know she was pregnant. Mirah knew time was against her side, rubbing her belly. She didn't know who the father was since her conception was so close to the time that she made love with James. What in the world was she going to do? James would never allow another man to raise his child. Mirah had to think of something and quick.

"Mirah, if you're up to it lets call my folks and tell them the great news."

"Don't you think you're rushing it," Mirah said. The last thing she needed was for his mother to come rushing up here. She knew the moment she found out she would be on the next plane from Cleveland.

"We can't wait forever," Bryce responded excitedly. He wanted to tell somebody of the incredible news.

"Bryce, you know the moment we tell your parents your mother will be here the same day. I'm not trying to be evil but we have our own problems to work through and we can't do it with our parents here. Why do you think I asked you not to call my mother?" Mirah asked him.

"Okay, you win," Bryce said kissing her on the lips. He definitely was not in the mood to be bothered with her pestering mother. He loved his wife dearly, but her mother, on the other hand, was a pain in the ass.

"Can I at least tell my best friend Kanai?" Bryce asked. "I'm going to explode if I don't get this off my chest."

"And you say women gossip all the time," Mirah laughed out loud. "You just make sure Kanai keeps this on the

DL," Mirah told him. "You know gossip can spread like wildfire," she added, poking him playfully on the chest.

"Only women gossip," Bryce said, tracing his finger over her lips. "Men don't partake in that mess. Why do you think we get along so well," he said. He parted her lips and slid his tongue in.

"So what are you saying?" Mirah asked pulling back. "Do you really believe that women are nothing but trouble?"

"When they are together, yes," Bryce replied.

"Bryce you are so crazy," she laughed, slapping him playfully on the arm.

"You know I'm right," he teased.

"Well, I'll never admit it," Mirah told him standing up.

"Hey, where are you going?" Bryce asked. He pulled her back into his arms.

"To the kitchen to get some milk. I'm thirsty."

"No you're not," he told her. "You're supposed to stay in bed."

"You are over exaggerating," Mirah told him. "The doctor said get plenty of rest...he didn't want me bed ridden," she told him sighing.

"Well just let me pamper you," Bryce said. His tone became serious. It was hard to contain the bulge in his pants while he unbuttoned her shirt.

"Bryce, what are you doing?" Mirah asked, playfully pushing him off.

"I want to make love to you," he replied with a series of kisses to her hardened nipples.

"I thought you just told me to relax." Mirah needed to find an excuse out of this. Just because she was back at home with him did not make everything perfect. Things were hardly back to normal and Mirah didn't know if they would ever be.

"Making love is the best relaxation in the world," Bryce told her. "Don't worry I'll do all the work," he said convincingly.

"Bryce, honestly I don't know if I am ready for this right now. We have a lot of things to work out."

"Baby, don't punish me like this," Bryce begged. "You're the only person I love and want to be with. Please forgive me."

"Bryce, I'm not blaming you for all our problems. I just don't want you to think that sex will solve all our problems and make everything okay."

"Baby, I know that," Bryce said taking her hand in his. "I just want to show you how much I love you. If you're not ready, I'm not going to push," he told her getting up.

"Bryce, where are you going?"

"To get you some milk," he winked as he walked out the room.

Mirah let her head fall back against the pillows and thought about what she was going to do. Unlike her husband, it really bothered her that she broke a special part of their marriage by sleeping with another man. Mirah knew this would weigh on her and she just decided it would be best to tell Bryce. Either he would accept her and the fact that this baby might not be his, or he could leave. Maybe this would truly test how much he loved her, she thought, wondering when and how she would tell him.

"You seem to be deep in thought." Bryce came back into the room and handed her a glass of milk.

"I just have a lot of things on my mind," she replied. She sat up on her elbows in thought.

"Well don't stress yourself out about anything," he told her.

"My thoughts exactly," Mirah responded. All this worrying wasn't good for her or the baby, she thought. She sipped down her whole glass of milk.

No matter what went on between them she still found her husband sexy while he undressed and was out of his clothes.

"Are you comfortable with me staying in here?"

"Why wouldn't I be? This is your house," Mirah replied.

"It's our house," Bryce told her before he slipped under the covers.

"Bryce all this was yours before we were together," Mirah told him. "I'm not going to lie, what woman wouldn't want all of this, but in the end if there is no love it's not going to make us happy."

"I agree," Bryce said, rubbing her stomach. "You tried to tell me but I was too blind sided to see what was truly important to me. Mirah, I'm so sorry for the pain I put you through."

"Bryce…"

"No, let me finish. Last time we said we would be open and honest about everything, and I didn't hold up to my part of the agreement. I truly love you and we can work this out," Bryce said, kissing her on the lips.

"It didn't hit me until it was almost too late. Mirah, I don't want to lose you," Bryce said. Tears formed in the corner of his eyes. Bryce truly meant those words.

Mirah began to cry herself. Bryce embraced her in his arms. How could she possibly try to work this out if she didn't know who the father of the baby was? For the first time in their marriage they were both regretful for the damage they caused. Although she loved James, she had made a commitment to her husband. If there was any way to work this out she had to try.

"Mirah, it's going to be okay," Bryce said wiping away her tears.

"But you don't understand…"

"Sssh, lets not discuss this anymore," Bryce said, seeing how upset his wife had become. "Whatever has happened up until now, I'll take full responsibility," he told her. He eased his lips over hers, "I miss being with you…being inside you," Bryce whispered softly in her ear.

Mirah knew it was wrong but somehow she thought making love with her husband would ease the tension, even if it were only for one night. She didn't refuse his kisses as she slid her tongue in and ventured into familiar territory. It had been so long that she forgotten how passionate her husband was. She ran her fingers inside of his silk boxing pajama pants. Her touch instantly made him rise; he eased down her gown to suckle on her firm breast. Mirah let out a series of moans while they continued in heated foreplay.

"Wait a minute," Mirah whispered. She reached over to her nightstand and fumbled. Bryce was surprised when she handed him a condom but she wasn't about to have unprotected sex with him after his dealings with Pamela Johnson. The thought of her making love with her husband made her want to choke. It was too late to change her mind, she thought, while Bryce slipped on the thin latex condom and then eased inside of her.

"I'll be gentle," Bryce, whispered in her ear. He moved in and out of her with slow, gentle strokes. Mirah just closed her eyes and tried desperately to get in the mood, but it just wasn't happening. She tried to hold back her tears. When it was over she turned over and silently cried herself to sleep.

Chapter 30

The next few months went by quickly and Mirah still found herself hiding the truth about her pregnancy from her husband and from James. She was actually glad her mother had come back into town to spend all her time preparing for the new arrival. Mirah welcomed the diversion, but Bryce was not happy that his mother-in-law had moved in and taken over his space again.

****

"Bryce, I need to go to the hospital." Mirah was frantic, she ran into the living room in tears.

"Honey, what's the matter?" Bryce asked, rushing over to her side.

"I started bleeding," Mirah replied. Bryce grabbed their coats; this couldn't be happening he thought.

"Where is my mother?"

"She went to the grocery store," he told her as he locked up the house. They quickly headed towards the elevator. Bryce was glad it didn't stop at every floor. They made it into the parking garage in a matter of minutes. He helped her into the car and maneuvered in and out of Manhattan's heavy traffic to the nearest hospital, where she had gone before a few months ago when she was in a car accident.

"Nurse, we need help immediately," Bryce called out as they rushed through the ER door.

Mirah was taken back to an observation room. They set up the ultra sound machine to see what was going on. She tried to relax but she couldn't shake the bad feeling. Mirah kept asking the doctor what was wrong.

"I'm sorry," the physician said cutting off the machine. "You are going to miscarry."

"Miscarry. No," Mirah cried in disbelief.

"Doctor, how could this be?" Bryce asked trying to comfort his wife. "We were here just a few months ago and listened to the baby's heartbeat. We've even followed up with our doctor frequently."

"I'm sorry, but at some point between your last visit your baby stopped developing. Your body realizes this now and has begun the process of expelling the fetus."

"I don't understand," Mirah continued to cry. "Bryce, do something. This has to be a mistake."

"Honey, I'm sorry," Bryce said, embracing his wife in his arms. He held her tightly while she continued hollering hysterically.

The doctor whispered something to the nurse and she quickly ran out of the room. When she came back they gave Mirah medication to help calm her nerves, and she miscarried naturally. It was nearly six hours of pain and the bathroom became her refuge.

Afterwards Mirah slipped into a deep state of depression. Her demeanor became cold and callous and she shut everyone out, including her husband. Mirah went into denial of what had just happened to her.

Over the next few days Mirah was doped up with so much medication that she constantly stayed sleep. She tried to stop the nurses from giving her so much medicine. Finally, she grabbed and pushed one of the nurses making her fall. She hated the way that medicine made her feel but after that incident they continued to flood her IV with more and they strapped her arms down to the bed in restraints. Mirah was actually relieved when her mother insisted on taking her out of here…away from this hospital and away from Bryce.

For the first time in over two years Mirah breathed a sigh of relief with no distractions. It felt good to be in the room she grew up in. She sat there curled up in the window ledge thinking back on her life. She couldn't believe her life had taken such twists and curves. Mirah had to get herself together. She knew in order to do that; she had to do what made her happy…not her mother, Bryce, not James, but Mirah. She had to take off this black mask.

Chapter 31

"Get out...get out of here," Mattie hollered.

Mirah woke from a half sleep. She heard her mother's voice and hurried down the steps.

"Mirah, please, I need to speak with you."

"The devil is not welcome, not in my house," Mattie yelled.

"Mom it's okay."

"Gal, go on back upstairs and let your mother handle this," Mattie said, rolling up her sleeves.

"Mattie!"

"Shut-up," she told Bryce. "You ain't about to ruin my daughter's life one day longer."

"Mirah is my wife."

"And she is *my* daughter," Mattie replied in a deep growl.

Mirah couldn't stand it any longer. "Mom please...I need to speak with my husband," she said, cutting in.

"Your husband! Bryce certainly has not been acting like a husband."

"Mattie, please, I didn't come here to upset you. I just need to speak with Mirah."

"Hmph! Lord, please help me," Mattie said, throwing her arms up in the air.

Mirah watched as her mother stormed out of the room.

"Can we talk somewhere private?"

Mirah had no choice: "My room," she said, as she headed up the steps.

"How are you feeling?"

"Better, now that I'm home. My mother said that you wanted them to keep me in the hospital."

Bryce gritted his teeth. "Mirah, I only wanted you to get better."

"And you thought I could get better with all those drugs running through me?"

"No, honey…I was just doing what the doctors thought was best. You've been through a lot."

"Bryce, I lost a baby. This is all your fault," Mirah cried.

Bryce just sat there while his wife vented. For once, he had to accept his part and deal with the truth.

"I told you to get Pamela out of our life. Why didn't you trust me? We could have built Whitaker & Associates on our own, remained in a happy marriage, and had a baby on the way. Now it's all gone. Pamela stole everything important to me."

"So I'm important?"

"You're my husband. Yes, I really wanted to do everything to make our marriage work."

"We can still try," Bryce said, taking Mirah by the hand.

"It's not that easy now."

"Marriage isn't easy. I know I've done things that hurt you but we can get past this. Pamela is no longer part of the equation. She has enough worries dealing with the files I sent to her lovers and to her father."

"Oooh…no you didn't," Mirah smiled.

"Yes."

"Get out!" Mirah could hardly contain her excitement.

"Is everything all right in there?" Mattie asked knocking at the door.

"Yes," Mirah replied. She opened the door to see a concerned look on her mother's face.
"Everything is fine."

"Well don't let that devil plague your mind," she hissed, looking at Bryce. "They certainly is right when they say money is the root of all evil."

"Not if you're using it in the right way," Bryce responded.

"Boy, don't get sassy with me. You're in my house. Sweet Jesus, the nerve of him," Mattie ranted angrily.

"Mom, please don't get upset."

"Mirah look at what this man has done to you. As much as I hate to say this, at least James truly loved you."

Mirah could see Bryce's skin turn beet red. The last thing she wanted was a feud between the two of them.

"Mattie, that is a low blow," Bryce said.

"Well it's the truth."

"The truth is, I'm married to your daughter. Mirah is still my wife and if you remember we took our vows before God and the family. If you really want to help you should not be encouraging Mirah to run away from her marriage."

"Oh Lawd…give me strength," Mattie said, fanning herself.

"Mom…"

"Mirah, get this man out of my house before I end up along side your father. You would just love that Bryce, right."

"Don't be ridiculous."

"That's enough, stop you two. I can't take all this bickering."

For a moment the room became silent and Mirah looked at the two of them.

"Mom, whatever decision I make, I need your support. Please let me speak privately with my husband."

"Not here, this man has been nothing but disrespectful."

"Then I'm going to have to pack up and move back with Bryce for the time being."

"Oh no...don't leave. Don't leave me here all alone," Mattie pleaded.

"If I stay you're going to have to respect my decisions."

Mattie could see the serious look in her daughter's eyes. "Fine," Mattie proclaimed.

She gave Bryce an evil stare, then turned and left the room.

"I'm sorry that happened," Bryce said. "The last thing I wanted was to get in a shouting match with your mother."

"I know," Mirah cried. "She can be overwhelming at times."

"Come back home with me."

"Bryce, I can't."

"Can you honestly look me in the eyes and tell me you don't have any feelings for me?"

Mirah was silent. "I thought so," Bryce said. "Please come back home."

"My home is here."

"No your home is with me," Bryce told her. Somehow Bryce had to convince her to come back with him. Between Mattie's meddling and James, he was liable to lose her forever.

"Now is not a good time to leave my mother alone."

"Stop making excuses. Mattie Jones can handle anything," Bryce said, throwing his hands in the air.

"Get that devil out of here," he laughed, mimicking her words from earlier before.

"Okay, enough with the jokes" Mirah smiled. "Why do you make it so hard to hate you?"

"Because you have a loving heart."

"Lately it doesn't feel that way."

"That's because I hurt you."

Should she tell Bryce about her affair with James? From the reaction he had when her mother mentioned his name, maybe it wasn't a good idea.

"Whatever happened up until now, let's forget and start over. I know I can make you happy."

Mirah didn't know what to do. Just an hour ago she had decided to make herself happy with or without Bryce or James. She had already given Bryce a chance to get their marriage back on track. How could she trust him again? Then again, how could she just walk out on her wedding vows? She married him for better or for worse, for richer or poor, to death do us part. Mirah took those vows seriously. There were too many people jumping into marriage, only to divorce. She did not want to be one of those statistics. What about her feelings for James? She loved him too. Was it possible to be in love with two men? She asked herself that question a thousand times. Of course she loved her husband but her relationship with James was on a deeper level. He knew her from within; they were soul mates. Unfortunately, circumstances directed their lives on different paths. Should she walk away from her husband to be with James? He would take her back with open arms; however, if she stayed with Bryce, any relationship she had with James would cease. James would not settle for a mere friendship when he was so in love with her. It would be too painful. What should she do?

"Mirah, I have some vacation time, come away with me."

"Bryce, we tried this before."

"No, we had too many elements around. Let's go away for a while, just you and me."

"Where?"

"You choose but you can't tell anyone our destination."

"You want this to be a secret?"

"Yes. I want us to try and work it out without any disruptions. Please give me one last chance."

How could she deny him that? "Okay," Mirah said.

"Are you serious?"

"Yes."

"Then pack your bags," Bryce smiled.

"Now?"

"Yes, I'll help you."

Bryce wasn't about to let this opportunity slip by. If he didn't act now she was liable to change her mind. He could see Mattie trying to persuade her not to go. No way in hell was he going to leave his wife alone with that woman. She was too possessive and Bryce was glad Mirah took after her father.

"I can't believe you want me to pack now. Where are we going?"

"I told you to decide. I can make the reservations on our way to New York. I'll go home, pack a quick bag, and then we'll be on our way."

"Just like that."

"Yes," Bryce replied.

Mirah didn't know how her mother was going to react. By the way things went earlier, she was liable to explode.

"Mom, Bryce and I are going away for a few weeks."

"What! Where are you going?"

"We don't know yet. We need some time alone to see where our marriage is going from here."

Mattie just stared at the two. "Fine," she replied.

Bryce was in shock. No turmoil from Mattie.

"You be careful, sweetie, and call me to let me know you're safe."

"Okay, I love you," Mirah said.

Mattie hugged her daughter and then watched her until they disappeared from sight. She came to the realization that she couldn't fight with the devil. She would leave that in God's hands.

Chapter 32

Mirah didn't know how Bryce did it but they were on their way to Montego Bay, Jamaica. His spontaneity was one of the things that attracted her to him.

"It's good to finally be here," Bryce said, as they checked into the resort.

"Yes, if you would have asked me this morning, I never would have imagined that we would be in Jamaica."

"Anything for you."

Bryce took their luggage and got everything settled in their room.

"So, what would you like to do today?"

"Relax," Mirah replied. "It has been a long day. Let's unwind and we can start our festivities tomorrow."

"Sounds good to me."

He went to the spa area in their room and turned on the Jacuzzi. After an hour of soaking in the hot water they crawled up underneath the covers of the bed.

"It's good having you next to me again."

"Is it?"

"Yes."

Silence washed over the room. Mirah saw the sincerity in her husband's eyes.

"Do you really love me?"

"Yes," Bryce answered.

"If we move on from here, how do you propose we do that?"

"First we have to build back the trust in our relationship. It's not going to happen over night but if you give our marriage a chance we can start tonight."

"Bryce, how do we trust each other again?"

"By opening up your heart. Let me love you," he said, kissing the softness of her lips.

"I'm scared."

"Don't be." Bryce continued planting kisses on her face. He gently kissed the top of her forehead, then both sides of her cheeks, then her lips again. He traced his tongue around the edge of her lips and when she opened her mouth, their tongues interlocked with acceptance. Bryce longed for this moment again. With everything going on in their life, he wasn't sure about the future of his marriage. When Mirah lost the baby he had been devastated. He was ready to throw in the towel because he wasn't sure he could deal with his own emotions let alone his wife's emotions. Their marriage had been on a roller coaster from the very beginning but much of it was his fault. He never imagined how lonely his life would be without his wife until she was almost gone. Bryce learned a valuable lesson in all of this: money could not buy love. He had plenty of women to spend, spend, and spend, but when it came down to it he never found true happiness until he met Mirah. She was so beautiful, energetic, and full of life. She knew what she wanted and didn't mind working hard for it. He should have trusted her from the beginning when she gave up her life and dropped out of college to help him build up his business. She gave herself completely to him and he broke the bonds of their marriage by having an affair with that scathing low life Pamela Johnson.

"You're so beautiful," Bryce said, working his tongue to her breast. "Let's make love every day that we're here in Montego Bay."

"Every day?"

"Yes. I want to replenish the love that you've been missing."

Mirah chuckled in amusement. She wondered why she was giving herself so easily to her husband. She should have made him work hard for her love, but somehow that didn't feel right. If she were going to forgive him then it would have to be with open arms. Mirah could not harbor resentment for the rest of her life; it wasn't in her nature.

"Bryce, I love you too."

Tears weld up in his eyes. Mirah had given him another chance to prove his love for her. He would make sure the third time around was a charm for her. He put all his will and emotions into making love to her. They both clung to one another as the intensity from their bodies heated the room.

****

Their time at Montego Bay was filled with activities. They dined in the finest restaurants, gambled in the casinos, and enjoyed walking along the "Hip Strip," where the island came alive. Mirah's favorite was diving in the beautiful waters to enjoy the marine habitat. The fish and everything beneath the waters were breathtaking. They even took a Jeep Safari trip and enjoyed seeing the rich land hidden by the natural terrain. Mirah was mystified by the falling waterfall and intrigued by the animals and the rain forest. What a sight, and she was able to catch it all on her video camera to have forever.

After they left Montego Bay, they continued their trip by going to the islands of Ocho Rios, Port Antonio, and Kingston. Jamaica was beautiful, but Mirah was ready to go home when the time came.

Chapter 33

Although they had mounds of fun in Jamaica, Mirah was glad to return to the bustling city of New York.

"We're home," Bryce smiled.

He was glad that his wife was by his side. They returned from their vacation with double the luggage, bringing back souvenirs for everyone.

"Mr. Whitaker, can I help you with your luggage?"

"Yes Paul, that would be wonderful," he told the attendant.

"Well you two go on ahead up and I will be there shortly after I take care of this gentleman."

"Great," Bryce replied, slipping him a twenty dollar bill. He and Mirah headed towards the elevators to go to his suite. "I'm glad we have the elevator to ourselves," he said, taking her in his arms.

He told his wife how much he loved her and kissed her until the elevator doors opened to the penthouse suite. He unlocked the door, swooped Mirah in his arms and carried her through the door like he did the first time they got married.

"Well, well, well…what do we have here?"

"Pamela, how in the hell did you get in here?"

"Shut up! I'll be the one asking all the questions," she yelled, pulling a gun out.

"Mirah, get out of here," Bryce said, putting her back down on her feet.

"No. You stay right there, bitch."

She pointed the gun at Mirah. "I must say it feels good to have the shoe on the other foot," Pamela laughed.

"What are you talking about?" Mirah asked.

"Don't play stupid. You remember the time you had a gun pointed at me while your husband and I were in the pool."

Mirah didn't respond. She stood there in shock staring at the crazed look in Pamela's eyes.

"This is between you and me," Bryce cut in.

"Didn't I tell you to shut up," Pamela said, pointing the gun at him again. "You should have never backed me into a corner. Why did you ruin my life? Bryce we could have had it all."

"No. You just wanted what you couldn't have. It has always been like that for you, hasn't it?"

"And what's wrong with that? I didn't see you complaining a few weeks ago when you were in my bed."

"Please put the gun down. We can all talk about this in a civilized manner."

"There is no more talking. You should have thought about that before you sent all those files to my father and his clients."

"I was angry. You caused us to lose our baby. Why couldn't you stop interfering in our marriage like I asked you to?"

"Why, Bryce, you never loved Mirah. She was just your showpiece. Of all the men I've been with I thought you were different. You were the only one I loved. Why couldn't you love me back? Why?"

"Because I love my wife, and you knew that. Now put the gun down. We can talk about this, just you and I. Let Mirah go…let me help you."

"No."

"Pamela."

The gun went off. Mirah watched as Bryce fell helplessly to the floor.

"Noooo," Mirah screamed, bending over to help him.

Mirah heard Pamela cock the gun again, but the police rushed through the doors and saved her life and arrested

Pamela. The attendant, Paul, rushed to her side as she held Bryce's bloody body in her arms.

"I love you," Bryce said in a faint whisper.

Mirah struggled to remain calm for Bryce's sake. "I love you, too. Help is on the way. Oh, Bryce, please hang on, everything is going to be okay," she cried, kissing him on the lips.

"I love you," Bryce repeated again. "Tell my family I love them too."

Those were the last words Bryce Whittaker ever said. He was pronounced dead before the ambulance had a chance to arrive.

The funeral services were held in his hometown of Cleveland, Ohio. Mirah sat in the front church pew, feeling like it was all some horrible nightmare. She cried throughout the entire eulogy. Bryce had a lot of friends and family. The church was filled to capacity with people even standing outside to say their goodbyes. His sister, Briana, went hysterical and his mother, Diane, fainted before the services were over. Mirah clutched on to her mother as she watched her husband being laid to rest. All in one year she had lost her father, baby, and now her husband. Mirah's body went numb. Why was this happening to her? Somehow she managed to make it through the day. Mirah and her mother stayed with his family for a week before returning to New Jersey.

****

It took Mirah weeks before she could go back to the home she had shared with Bryce. It helped that his parents and Briana traveled from Cleveland to help go through his things.

The penthouse was virtually spotless as she walked around. You would have never been able to tell a murder had ever taken place within the walls that Bryce once called home. The place was inundated with flowers and cards. Mirah, Diane, and Briana cried as they read through each one. Bryce's former employer and all the colleagues he had worked with sent their condolences. Mirah was stunned to see in the stack a card from the Johnson family. At the bottom she read the hand written portion:

We are truly sorry for the trouble our daughter has caused. No amount of words can express how devastated your family must be. We are trying to cope through this ordeal ourselves because we never imagined we raised a daughter who could have committed such a heinous crime. Our heart goes out to you for the loss of your husband.

Regretfully, The Johnson's

Mirah dropped the card to the floor. Briana picked it up, read it, and then gave it to her mother.

"You know, my brother really loved you."

"I know," Mirah cried.

"Bryce confided in me the problems you all were having. He was truly sorry for putting you through this."

"Briana, he should have left that crazy woman alone. I begged him. If he had, he would still be here with us."

Briana nodded and embraced Mirah as they cried in remembrance of Bryce. They stayed in New York a month while they wrapped up his affairs. When they left, the place they had once called home was empty. Mirah took a last stroll through the place remembering all the good times they shared together. When she was done she locked the door and headed off to a life all alone.

Epilogue

One year later Mirah was just beginning to move forward with her life. She had her hands full with Bryce Williams Whitaker Jr. and enrolling back in school. Mirah also spent a good portion of her time in the courts making sure Pamela received the punishment she deserved for murdering Bryce. She tried to pull an insanity plea, but Mirah made sure the jury saw her for the scathing person she was. She also wanted them to see the baby growing inside her, a baby that would never know his father. When the trial was over, Pamela Johnson received life in prison without parole. It gave Mirah some comfort knowing she would spend the rest of her life behind bars, a fitting punishment for the trouble she caused. Mirah even took her to civil court and sued Pamela for all her assets. Mirah walked away with a large settlement, not to mention the large amount that was left from her husband's estate. No amount of money could ever replace a life but Mirah vowed she would make good with what she was left of it.

"Are you okay?"

"Yes," Mirah told James.

She handed James the baby and went into the kitchen to remove their dinner from the oven. James had been a lifesaver. He never questioned or pushed her about the last days she was with Bryce. Obviously, he knew they had decided to give their marriage another try since she had the baby, but he never faulted her for that. In fact, Mirah was glad she had made the decisions she had. She could not fathom the thought of Bryce living his last days alone. Instead, they spent their final days of marriage together as a happy couple. Mirah relived their days in Jamaica often, looking at the videotape she had of their time together.

As for Whitaker & Associates, Mirah decided to keep her husband's business alive. Bryce had worked so hard for it, even compromising his ethics by having an affair with Pamela, the woman who took his life. Not knowing the ins and outs of the business, Mirah offered Bryce's workers, Sheila Hendricks and Raymond Orr, full partnership. Not a bad incentive for someone who was just getting his or her feet wet in the workforce. They had always been loyal to Bryce, and they were down right hard workers who earned this opportunity. Mirah put up front all the money for the merger but it was an investment that was well deserved. The company could continue to grow and she knew her son would always have a piece of the business his father had started.

"You've barely touched your food. Are you sure you're okay."

"Tomorrow will be a year since Bryce was buried," Mirah answered.

"Would you like to put flowers on his grave?"

"Yes, but he's laid to rest in Cleveland."

"Well let's pack up and hit the road. I'll drive you to Cleveland. You need to put closure on this chapter of your life."

"I know. With the baby and all the court hearings it has been a difficult year."

"That's to be expected. Last year you had an extremely difficult time with losing your father, your first baby, and your husband."

"James, you've really been understanding."

"I know Bryce and I weren't on good terms but we did share one thing in common, our love for you. I love you and have from the first time I laid eyes on you. We're soul mates."

"Yes we are," Mirah replied, with tears clouding her eyes.

"Look, you know I want to be with you. Things have been pretty rough but life has brought our paths back together again."

"It's just been difficult putting the pieces back together."

"I know but you have to move on for yourself and Bryce Jr. It's not healthy having your life in constant chaos."

"You're right. Please give me a little more time. I really appreciate how patient you've been with me."

"I'll give you whatever time you need as long as you promise me you will not run off and marry another man."

Mirah smiled. "Of course not," she said, kissing him on the lips.

"Good, now let's get ready to go."

****

Hours later Mirah was back in Cleveland, Ohio. It was late but she took the car and headed over to Bryce's family house. They were overjoyed anytime they were able to see their grandchild. It gave them comfort that the memory of their child would live on through his son. Mirah wanted to make sure that Bryce Jr. always had ties to his father side of the family and together they would make sure that he had the proper upbringing that his father would have wanted him to have.

The next morning Mirah stood over Bryce's headstone. She laid the flowers down and then said a silent prayer. The sun was just beginning to cascade its beautiful rays.

"Bryce, this is your son," Mirah told him.

She smiled thinking back to their past. "You know you were always full of surprises. I guess you had a plan on our last days in Jamaica when you insisted that we make love every day."

Mirah knelt down and ran her hand across the headstone.

"I'll miss you and know that I'll always keep a special place in my heart for you."

Mirah picked up her son and headed back to the car. She was finally able to bring closure to this chapter in her life and move on.

The Black Mask.

ABOUT THE AUTHOR

Kimberly McKenzie was born and raised in Cleveland, Ohio. She graduated from Wright State University in 1997, with a Bachelors of Arts in Political Science. Kimberly always enjoyed a good book. She started writing a year after finishing college in 1997, after reading an African-American historical romance novel. The challenge of writing her first book soon became more than a hobby, and to date Kimberly McKenzie has completed four soon to be published novels. Kimberly enjoys spending time with her husband, son, and family. She works in the healthcare industry and would like to get her Master's Degree in Information and Computer Science. Kimberly also enjoys working on database and web design.

COMING SOON
"THE BACHELORS FOOL"
(Enjoy the 1st chapter)

Ken could not breathe; the cold gun barrel was rammed down his throat. Tears of anger fell from his eye.

"Yeah, bastard, it don't feel good, do it?" Sheryl asked.

Ken did not respond.

"Answer me," Sheryl said, removing the gun from his throat and slapping the hard metal against his face.

"And give you the satisfaction? Never," Ken responded, feeling the blood rush from his face.

"Get up," Sheryl screamed. "You're going to pay for leaving me and our daughter."

"Can you blame me? You've been nothing but abusive, intolerant and crazy. I never should have married your crazy ass in the first place."

"Oh really! You didn't say that shit when we had sex last week. And now that you have a new wife, you think you can conveniently get rid of me?"

"Sure do. The sex was merely a quick fix. I just wanted one last farewell to all the misery you put my ass through."

"You son of a bitch," Sheryl spat.

Ken laughed. He felt exhilarated to finally be able say what the hell he wanted. For eight years he put up with her bullshit. Every day of their marriage, they were either fighting or she was laying her hands on him. If he had defended himself, he knew he would have been in jail for murder, so he just took her bullshit day after day until he could take no more. When she bluffed one day and said she was moving out, he helped her ass pack. It felt good getting her out of his home; if it wasn't for their daughter, he would have had Sheryl permanently out of his life.

"Why, Ken? How could you marry someone else so quickly? We haven't even been divorced two months and you already have someone in the home we picked together."

"The same way I married my new wife is the same way I married you, so I don't understand your question."

Sheryl just stood there, tears forming in her eyes. She loved Ken despite whatever problems they had but she would be damned if he would just abandon her and their five year old daughter Katrina. She gripped the gun, pointed, and squeezed the trigger.

Ken jumped up from a pool of sweat. He looked over at his wife Tamia to make sure this horrible nightmare was just a dream. Tamia was sleeping peacefully next to him. She opened her eyes at his sudden movement.

"Is everything all right?"

"Yes, baby, I just had a nightmare," Ken responded.

"Want to talk about it?"

"Not really. You go back to sleep," he said, kissing her forehead. It was 3:30 a.m. and he did not want to upset her with talk of his ex-wife Sheryl.

"Are you sure," Tamia asked, running her hand along his sweaty forehead.

"Positive," he said, wrapping his arms around her. "I love you; I love the way you feel laying up against me," Ken whispered, as his shaft became rock hard.

"Now how am I supposed to go back to sleep?"

"Good question," Ken responded, lowering his lips to meet hers.

"Umm, I love the way your tongue feel against mine," Tamia said.

She let her husband's tongue intertwine with hers as she massaged the hard shaft bulging from his legs. Tamia let her head fall back to the pillow as his lips made their way down to her hardened nipples. He then ran his tongue down to suckle the flowing juices between her legs. When she could hold it no more, she released and then positioned his swollen muscle to relieve his build up. Relaxed, they were both able to drift back to sleep.

****

Ken was excited about the morning activities. He was going to pick up his daughter Katrina and she would be joining his new family for an outing at one of the large theme water parks.

"What time are you picking Katrina up?" Tamia asked.

"I thought we'd pick her up on our way to the park," Ken responded, sipping his morning cup of orange juice.

"Are you kidding me? I'm not trying to ruin my day by dealing with your ex-wife."

"Tamia, you're going to have to deal with her sooner or later. You knew the deal when we got married. I know it's difficult having a ready made family, but I love my daughter and I will not put her in the middle of any family rivalry."

Tamia just shook her head. Her day was already starting to turn downhill. Ken had always talked about how crazy his ex-wife Sheryl was and for the world she could not understand why he wanted to put her smack dead in the middle of it. She didn't want to be bothered with her or his daughter Katrina. The last time Katrina was over, she gave Tamia hell. She was rude, smart-mouthed and knew way too much about things for a five year old. If Tamia had her way, she would straighten that child up real quick, because the road she was taking she would undoubtedly be just as crazy as her mother when she grew up. How in the world did Ken ever bring that woman into his family? People said that opposites attract, but damn, their past relationship was way off the charts and that's exactly why it was in the past. Sheryl was one nutcase of a woman.

"Are you ready to go?" Ken asked.

"Sure, why not."

"Tamia..."

"Look, you're making a huge mistake," Tamia said, cutting his sentence off.

"And everyone told me I was making a big mistake by marrying you two months after getting divorced from my ex-wife," Ken responded.

"What's that supposed to mean?"

"It means sometimes we have to make sacrifices. I made a big one being with you, so I expect the same loyalty in return."

"Well who said we should not have gotten married?"

"Let's not go there," Ken said, thinking about how upset all his family and friends had been over his marriage to Tamia.

"You brought up the subject."

"Yes, but it was only to point out the sacrifices I have made to be with you. Now come on, I don't want you getting all upset. We're a family and that includes my daughter Katrina. Let's head out so we can pick her up."

"Fine," Tamia said angrily.

Tamia had a straight up attitude from the moment she set foot in the truck. Ken looked over at her and brushed her lips with the tip of his hand.

"Oh, you think your loving can resolve everything?"

"It must be good or you wouldn't have bothered to be with me and all my *so called* baggage."

"Funny," Tamia smirked, while they merged onto the highway.

The Florida weather was absolutely perfect that time of year. It was sunny with a nice breeze for a mid-September day. It was pleasant to have the breeze caress her face rather than the cold air conditioner that was needed during most of the hot days they got.

"We're here," Ken said, pulling up to the apartment building.

"I'll just wait in the car while you go get her."

"No, we're both going. Now come on," Ken said, opening the passenger side door.

Reluctantly, Tamia got out and followed her husband up to the fifth floor.

"Oh, no, you didn't bring that heifer over to my place," Sheryl said, standing at the door.

"Sheryl, what is your problem?" Ken said, in a scolding tone.

"My problem is I don't want your new wife no where near my place. How ass backwards are you going to get?"

"Now, let's not start on a rampage," Ken told her. "I thought it would be good for you to meet my wife. She will be spending a lot of time with our daughter."

"Yes, *our* daughter, the one we made together when you stuck your dick up me."

"Oh my goodness, Ken, I am going to wait downstairs," Tamia gasped.

"Since you're up here bitch, you might as well stay so we can get a few things straight," Sheryl said, pushing the door closed.

Sheryl didn't give either one of them a chance to respond to her remark.

"Now, first of all, how do you like having my leftovers?" Sheryl asked.

"Sheryl..."

"Shut the hell up Ken. You wanted me to meet this heifer, so let me talk," Sheryl interrupted.

"Let her say what she has to," Tamia said.

"No, I'm not about to let her speak to you in this kind of tone."

"Fuck you, Ken. I'll speak in whatever damn tone I want to. If you think you're going to get our daughter and play the happy family, you're dead wrong."

For a brief moment the room fell silent. Sheryl smiled.

"Now, as I was saying, if you want my leftovers, fine. Just know that Ken and I fucked in every inch of that house that you now call home."

"Excuse me?"

"You heard me right. Every inch of that house has been claimed with my DNA."

"And what does that have to do with Katrina?" Tamia asked upset.

"This new wife of yours is a stupid one at that," Sheryl said, rolling her eyes over to Ken. "It means that we fucked on every inch of that house, dummy. How do you think Katrina got here?" Sheryl said, shaking her head. "Just know that every time you look at our daughter that my legs were spread all over the house that you're living in."

"This is nonsense," Ken interrupted. "Where is Katrina? We're ready to go."

"Don't interrupt me you selfish bastard. You were bold enough to bring this woman in my house so deal with what I have to say."

"I'm going to ask you again, where is Katrina?"

"Don't worry about where she is at. You weren't worried about her when you were running up and down that highway visiting this piece of trash," Sheryl ranted.

"Look, if you don't get my daughter…"

"What?" Sheryl said, jumping like she was going to hit him.

Ken jumped back from his ex-wife's sprawling hands.

"Yeah, still a wimp," Sheryl laughed.

"I don't see anything funny," Tamia cut in. "You played these silly games with Ken, but don't think I'll let you put your hands on me. I'll whoop you until there's no tomorrow," Tamia said, rolling up her arm sleeves.

"Ghetto fabulous," Sheryl clapped. "The cherry don't fall far from the tree. You better be careful because just like Ken up and left me, he'll do the same thing to you."

Tamia just rolled her eyes. She would not stand here and be humiliated any longer.

"Let's go," Tamia hollered.

"Where is Katrina?" Ken asked for what seemed like the thousandth time."

"She's not here. Do you think I would let her go to your perfect little family outing?"

"It's my visitation weekend?"

"The hell with your visitation weekend," Sheryl scolded. "You should have thought about all this when you deserted our family. If you think I'm going to sit here and be cooperative, you have another thing coming, you idiot."

It took all Ken's strength not to haul off and punch Sheryl. He didn't resort to violence when they were married and he was not about to do it now. He had too much going for himself to be sitting in jail over her.

**THE BACHELORS FOOL
COMING SOON**

Printed in the United States
102437LV00001B/139-300/A